Debbie Ellis
~2022~

Awakening from Terror

~~~~~~~~~~~~~~~~~~

Debbie Ellis

Blackbird Wings Publishing, LLC
~~~~~~~~~~~~~~~~~~

This book is a work of fiction. Names, characters, organizations, places, events, dialogue, and incidents are either products of the author's imagination or are used fictitiously. Any resemblance to actual events or persons, living or dead, is entirely coincidental.

Published by Blackbird Wings Publishing, LLC
ISBN: 978-1-7329772-0-4

Author website Design by Tony Morris

~ Dedication ~

I dedicate the books of the Awakening Series: Awakening from Terror and Awakening to Peace, to my many sisters who have suffered from domestic abuse, both physical and emotional, from the hands of the personality disordered, the narcissists, sociopaths, and psychopaths. Thank you, Karen Shaw, for your treasured friendship and for starting the life-altering support group that has helped thousands of victims heal and grow. From our sisterhood, I thank you all for gifting me your support, friendship, and love.

For my younger sister, Becky, who was murdered by her abusive boyfriend in 2001, I pray you are resting in peace. This book is especially dedicated to you.

Special thanks go to my beloved family, my amazing children and precious grandchildren. Many thanks go to Andrea Foster and my fellow writers in Creative Quills, as well as my brilliant nephew, Tony Morris. Your knowledge has been invaluable. Thank you, Katrina Conn and Karen Bullock, for believing in me when I didn't believe in myself. I would never have finished writing this novel without everyone's encouragement and support.

Chapter One

~ April 8, 1992 ~

She smelled like a Fuzzy Navel. There had been a lot of traffic behind the bar, and Marcy ended up wearing peach Schnapps and orange juice when the cocktail waitress, Vicky, tried to mix the peachy drinks. Instead, she only managed to slosh the fruity concoction onto Marcy. The tired barkeep thanked Vicky for her efforts, shooed the waitress to the other side of the bar, and cleaned the spilled vodka and juice. As one of the bartenders of *Molly's Shamrock Pub,* Marcy had poured a lot of drinks that night.

There had been a lively crowd composed of regulars, as well as a dozen truck drivers who had parked for the night across the street at the truck stop. With bent elbows, patrons of the pub would lean their drunken frames onto the bar's padded front while nursing their mixed drinks, whiskeys, and ales. Marcy was exhausted, but she bagged all the empty beer bottles and polished the oak bar's worn, marred counter until it shined. Shutting off the jukebox, she cut off Billy Ray Cyrus in mid-chorus as he sang *Achy Breaky Heart.*

After restocking the liquor bottles and washing the glasses and mugs, she was finally ready to make her way home. The other bartender, Janice, had left an hour earlier, which was against the owner of the pub's rules. Molly Brennan, owner of the busy establishment, had lectured her employees and staff about safety and advised them to never close the pub or go outside alone in the evenings.

Janice sometimes suffered from migraine headaches, and Marcy had sympathized with her misery. The ear-splitting music and dense cigarette smoke had triggered an excruciating headache for Janice. Her pain and nausea had become progressively worse, so Marcy suggested Janice leave early and assured the ailing co-worker she would be fine closing the bar by herself.

I can't wait until I can quit this job and teach full time. Only a few more months, she thought. She was a student at the community college by day and a bartender by night. Marcy was excited to follow her calling. She loved children, and she'd decided to pursue a career in teaching. Marcy was anxious to trade the pub full of rambunctious drinkers for a classroom full of rowdy youngsters.

From under the counter, she pulled out an old rotary-dial telephone and called her roommate, Sandra. She envied her roommate's new Motorola cellular phone that was a luxury to many. She hoped to have enough money saved up to invest in one of the convenient gadgets in a few months. Sandra was a night owl, and Marcy knew her friend waited up for her. She heard her roommate pick up her call.

"Hi Sandra! What's up?" asked Marcy.

"Not much… I spoke to Daniel earlier. He didn't make it tonight for our date, so I've been hanging out alone and watching *Roseanne* and reruns." Sandra's voice held an exasperated tone, and Marcy wondered if her friend had picked another loser as her next boyfriend.

Sandra had an uncanny ability to choose cheaters, liars, and deadbeats. She seemed to be a magnet for contemptible bums, and Marcy wondered when she'd meet this new guy, Daniel. Other than his first name, she didn't know anything about him, and her roommate seemed tight lipped about her new love interest. Maybe Sandra was afraid she'd jinx the relationship, or she didn't want to hear the protective warnings from her roommate. Marcy thought her auburn-haired best friend deserved much better than what she settled for in boyfriends.

Marcy smiled as she heard the nasal voice of Roseanne Barre on her roommate's television in the background. She told Sandra she was headed home and hung up the phone. She loved living with her best friend in the chic, loft-style townhouse with its interior of bricked walls, and modern décor of chrome and glass. Sandra had purchased and furnished the cool, yuppy home a few months before Marcy moved in with her. Sandra had even decorated her best friend's bedroom in the trendy seafoam green color she knew Marcy loved.

She hurried to leave the pub, anxious to shampoo her hair and rid her curls of the rancid odor of the thick cigarette smoke that had smothered the pub like California smog. After turning off the green, blinking neon light, which was shaped like a four-leaf clover by the front door, she wrapped herself in her warm puffer coat. She pulled out the pub's door key, plus her heavy keyring which tended to weight down her purse like a brick and walked outside locking the pub's door behind her.

Pulling the fur trimmed hood over her blonde head for protection from the night's frigid wind, she scurried to her old car in the parking lot. Oklahoma nights could be harsh in early April, and she kept her head down to block the northern gusts. Smiling, she thought of one of her mother's favorite winter expressions: *It's so cold, I saw a politician with his hands in his own pockets.* After quickly jumping behind the steering wheel of her blue 1980 Ford Pinto, she blew onto her hands to warm them.

Turning the key in the ignition, Marcy's stomach dropped when the car made a clicking sound and refused to start. She was tired of the old heap giving her grief and was anxious to trade in her unreliable wheels for something new. Marcy hoped nothing was seriously wrong with the Pinto, and she grudgingly climbed out of the car. Diesel fumes from the nearby truck stop wafted towards her. Walking to the rear of the vehicle, she opened the hatchback and looked for the flashlight given to her from her father for just this sort of occasion.

She gave a little yelp and nervously jumped when she unexpectedly heard a man's deep voice behind her. "Need some help, Miss?" he politely asked. *Hmmm, he doesn't have an Okie accent, and he has a slight lisp.* Marcy thought she'd heard his voice somewhere before.

Looking up at a friendly face, she felt relief. He appeared to be around her age, was at least a foot taller than her petite five-feet three-inches, and she was grateful for any assistance he might offer. She informed the good Samaritan of her frustrating dilemma, and he said he'd be glad to look at the car. The man pulled on a pair of oil stained leather gloves from his coats pocket and lifted the hood.

Marcy held her flashlight, so they could look at the engine better. With the improved lighting, she was able to get a clearer view of the dark-haired man. She recognized him as one of the patrons who'd been sitting at the bar earlier. She had served him draft beers and tequila shots that night. She remembered the western shirt he wore, a *Mo Betta* American flag design. Lots of patrons wore *Mo Bettas*. The colorful shirts, designed by Maury Tate, an Oklahoma calf roper in professional rodeos, seemed to be worn by half the men who frequented the pub since Garth Brooks began wearing and promoting them on his album covers.

Gazing at the large, cavernous parking lot, she suddenly noticed there were no other vehicles parked in the area. "You look familiar. Were you in the bar earlier tonight?" she asked with an uneasy feeling slowly crawling up her spine.

"Yup, I was. Had a few beers. Looks like a loose battery cable," he answered, and she could smell the alcohol on his breath. She noticed he'd removed a small screwdriver from the pocket of his thick parka and was tightening one of the cables on the battery's acid-crusted post. He looked at her and smiled, but the smile didn't quite reach his eyes.

Intuitive warning bells caused pebbly goosebumps to cover her arms beneath her warm coat. Looking into his dark, hooded eyes, she thought they appeared reptilian and predatory. He didn't blink. She was being sized up as his prey.

"I think I'll just go back into the bar and call my roommate. I'm sure she won't mind coming to pick me up," Marcy said, as she quickly backed away from the front, moving towards the driver's side.

Like a viper striking after its mark, he slithered and followed. She opened the door to retrieve her purse and keys. Leaning inside, she felt a strong shove causing her to dive headfirst over the car's center and emergency brake between the front bucket seats. She gasped in pain when her forehead hit the inside of the passenger door. As her purse and flashlight hit the front floorboard, she felt her long hair being yanked, and her head whiplashed backward. She became dizzy as he overpowered her.

~~~~~~~~~~~~~~~~~~~~
~~~~~~~~~~~~~~~~~~~~

Sadly, the fraudulent good Samaritan never had intentions of assisting Marcy. Angrily cursing because the driver's seat was pushed forward too far for his long legs to fit, the evil man adjusted the seat and folded his tall body back inside the little car.

Red splotches were beginning to stain her slender throat. Her breathing was shallow and diminished, but his was labored from rending Marcy unconscious. Slowly exhaling, a lecherous smile spread across his face. He was surprised at how easy it had been to loosen the battery cable to incapacitate the Pinto. *Thanks for parking in the most poorly lit area of the parking lot, Marcy. You made it convenient for me to sabotage your car.*

He twirled and loudly jangled the heavy set of keys with the Pinto key fob and letter "M" keychain. Thinking the red, white, and blue key and fob matched his shirt, he decided to hang onto the keys and keychain as a memento.

The brutal psychopath considered himself funny and quite clever. He snickered, baring his teeth as his loud laugh became more of a roaring guffaw, echoing inside the confines of the car.

Hovering over her, he taunted the motionless young woman. "Your roommate can't pick you up, Marcy. She's too busy watching *Roseanne*."

Chapter Two

~ April 5, 2018 ~

Tessa Ryan couldn't resist. On her drive to work, she pulled into the parking area by the Cedar Trails walking path. The dark-haired young woman stepped from her car, looked toward the eastern sky, and gazed in awe at the early morning shades of pastels. Breaking over the horizon, lavender, peach, and bright pink, cotton-candy floating clouds seemed to part aside for the beams of sunlight piercing from the glowing sun.

Glancing around, Tessa noticed there was no traffic on the street, and she savored the private moment of solitude. Raising her arms toward the heavens, she breathed deep of the fresh air and began to praise God for the beauty bestowed upon her morning of the picturesque view.

"Thank you, Lord. What an amazing artist, painting the skies with your glorious brush and palette." She closed her eyes, kept her arms raised and continued praying.

"Please work through me this day, Lord. Let me be an instrument for you. Help me to have strength and compassion. Help me to see, to hear and do Your Will and not my own. Amen."

Tranquil thoughts and the sun's warmth soothed her as she climbed back into her car.

Ten minutes later, Tessa clocked in at the medical clinic where she worked as a registered nurse. She greeted her co-workers, Angie, the receptionist, and Sara, another nurse. Her special moments of early morning prayer had given her a feeling of peace, and she hummed as she began her tasks. As per her usual routine, she glanced at the list of patients to be seen that day.

Tessa commented to her co-workers, “I wonder how Mr. Sanders is doing? We haven’t seen him in several months.”

Mr. Thomas Sanders was one of their favorite patients. At eighty-four years young, he was still spry and fit for his age. At his last visit, he’d been having a few issues with his arthritis. Less than a minute passed, and the phone rang. Angie answered the call. With widened eyes, she spoke to the caller saying, “Hello, Mr. Sanders. Yes, I’ll be happy to help you schedule an appointment.”

A few minutes later, Angie looked at Tessa, smiled and curiously asked, “How do you do that? At least once a week, you freak me out, Tessa. You’ll mention a patient or someone, and they either call or show up here within minutes. How do you do that?”

“I have no idea, coincidence probably. For some reason, someone will cross my mind… like we’re on the same wavelength, I guess.” Tessa shrugged her shoulders, picked up a box of supplies and began stocking the shelves with tongue depressors and rolls of gauze in the clinics supply room. Angie and Sara glanced at each other, always surprised of their co-worker’s unusual ability.

Tessa’s workday was pleasant until the last patient walked into the lobby. She immediately noticed the young woman’s arrival. Her name was Elise, and this afternoon’s visit wasn’t the first time the quiet mother of two walked into the clinic in pain. Fresh bruises marked her arms and a blackened eye was noticeable, even though there was a half inch of makeup applied. As usual, Tessa suspected the bruises were from the brutal courtesy of the young woman’s abusive husband. Although Elise always had a flimsy excuse for the injuries, Tessa saw the fear and anguish in her eyes. She noticed the timid girl try to hide telling marks as she tugged on the sleeves of her blouse. The prayer warrior silently prayed for comfort and healing for the blonde girl who wore enough makeup to rival an actress in a Broadway theater.

Leaving work an hour later, Tessa felt conflicted. Her emotions ran high, and she felt furious at Elise’s abusive husband. She was concerned for the young, battered wife, for whom she’d scheduled a scan at the hospital for a suspected fractured wrist. Recalling the discolored marks on the patient, Tessa’s righteous anger caused her teeth to clench, and her hands tightened on the steering wheel as she drove home. As a nurse, she occasionally saw victims of domestic abuse, but the injustice of this case seemed to ignite her Irish temper. In Tessa's opinion, any spouse who deliberately hurt the other, whether physically or emotionally, should be held accountable.

Interrupting her angry thoughts, Tessa's cell phone rang as she pulled into her driveway. The caller was her friend, Kyra, whom she'd met two years prior. Kyra was the realtor who'd located the Craftsman style house where Tessa now lived. They'd become close friends after closing the purchase. She loved her little house and had worked hard to make the cottage charming. On the phone, Tessa agreed to meet Kyra at their local gym, *Tony's Fitness Center,* and join her for a workout. They were trying to catch up to their mutual friend, Rachel, who was a bit of a fitness junkie. Changing from her nursing scrubs to yoga pants and a tank top, she hurriedly grabbed a jacket and left to meet her friend. A half hour later, Tessa transferred her anger from witnessing the blonde patient's pain, onto the gym's equipment and her work out.

"Feel the burn?" asked Kyra, as she steadily marched up and down on the stair stepper with sweat dripping down her flushed face.

Tessa was on the leg extension machine, working her quads. She grunted as she finished her reps and stood with quivering, protesting leg muscles. She and Kyra ended their exhausting work out with a slow paced walk on treadmills. She briefly told her friend about the bruised woman from the clinic.

"That's horrible, Tessa. I'd like to give that jerk husband a taste of his own medicine." Kyra made a fist and looked the way Tessa had felt before coming to the gym.

"I worry about the children in such a miserable household… those poor kids." Tessa said with a frown. She was suddenly extra grateful for being blessed with two loving parents. She was one of the lucky ones whose parents loved and doted on their children, as well as adored each other. She reminded herself to call them when they finished their workout.

Kyra commented, "What's wrong with men these days? Seems like all I meet are losers, and the lies they tell, oh my gosh! One guy I met on that new dating site told me lie after lie, but nowadays, we can check them out, thanks to *Google*. They can't get away with their deceptions quite as easily as they used to. I told him, no way buddy… that dog don't hunt. I confronted him with the truth, and I haven't heard from him since."

"I'm sorry, Kyra. You deserve better." Tessa sympathized.

At her home later, she indulged in a steamy soak in her clawfoot bathtub to pander her achy muscles. Afterwards, she pulled on sweatpants and a soft pink t-shirt and plopped onto her *dragonfly chair*, which had been aptly named by her four-year-old niece, Sophia, because the upholstery fabric had dragonflies landing among colorful flowers printed on a light green background. Tapping her parent's number into her cell phone, she hoped her mother picked up.

On the second ring, her mother's cheerful voice answered, "Hello, beautiful Daughter."

Tessa told her about her day and how much she appreciated her parents and the love they'd lavished on her and her two siblings, Trisha and Trevor. She asked her mother what the secret was in having a happy marriage.

"Oh Tessa, it hasn't always been rainbows and unicorns. Your father and I have had our moments, but we made it a point to never argue in front of you kids. Plus, we truly love each other, even with our crazy quirks. Over thirty years of marriage and lots of life lessons thrown at us, we've managed to make it work."

"Well, Mom, I want a marriage like yours. That is, if I ever find anyone I even want to date. Am I being too picky?"

Her mother answered, "No, you're not. Never settle for anyone who doesn't have strong integrity and morals. You deserve the best, my sweet girl. Never settle for less."

After enjoying another ten minutes of inspiration with her mother, she began feeling settled. Once she'd ended the call, she breathed a relaxed sigh. Being an avid reader, she picked up the new novel purchased at the tiny bookstore in town named *Rays of Sunshine Books*, owned by a local author whose first name was Ray. After barely finishing a chapter in the novel, Tessa gave in to her exhaustion, decided to call it a day, and made her way to bed. She slept for a few hours before awakening from the terror of a horrendous nightmare.

Vaulting from her bed, Tessa landed firmly on her feet. With arms outstretched in a defensive stance ready to do battle with the world, her eyes rapidly searched her bedroom which felt unfamiliar. Her racing heart felt ready to charge out of her chest. Tessa had awakened from another night terror which created a tidal wave of panic and anxiety. Her frightening dream was fresh in her mind as she gasped for air. *Deep breaths*, she thought, *deep breaths*.

"It was only a bad dream," she muttered aloud, trying to calm her quaking limbs. She turned on the lamp sitting on the bedside table. Looking at the clock, she was disappointed to see the time said four o'clock in the morning. She knew going back to sleep would be impossible, so she picked up the dream journal used to track the disturbing images which sometimes haunted her nights. Fortunately, they were rarely as harrowing as this one.

Recalling the ghostly, pale face of the blonde woman from the nightmare, who looked to be in her twenties, Tessa closed her eyes. In the dream, she could hear the woman speak to her, telling her about her *mistake*. The woman appeared to be standing behind a bar in a club with dozens of liquor bottles neatly positioned on shelves behind her, and a green neon light shaped like a four-leaf clover blinked beside the girl. With anguished green eyes, the woman seemed to be looking directly at her.

"Serving those drinks to that man and trusting him was the biggest mistake of my life," she told Tessa.

Suddenly, the blonde woman was no longer in the bar. In the blink of an eye, she seemed to be standing outside, near a lake, or large pond, with a thick grove of tall trees surrounding the area. The woman pointed to the black water, keeping eye contact with her.

"There… that's where I am. I'm at the bottom of the lake. That's where he put me." Her pleading eyes peered at Tessa with a sad haunting grief.

She felt the woman trying to convey her demise. In the dream, Tessa had even felt the cold lake waters circling around her ankles, then her whole body. She couldn't breathe. Wincing, Tessa groaned as she remembered feeling an intense, sharp ache in her chest.

Tears now fell from Tessa's blue eyes as she flashed back to the woman's mournful plight. *Who is she, and what happened to her? Who was the man who hurt her… who had murdered her?*

Tessa wiped tears from her cheeks. After writing detailed notes and closing the dream journal, she continued rubbing the left side of her chest unable to forget the pain. She shuffled into her small kitchen and turned on the coffee maker. Setting her favorite mug underneath the Keurig, she pushed the button and breathed deep. The familiar, aromatic brew began filling the blue mug, and her tense muscles began to relax for the first time since waking.

Sipping her caffeine, she glanced at the cheerful kitchen with its white painted cabinets and colorful, braided area rug. The old oak floors had been refinished and shined. Granite countertops held yellow and blue canisters, and there were potted starter plants with their tiny shoots peeking out of the dirt sitting in the windowsill. Every spring, Tessa added flowers to her home's expanding backyard garden. The fresh cup of hot coffee and the bright, warm kitchen couldn't soothe the bleak residual effects of her dark dream.

Carrying the steaming mug to the next room, she flipped on a lamp. She sat on the overstuffed dragonfly chair, curled her legs beneath her, and settled into her comfortable space. With eyes closed, she recalled more details of the haunting dream. The woman's hair was a honey blonde with highlights, and she wore a dark green blouse and jeans. The old fashion style of her clothes and hairstyle insinuated the time was from perhaps the late 1980's or early 90's.

Was she murdered decades ago? Tessa deliberated. The tragic images in her mind were still strong, and for the umpteenth time she wondered why she experienced the ghostly dreams. *Why me?* It mostly felt like a curse, yet fortunately, she also had dreams that were pleasant ones.

Since her childhood, Tessa had experienced unique, unconventional dreams. Sometimes after a nightmare, she would pray for the dreams to stop, begging God to take away what felt like a burden. Many of the dreams were premonitions, warnings and glimpses of the future. Some of the dreams, such as the recent nightmare, appeared to come from past times.

The rich hazelnut coffee helped wake her and clear her troubled mind. She turned off her alarm before it began its annoying beeping and began getting ready for her busy day. After a hot shower, she donned her light blue nursing scrubs and brushed through her brunette mane. Looking into the mirror while tying her long hair into a ponytail, she noticed her face was pale. She sighed and thought how night terrors, such as the one from earlier, seemed to drain her energy physically as well as mentally.

She filled her travel mug with another dose of hazelnut brew, grabbed a cranberry-almond protein bar, walked into the garage, and hopped into her car. Opening the garage door, she backed out into the street. The night terror seemed to hover over her as she drove to work.

Arriving at the medical clinic, Tessa clocked in and walked into the lobby to straighten magazines and unlocked the front door. She turned on the flat screen television that was anchored to the wall. The Channel 10 news program was on, and the local TV journalist, Linda Cutter, wore a serious expression. Along the bottom of the screen, read *Breaking Report*. With trepidation, Tessa turned up the volume to listen to the morning's breaking news.

The camera cut to a handsome blonde reporter named Brad, standing in front of a wooded area outside the town's city limits. The cameraman zoomed behind the reporter toward the backdrop of the community's local lake which had bright yellow barricade tape reading *Police Line Do Not Cross* alongside a fishing boat and the shoreline. There were divers in wetsuits near the lake, and there seemed to be lots of bustling activity. There were several uniformed police officers, and a medical examiner's van had pulled up beside the organized, solemn scene. The camera panned back to the reporter as he interviewed two men who wore fishing gear and caps.

One of the fishermen identified as Sam Schmidt stated, "We just wanted to wet a line this morning. Finding a body in the lake was the last thing we expected."

The men went on to explain they'd been fishing at Crampton Lake, when Sam's fishing hook had caught on something heavy. Assuming it was a log or tree branch, the fisherman carefully reeled in the line, however it was not a log. He had reeled in a badly decomposed body. The fishermen's unblinking eyes and pallid faces indicated their shock. Clearly, they had gone through a traumatic experience.

Tessa felt her knees weaken, and she quickly sat on one of the chairs in the lobby feeling vibes of *déjà vu*. It had happened again. Her nightmare was coming true. The dream had been a terrible premonition, and she felt a knot in her stomach the size of a bowling ball. *Deep breaths*, she told herself, *deep breaths*.

She shakily made her way to the small nurse's station, feeling distressed. Minutes later, she listened to Angie speaking with a patient, who had a deep voice with a slow Oklahoma drawl, in the front of the office. Tessa tipped her insulated mug and swallowed the last drop of her coffee. Trying to be braver than she felt, she threw back her shoulders and decided to get on with her day.

The man who Angie spoke with was a patient from a few weeks earlier who asked if he could be worked into their morning's schedule. Angie asked the man if his insurance and address was the same as his previous visit, and he confirmed his personal information had not changed. Tessa had noticed earlier on the clinics schedule that the first patient had cancelled their appointment. She walked into the front office and told the man they could see him, and he scribbled his name on the patient sign in sheet. She noticed he was limping and appeared to be in pain, so Tessa asked him what had happened. She motioned him to a leather chair positioned by some medical instruments, so she could take his vital signs. He removed his jacket, so she could check his blood pressure.

He was a tall man with graying hair at his temples, and he sported a full gray mustache. As he took off his windbreaker-style jacket, she noticed large, capital letters reading MPD on the back. A gold badge was attached to his belt, and he also wore a shoulder harness with a revolver tucked inside. Realizing her patient was obviously a police detective with the Morrigan Police Department, she wondered if he was investigating the body discovered by the fishermen.

As she wrapped the blood pressure cuff around his upper left arm, he told Tessa, "I've had a clumsy morning. Hopefully, I haven't broken my ankle." He went on to tell her he'd tripped over a tree root in some woods. Hairs stood up on the back of her neck as she remembered the dark woods in the news report by Crampton Lake; the same woods she'd seen in her bad dream.

She glanced at his chart, reading his name was Craig Taylor, forty-one years old, and she noticed his blood pressure was elevated. Tessa continued taking the patient's vital signs and noted them in his chart. As quickly as possible, she excused herself and told him the doctor would be with him in a few moments.

Tessa knew his being there was no coincidence. Between her disturbing nightmare and Detective Taylor limping into the doctor's office, she had no doubt the woman with honey-blonde hair from her dream was the body found by the fishermen. She'd been forewarned, but she didn't know why. Feeling overwhelmed and desperate to do the right thing, she prayed for guidance to help the woman from the watery grave.

Somehow, she had to find a way to speak to the police, and not appear to be a demented lunatic. She wasn't sure how to share the information from her dream, and she didn't think she'd be taken seriously. Deciding to try gathering information about what had happened that morning in the small town's recent nefarious development, she knew she'd need to be careful lest she seem like a crazy woman.

She leaned into Dr. Redman's office doorway and told him his first patient was ready to be seen. Dr. Mark Redman was a pleasant man and a talented, caring doctor. He was fifty-five years old, tall and slim, with kind hazel eyes and had a thick shock of dark brown hair. He'd started his medical practice in Morrigan, Oklahoma almost twenty-five years prior. Rising from behind his desk, he smiled and made his way toward his first patient for the day.

Minutes later, Dr. Redman walked out of the exam room and asked Tessa to call the hospital for their patient and schedule an ultrasound on his ankle. The doctor suspected the injury was a bad sprain but wanted to verify that it wasn't anything more serious.

Detective Taylor wore a pained expression when Tessa strode into the exam room and handed him the appointment card with the orders to be taken to radiology. She tried to think of a way to approach him about the body found in Crampton Lake. She decided to be direct and nervously asked him if he was investigating the news report she had listened to earlier from the lobby's television.

He replied, "Yes, I am as a matter of fact. When the fishermen called the police station this morning, it was early. My partner and I responded and ended up hiking through the woods to get to the location. We couldn't see well in the dark. That's when I face-planted, tripped over a darn tree root and rolled my ankle." He caught himself before saying too much, "I can't talk about the case, of course."

"Oh, of course… I'm sorry if I seem nosy. Not trying to gossip or anything like that. I just wondered," Tessa stammered. "I heard the woman found might be a victim of a crime from the '90s. I heard something about a young woman who went missing years ago." She shrugged.

Well, that certainly got the detective's attention. With his baritone voice and slow drawl, he asked, "Why would you say the body is a woman, and that it was a crime from the '90s?" He stood up, leaned on the chair for support for his injured ankle, and looked at her with inquiring eyes.

"I think I heard about a case from a long time ago, from the late '80s or early '90s. Maybe I'm getting it mixed up with something else." Tessa stuttered, began feeling panic, and decided asking any questions of the detective about the case had been a bad idea.

She opened the door to leave the exam room as Angie walked by, and she told Tessa the next patient was ready to be seen. Tessa smiled at the detective and told him she hoped he felt better. As she walked to the lobby, he stared after her with his eyebrows pinched together. She had a feeling her discussion with Detective Taylor wasn't concluded, yet she had to find a way to get more information concerning the discovered body from the dark water. She quickly walked down the hallway before the detective could ask her anything else and opened the door to the front lobby. She called the first name of the next patient.

~~~~~~~~~~~~~~~~~~~~

Craig Taylor always trusted his gut, and his gut told him Tessa, the cute blue-eyed nurse, knew something significant about their investigation, yet he couldn't see how that was possible. She seemed extremely uncomfortable when she asked him about the newly developing case. *She was nervous as a long-tailed cat in a room full of rocking chairs,* he thought. They were in the early stages of the investigation, so the fact she'd referred to the body as being a woman when she had asked if he was working the case seemed odd. No one had been informed yet if the body was male or female.

What was that remark about her hearing of a woman being a victim from the '80s or '90s? If there is an old rumor or story from an unsolved local murder of a woman from decades ago, Jack and I need to find out what the story is about.

He shrugged his shoulders and limped out of the waiting room lobby to his work assigned silver Dodge Charger parked in front. He was relieved they'd been able to work him into their schedule, and Doc Redman had given him a prescription for the pain. Grateful that his left ankle was the one hurt, and not his right which he used to drive, he carefully pulled out of the parking lot and
~~~~~~~~~~~~~~~~~~~~

headed to the Morrigan Regional Hospital to have his swollen ankle scanned. It hurt like a beast.

He was anxious to get back to the crime scene even though he had confidence in his partner's abilities. Detective Jack Parker had been assigned to work with Craig almost a year ago, and he was impressed with the kid's work ethic. The young Jack Parker was only twenty-nine years old, but he had a level head and good instincts. The new detective was an asset to the Morrigan Police Department.

Working with Jack was also a pleasant change from his last partner, Ben Reed. Ben was demoted after his poor job evaluation, and Jack was quickly promoted. He had been a lousy detective, and even though he could never prove it, Craig suspected Ben was on the crooked side of the law. He was confident that his lazy ex-partner was involved in some shady deals.

When Craig passed the ex-detective in the hallways at the police station, he often caught Ben glaring at him. What he didn't know was that Ben Reed held Craig responsible for his demotion and vowed to get back at him. Ironically, Craig had not been the one who had reported the ex-detective. Instead, Police Lieutenant Darrell Johnson had been the one who had noticed Detective Reed signing into the Evidence Room, supposedly to check on an old case. Shortly afterwards, some drugs had gone missing, which resulted in a local drug dealer avoiding indictment. Suspicion of the drug theft as well as poor performance reviews and accusations of using excessive force were the reasons for Officer Reed's demotion. He'd been fortunate that he hadn't been fired. Rumor around the department was Lieutenant Johnson had shown last minute mercy for Ben because he'd been his coworker many years prior, before either of them had joined the police force.

~~~~~~~~~~~~~~~~~~~~

Staring out at the calm lake waters, Detective Jack Parker sighed and silently prayed for strength and knowledge. *Lord, please help us with this tragic case.* Witnessing the plastic-wrapped, deteriorated remains of the discovered corpse tugged on his heart. The skeletal remains had been someone's child, perhaps someone's spouse, and he silently prayed for the family of the victim. Clearly,
~~~~~~~~~~~~~~~~~~~~

the case was a homicide, and he suspected the body had been in the lake for many years.

The cruel, ruthless brutality of mankind never ceased to amaze him. Someone had gone to a lot of trouble to wrap and weight down the body. They probably never expected their crime to come to light, and Jack also felt badly for the two unfortunate fishermen who had come across the water-ravaged remains.

Stretching to his full six-feet four-inches, he looked upwards into the clear morning sky and gave another heavy sigh. Slowly making his way along the driftwood littered shoreline toward the moored fishing boat at the lakes small dock, he listened to the lapping water gently roll onto the beach. Anguished memories of his years in Afghanistan flashed through his mind. Jack had seen a lot of grim and appalling scenes as a Marine in the military. At the young age of eighteen, the freshly graduated young student had signed up to fight for his country. He was forced to grow up fast, and years later, the many horrifying memories from his days as a soldier continued to haunt him. The ringing of his cell phone in his jacket pocket shifted his thoughts from the decayed body and haunting military memories.

"Hey, Craig. How's the ankle? What did the doctor say?" Jack asked.

With his slow drawl, Craig answered. "Looks like I'm gonna live, and I was lucky to get into Doc Redman's office. Just left radiology, and fortunately, nothing is broken. I'm dropping by the pharmacy to get a prescription of Norco filled, and an ice pack. Then, I'll head out to the location. Are you still there? Thought I just heard crows hollering in the background."

Jack answered as he gazed into the bird-filled sky, "Yes, the blackbirds are cawing like crazy. I'm getting ready to head back to the office, so I can meet you there. The M.E. left with the *vic's* body about a half hour ago." He watched a black Dodge pickup truck with *Crime Scene Investigator* written on the back doors of the truck's camper shell. "The techs will be finished up soon, and there isn't much more we can do here."

"Did the M.E. volunteer any information about the body? Like if it's male or female? Or how long it had been in the water?" Craig asked.

"No, he didn't, but he said he should have a few details by tomorrow and will call us." Jack said, hoping they were informed soon.

"The nurse at Doc Redman's made a couple of odd comments, and I can't stop wondering what she was getting at. It's kind of nagging at me. She asked if I was working the case of the *woman* found at the lake, and she asked if it was from a crime from the '80s or '90s. I asked why she thought the body was a female, but she hem-hawed and avoided answering. I can't help but feel in my gut that maybe she's heard something regarding an old, unsolved crime. Worth checking out, and once we have a more definitive description from the M.E.'s office, we can search for missing persons matching the body."

"Yeah, I'm quite curious. By the way, Lieutenant Johnson wants to talk to us about another new case. Karla Rogers called in this morning and reported two of their show heifers were stolen from the Rogers Ranch. Those show cattle are expensive, worth tens of thousands a piece. That's the second report of stolen cattle in the last month in our area. Depending on what we find out tomorrow, he might hand off the case to someone else. I have a feeling this investigation will keep us busy." Jack hoped they weren't assigned the stolen cattle case. He preferred focusing solely on the homicide.

"Interesting. Well, Jack, my script is ready, so I'm heading to the PD now. Meet you back at the office, and in case I forget later, can you drop me off at my house after work? Just driving a few blocks has my leg screaming."

Jack answered, "Of course, I can, and we'll plan on riding together in the morning, as well. I'll even let you buy me breakfast."

Jack looked up to his partner, almost like the big brother he never had. Craig seemed to have an unusual instinct when it came to details. In the cases they'd investigated together in the last year, when he told Jack, "I've got a feeling…", Jack took notice. So, if there were an unsolved cold case of a woman missing, or murdered, he trusted Craig would lead them in the right direction.

Smiling, Jack thought how his partner had a unique voice, and he got quite a kick out of listening to him. His slow, deep drawl was a cross between the cartoon character, Eeyore, and Sam Elliott. Fortunately, with his full gray mustache, he looked more like the actor than Eeyore. Jack knew he had a lot to learn as a detective, and he was glad he had Craig as his mentor and friend.

Chapter Three

Contemplating her brother's incompetence, Selena Hayes slammed her car door in sheer exasperation. Matthew and Jeffrey were lucky they were her brothers, or she would have already cut them loose. She stood on the graveled overlook alongside the highway and gazed at the view with rolling hills and a breathtaking sunrise peeking over the thickly wooded bluff.

Closing her eyes, she listened to the symphony of cooing doves and early morning songbirds. She breathed deeply of the clean air of the Oklahoma countryside. Opening her eyes and appreciating the peaceful view, she came to a decision. Her brothers would be ordered to leave town immediately and lay low before they destroyed all she had accomplished with her organization. Their latest botched job involved their use of poor judgment when stealing unique cattle which would be risky to sell.

Walking back to the sapphire blue Mercedes-Benz convertible with purpose in her step, she climbed inside. The sporty roadster was new with a car dealership's paper tag bolted on the back bumper. Once settled on the plush, white leather seat, she pushed the start button on the console dash with a long red fingernail. The V8 turbo-engine roared to life. She swung the two-seater onto the entrance ramp and eased onto the highway. The roadster made heads turn, but Selena would have gotten second looks, even if she was driving a rusty old van.

She stood five-feet ten-inches tall, and wore her bleached, platinum hair severely slicked back in a long straight ponytail. Not many women could pull off the sleek hairstyle, but it accentuated her high cheekbones and delicate features. Gunmetal gray, Gucci framed designer sunglasses concealed her dark gray eyes. They were cunning eyes that could spot a weakness in someone with a mere glimpse.

Exiting off the highway and onto her street, Selena drove into her garage and closed the door behind her before stepping out of the Mercedes. She pressed the alarm code on the security keypad going into her house, and the door clicked open. Her red-soled Louboutin high heels barely made a sound as they gently tapped along the polished floor. Long legs wearing skinny jeans carried her into the ultra-modern house.

Twelve-foot ceilings and glassed-in walls with long windows revealed the waking city. Selena looked from the cityscape to her diamond-encrusted Versace watch and noted her brothers were late again. She sat down at her glass-topped desk and made herself comfortable on an armless, gray leather chair. From her burgundy Prada bag laying on the clear glass desktop, she looked inside.

Withdrawing her Walther PPK .380 pistol, she checked to make sure it was loaded and ready. She'd received the gun from her late father, and even though she could have carried a more modern gun, she preferred the old model. Her red-stained lips grimaced and became a sad, crooked smile as she fondly thought of her deceased father. He'd taught her all she knew about the business, and she hoped he approved of her efforts to keep the family business growing from wherever his afterlife might be.

Her doorbell rang, and she waited for Ivan to answer the classical chime, ringing from the front door. It rang again, and Selena stood, adjusted her short-waisted jacket and tucked the pistol into her pocket. The other jacket pocket held two bulky envelopes. Walking through the stark, white painted rooms with expensive abstract art gracing the walls, she glanced at the security monitor revealing the men standing outside. She tapped the monitor which unbolted the tall eight-foot door.

The oversized door silently glided open, and Jeffrey and Matthew Hayes sauntered into their sister's tastefully decorated, modern home. She didn't smile as she waved them inside to her front room toward an L-shaped couch. She asked them to sit down.

She faced them, perching herself on a tufted retro-style chair. Ivan Barnes, a bulky man with no neck, considered by some to be Selena's bodyguard, appeared in the hallway, standing nearby in case she needed him.

Jeffrey nervously asked his sister, "Got any coffee brewed, Sis? I could use some caffeine."

Her cold gray eyes bore into him, and she told her round-faced brother with his noticeable overbite, "There's no time for that, Jeff. You and Matthew need to get out of town right away. My little birdie at the MPD told me early this morning that your names have been mentioned lately. I've already arranged things with Jimmy in Dallas to keep you guys under the radar. There's no time to discuss it… just do it, and don't speed. Last thing I need is you guys getting pulled over for a speeding ticket and end up being arrested." Selena could tell her brothers weren't keen about her orders.

She handed them each an envelope filled with cash and told them to drive to Oklahoma City to trade out Matthew's truck with a friend of hers who had a car dealership. "Jimmy has a brand new, black Tahoe waiting for you guys. You royally messed up when you grabbed the cattle from the Roger's Ranch. Word has it someone spotted you guys in that area, and why in the world would you grab show cattle? You should know it's too risky to try and sell those kinds of cows. You've made several mistakes lately. As usual, you idiots get in a hurry."

Jeff blanched and responded, "I told Matt not to take the show cattle, but he doesn't listen to me. Because they were so gentle and could be led out of their pen like dogs, he thought it was funny… and easy to load them in the trailer."

Matthew frowned and defiantly grumbled, "Shut up, Norbert. Selena, I need to go back to Mineral Springs and pick up Brianna. Then, I can go to Dallas, but I need to take care of some things first."

"You aren't listening, Matt. You do *not* have time to go back and get your girlfriend. You'll barely have time to swap vehicles. The Chief of Police in Morrigan has someone ready to I.D. you guys. Your pickups tag number was reported."

~~~~~~~~~~~~~~~~~~~~

Even though he was used to his brother's jeering mockery, Jeffrey felt his anger burn when his arrogant, cruel brother called
~~~~~~~~~~~~~~~~~~~~

him *Norbert.* As children, both Selena and Matthew had shown him extreme malice and humiliation every opportunity they had. He was often the butt of their jokes. They would mercilessly tease him about his protruding front teeth. They had nicknamed him *Norbert* from the '97 cartoon character from *The Angry Beavers.* Selena and Matthew were closer in age and always treated him like the bothersome little brother, even as adults. A big part of him wanted to move far away from his mean-spirited siblings, but he'd never had the opportunity. *One of these days…* he thought.

~~~~~~~~~~~~~~~~~~

Selena's cell phone vibrated in her pocket, and she took the call. Her steely eyes hardened as she glared at her brothers and listened to the caller. They squirmed as they sat on the couch under her cold, penetrating stare.

Hanging up the call, she slowly said, "Change of plans. Give me back those envelopes." She motioned for Ivan Barnes, her devoted employee of ten years, to join them in the front room.

Jeffrey immediately pulled the envelope from his coat pocket and handed the envelope to her, but Matthew wouldn't give his to Selena.

As she glowered at her brother, she warned, "Matt, am I gonna have to take off my earrings?"
~~~~~~~~~~~~~~~~~~

Chapter Four

~ April 5, 2018 ~

Lying on the old, squeaky creeper, James Ryan noisily rolled out from under the 289 V8 engine of the nearly finished, restored 1965 Ford Mustang. Anxiously counting down the days until his daughter's twenty-sixth birthday, he and his wife, Carol, planned to unveil their surprise gift to their youngest daughter, Tessa.

The car had been painted a couple of weeks before at his high-school friend Walt's auto-body shop. A month ago, Tessa had unwittingly picked out the color, not realizing her parents planned on giving her the sports car. She thought she was choosing for her father, who often rebuilt and refurbished cars, so she inadvertently chose *candy-apple red* as her own car's shiny new color. The interior, with newly upholstered black leather seats, had been completed a month ago. James was happy with the improvements thus far on the little Ford.

Fortunately, there was only a small amount of rust on the body. The frame was straight, but the engine had needed totally rebuilt. He hoped the car lasted Tessa many years and was dependable as well as fun to drive. His hard-working girl deserved some fun in her life. She'd been dedicated to school and her career without allowing herself much entertainment.

As he rolled off the old creeper, he felt his complaining joints noisily balk, and he struggled to his feet. He thought he must have rust in his back and knees. Over forty years of laborious farm work and countless hours of being a wrench monkey, as he jokingly referred to himself, had taken a toll on his fifty-nine-year-old body.

Slowly stooping over and picking up the scattered tools, he wiped grease from the wrenches and placed them in an orderly fashion inside a rolling metal tool cabinet. After wiping his hands on a red shop towel, he hobbled to his workbench and used his bone-handled pocketknife to slice open the seals of the awaiting cardboard boxes holding the exhaust system. He knew Tessa wouldn't want anything too loud or noisy, but the new exhaust would make the Mustang hum. The three-chamber design would give the sporty car a throaty purr. With a foil wrapped antennae, his old Zenith transistor radio battled static while sitting in the windowsill, so James adjusted the tuner and began humming along to the crooning of George Strait singing *All My Ex's Live in Texas*. Like a kid on Christmas morning, he grinned and tore into the boxes.

James and Carol lived in Mineral Springs, almost thirty miles from Tessa. Her home base was now in Morrigan. The town of Mineral Springs was a small, bustling community, while Morrigan was over double the size of the neighboring town. They were located inside the northeastern corner of Oklahoma, near the Quapaw and Osage Native American Indian reservations. Nestled along the Neosho River, the area was considered to have been part of the Indian Territory.

With his Irish heritage, James had a dusting of freckles, gray streaked, wavy auburn hair and blue eyes, while his wife, Carol, had dark brown eyes and black hair, with a few recent, white strands framing her attractive face. Carol's ancestry came from the Quapaw Indian tribe. Tessa had inherited traits from both her parents. Her thick mane of long hair was dark, and she had James' bright blue eyes.

Thirty years ago, James and his wife were blessed with their first child, a son who they'd named Trevor. He had his mother's eyes and his father's dark auburn hair, and so did his younger sister, Trisha, who was born two years after Trevor. Their youngest offspring, Tessa, surprised them with an early arrival almost twenty-six years ago. James would never forget that cold, spring morning on the eighth day of April in 1992.

~~~~~~~~~~~~~~~~~~~~

~ April 8, 1992 ~

Strong, northern winds were howling that morning, and the low-hanging building clouds on the horizon were dark and ripe with oncoming spring showers. His mother-in-law, Lucille, showed up on his and Carol's doorstep, grinning from ear to ear. A gust of wind whipped her long silver braid around her slim frame, and she proclaimed, "This is the day Tessa Gail greets the world. She'll be a blessing to all who will know her."

He was used to Lucille's unusual announcements, which were always correct, so he immediately made sure Carol's small suitcase and a diaper bag, which his wife had already prepared for the hospital visit, were loaded in their Chevy Suburban. His wife, looking round and miserable, waddled into the kitchen where he and Lucille drank cups of strong black coffee. After hearing her mother's surprising prediction, she shook her head.

~~~~~~~~~~~~~~~~~~~~

"Mom, I'm sorry, but I think you might be wrong about this one. I know you've been extremely on target other times, but I feel fine. I've even been doing extra cleaning the last couple of days," commented Lucille's daughter, as she rested her arms on top of her enormous stomach.

Carol was skeptical of her mother's unanticipated prediction. She had felt energetic earlier that morning, although she hated to admit she was quite tired from all the extra cleaning and a moment of nausea had briefly nudged her as well. Her due date was over three weeks away, and there hadn't been any complications or signs of labor. There had been a few mild contractions, but she considered that normal. She rubbed her hard belly and flinched, feeling her little one apparently kicking her kidneys like they were soccer balls into the goalposts of her ribcage.

Lucille only smiled at her daughter's skepticism, and said, "I'll wake and dress Trevor and Trisha. We'll be waiting in the Suburban for you."

She walked to the young children's bedrooms and began hustling them to get dressed. Fifteen minutes later, Lucille pulled a package of powdered donuts from the pantry and poured milk into plastic cups with lids. She and the two children, who rubbed their sleepy eyes and yawned, walked to the gold-colored SUV parked in the driveway and climbed onto the backseat.

Carol watched her mother with arched eyebrows, shook her head and said, "My mother is losing her mind. For one thing, we don't know if this baby is a boy or girl, so it might be a James, Jr. instead of a Tessa. And, two, it'll probably be another month before it's born. And three…" Carol sucked in a deep breath. Surprise and pain clouded her brown eyes. Her stomach seemed to tense and clench, and she gazed at her husband looking extremely astonished.

Glancing down at the puddle on her kitchen floor, she moaned, "Oh no! James… um, my water just broke. This baby is an early bird. Get my bag, and let's get to the hospital!"

"We're way ahead of you. Bags and kids, and your mother, are loaded and ready to go."

Within minutes, the entire family was piled into the big Suburban rushing to the Morrigan Regional Hospital to celebrate the delivery of Tessa Gail Ryan. In the backseat, they all laughed when Lucille, aka Grandma Lucy, casually commented, "I told you so."

~~~~~~~~~~~~~~~~~~~~

~ April 8, 2018 ~

On Sunday afternoon, the eighth day of April, the Ryan family gathered to celebrate Tessa's birthday on their small family farm. Trevor and his wife, Kate, with their two young ones, Emily and Cooper, as well as Trisha with her husband, Caleb, and their little girl, Sophia, enjoyed each other's company. They dined on barbeque ribs and brisket, potato salad, and baked beans. A large decorated chocolate cake, with twenty-six pink candles, had been devoured. Tessa had excitedly opened presents from her family, and she mistakenly thought the party was winding down. James
~~~~~~~~~~~~~~~~~~~~

nonchalantly slipped outside to the garage built next to the farmhouse, and Carol asked for everyone's attention.

"Listen up, everyone! Tessa, we have one more gift for you, Daughter, but we need to go outside, so you can open it." Carol mischievously grinned at her youngest child, opened the back door, and everyone eagerly followed her outside.

The birthday girl was puzzled, although her family members were clued in on the big surprise. Following their mother, they heard the revving of an engine, and James proudly drove the shiny red 1965 Ford Mustang out of the double car garage. His face beamed at his twenty-six-year-old baby girl, and her blue eyes bulged with shock.

Shifting the gently rumbling V8 into neutral and setting the parking brake, the sporty car idled with a solid, humming rhythm. James got out and held the door open, motioning for Tessa to come toward her birthday present. With happy tears floating from her eyes, she ran to her father and wrapped her arms around him. After hugging her mother next, she laughingly looked at her siblings and their children and shook her head.

"You all knew, didn't you?" she teasingly accused, with her hands on her hips. Without waiting for an answer, she sprinted to the glossy red car and took her place behind the wheel. James gently shut the car door and walked to the passenger side.

"Let's go for a ride, Princess!" he happily said, and Tessa didn't need to be told twice.

"Put on your seatbelts!" ordered a smiling Carol.

Shifting into first gear, she slowly lifted her left foot off the clutch, and the sporty car unhurriedly purred down the winding driveway. Pulling onto the blacktop-road, Tessa picked up speed and shifted gears. She adoringly looked at her generous father.

With love shining bright in her eyes and a quivering voice, she said, "Dad, this is the best present anyone could ever ask for. I can't believe this is happening! You're the best father in the world."

She leaned her head out the open car window and began whooping and yelling. Enthusiastic happiness rolled off the birthday girl as she shifted into third gear.

"Watch your speedometer, Tess!" James suddenly wondered if he should have given his fearless daughter a four-cylinder car with less power, when the Mustang bolted forward, and his right hand automatically clutched the chrome door handle. Back at the farmhouse, her family watched and pointed, and roared laughing as they heard Tessa loudly whooping and hollering over the sound of the gently rumbling engine.

By the end of the evening, Tessa had given everyone rides up and down the blacktop road, and she even let Trevor have a turn driving the sporty little Ford. Before leaving her parent's home, Tessa swapped car keys with her father. Her old Chevy Malibu needed a lot of work, but James knew he could invest a few hundred dollars and labor and easily sell the car with a profit. He'd gifted it to her when she started nursing school several years ago. He'd been worried about its reliability the last couple of months, noticing a few clacks and screeches from the little car when Tessa would visit them on the farm. He thoroughly enjoyed taking vehicles that needed a mechanic's attention and giving the cars a second life. He'd earned a lot of money and saved many vehicles from the car crusher and salvage yards over the years with his hobby.

As the Ryan family members gathered their children and jackets, lots of hugs and love were shared among them. Tessa picked up her brother's two-year old son, Cooper, and her nephew gave her a tight embrace. She suddenly recalled the first time she saw her nephew several years ago. She flashed back to that intriguing day.

Trevor and his wife had announced the delivery of their newborn baby girl. Tessa had raced to the hospital to welcome her beautiful niece, Emily, to the family. As she sat with other family members in the hospital room admiring the new addition, Tessa looked at her brother and said, "Your next baby will be a little boy, and he'll have a head full of blonde hair." The random, yet profound thought and vision of a blonde baby boy, belonging to Trevor, had come to Tessa completely out of the blue.

There was an awkward silence as her brother and his wife glanced at each other. Her brother commented his wife had undergone a procedure after the baby's birth. She was unable to have any more children. Tessa shrugged and didn't say anything else. Yet, she knew in her heart she would one day have an adorable blonde nephew, and Trevor would have another child.

Two years after her prediction of a nephew, her brother and his first wife decided to divorce. Unfortunately, they had grown apart, and their marriage couldn't be saved. A few months later, her brother met a lovely blonde-haired girl named Kate. He remarried, and the following year a baby boy was born. The sweet bundle of joy, named Cooper, was very blonde, just as his Aunt Tessa knew he would be. He looked exactly as she had seen him in her mind three years before.

Smiling at the fond memory, she handed Cooper to his mother, and Tessa began loading her presents into the back seat of her new coupe. Her brother looked at her with curious eyes.

"So, what are you going to name this one? You named our old farm truck we drove to school Ernest, and you call my black and silver dually, Shamu." Trevor couldn't wait to hear what his baby sister had come up with this time.

"Oh, I already have it figured out. Her name is *Mabel*."

"Mabel? After my mother, your grandmother?" James chortled and slapped his knee.

Tessa calmly added, "Of course. Grandmother was a beautiful red-head, and this red beauty deserves an outstanding name. So, *Mabel* it is."

~~~~~~~~~~~~~~~~~~~~

She was an ugly crier. Blubbering happy tears, Tessa sat in her garage, in her car named Mabel and bawled with big, racking sobs. Clutching soggy tissues in her hands, she wiped her leaking eyes and searched in her purse for more Kleenex. Loudly blowing her nose and taking a deep breath, she looked upwards, and sighed a thankful prayer. She lovingly ran her hand along the custom designed, black leather seats, with the embossed Mustang Pony's loping across the plush upholstery. Wood grain and chrome accents graced the interior, and she was impressed with her father's hard work and talent of restoring the sporty car to its original beauty.

She smiled, looking forward to giving rides to her co-workers the next day in her new wheels. She'd already called her friends and arranged lunch plans to show them her treasured birthday gift from her generous parents. Tessa and her friends, Rachel and Kyra, were dubbed *The Three Amigas.* The trio had been lovingly named by her father, and the nickname had stuck.

Not wanting to leave the warm cocoon of the shiny red car, she wondered if it would be too weird if she slept there that night. She laughed at herself and inhaled another deep breath of the upholstery's new-car smell, then opened Mabel's door and walked inside her house.
~~~~~~~~~~~~~~~~~~~~

Chapter Five

After finishing her shift at the doctor's office late Monday afternoon, Tessa dropped by the *Biscuit Hill Diner*. The busy diner literally sat on top of a small hill and was well known in the area as having the best biscuits and homemade pies around. The menu had lots of homestyle dishes, and a busy clientele filled its red vinyl covered booths from the minute the diner opened at six o'clock in the morning until the *Closed* sign was hung on the front door at night. Tessa decided to order something to go, and the new salad with grilled chicken and steak on the menu seemed healthier than some of the other dishes. She had been trying to eat cleaner and healthier for the last year, which was difficult since her sweet tooth caused daily cravings for chocolate. She'd also been getting more exercise.

She'd started taking a class a few weeks ago with her friends, Rachel and Kyra. They'd talked her into joining them in a self-defense class. It had been Rachel's idea. The pretty dark-haired girl was the most athletic of the three friends, *The Three Amigas*, and she often encouraged Tessa and Kyra to join her running and going to the gym. At the time Rachel suggested taking the class, just spending time with her friends seemed like a good idea to Tessa. After a couple of classes, Tessa found she enjoyed the workouts, and she felt much healthier and even more confident.

While waiting for her salad to be prepared, she glanced around the quaint diner and noticed it seemed busier than normal. One of her father's friends, Walt Kramer, plopped himself on the barstool next to Tessa. With a big, toothy smile, he spun sideways on the barstool and asked her how she and her parents had been and began chatting.

"How's the Mustang running? Are you enjoying it?" he inquired of her new car.

"Walt, I absolutely love Mabel! You and Dad did such an amazing job restoring that car."

He grinned, and said, "Mabel, huh? It was a fun project. Hey, did you hear about Tommy and Sam's big catch at Crampton Lake last week? Sam said it scared the tar out of them." Walt had talked to his friends who were the fishermen from the tragic discovery from the lake waters.

"Yes, I saw the news report. Sounds like it was a terrible thing." Tessa hoped Walt had some information about the case that wasn't idle town gossip. "Do the police know who the victim is?"

"No," replied Walt, "but Sam told me the body had been wrapped in plastic and duct tape. Looked like it had been down there for a long time. There was a nylon rope wrapped around the body's feet that must have been tied to something heavy like a rock or concrete block. The rope must have come loose, and the body had risen towards the top of the water. At first, he thought he'd hooked a log, then seeing the muddy plastic floating towards him while reeling it in he thought it was garbage somebody had thrown in the lake. When it got closer to the boat, they realized it was a body… in very bad condition."

"So, do the police know if the body was a man or woman, adult or child?" Tessa asked.

"The police aren't saying right now, but Sam said he thought he saw a woman's shoe in one end of the plastic. Might have been a woman. There should be a news report soon with more information, I'd think." Walt seemed troubled and quietly asked, "Who would do such a thing? Wonder if whoever did it lives around here?"

The waitress handed Tessa a takeout container holding her salad. She paid for her dinner, but her appetite was gone. Thinking about the poor woman from the dark water and her bad dream a few nights before made her feel anxious. She told Walt, "I hope whoever the culprit is will be caught and punished soon. I'll be praying for the victim and the family."

She slowly walked out of the diner and made her way outside to Mabel. As she drove down the tree-lined street toward her bungalow-style home, she admired her neighbor's houses and meticulously tended lawns. Two years ago, she had bought her 1930's Craftsman style house, and the previous owners had done an outstanding job renovating and modernizing the house while retaining its original character. Tessa had added her own decorating touches to the home, making it her own.

She pulled into her long driveway that ran along the south side of the house. The garage had been added to the enclosed porch which ran off the kitchen. They had retained the Craftsman style of the house with the new garage's wood-stained doors. There were glass-paned windows on the upper part which matched the oak, wood-stained door on the front of the house. A long, veranda porch that ran the length of the front had four wide columns supporting the porch and a gabled roof. The previous owners had painted the house a woodsy light green and trimmed it in white.

They'd planted rosebushes underneath several of the windows. One of the rosebushes situated under the long window in Tessa's office, which had been the daughter's bedroom of the previous owners, now boasted gorgeous blossoms on a tall, luscious rosebush and trellis. Tessa smiled, remembering the story of the girl's protective parents. When the soon-to-be parents knew they were pregnant with a girl, they had planted the thorny bush in front of her long bedroom window to discourage her from slipping out the window in her teenage years. Tessa wondered if the parents had been wild teenagers. They'd picked the thorniest type they could find; a large hybrid named the Double Knockout with dark pink blooms. By the time the girl became a teenager, the blood-letting thorny rosebush had flourished to over eight feet high. When sitting at her desk, Tessa enjoyed gazing out the long window at the stunning, blossom covered trellis.

She decided she would eat later and placed her salad inside the refrigerator. Changing from her work scrubs into leggings and an OSU t-shirt from her nursing school days, she walked barefoot onto her front porch carrying a novel she'd been trying to finish for the last week. She settled onto the thick cushion on the seat of the hanging swing situated on the left side of the porch. The other side held two wicker chairs, with fern plants hanging over them from the porch's rafters. Swinging back and forth, listening to the swing creak, she tried to relax. She was quite tired from her lack of sleep the last few nights and the busy day at work. Thoughts of the woman found in Crampton Lake had kept her muscles tense for days. Tessa felt perplexed how to approach the police, about what she had seen in her dream.

Suddenly, she sat upright, alarmed and curious when she spotted three large dogs trotting on the sidewalk toward her house. They were beautiful, whitish-silver German shepherd dogs, and one looked a bit smaller than the other two. They looked healthy and well fed, so she knew they weren't strays. She hoped they returned to their home before the dog catcher spotted them and hauled them to the dog pound. They stopped at the end of the sidewalk leading to her house and looked at her. One of the larger dogs tipped its head sideways and seemed to smile.

Tessa laughed, and the dogs walked right onto her porch and sat at her feet. She loved animals, and she'd always had a way with them. She wasn't surprised that a dog would approach her, but three of them seeming to make themselves at home on her front porch was unusual since she didn't know the animals. All three had kind amber eyes and a gentle demeanor. She stroked their shiny silver heads and spoke to them as though they were old friends. After half an hour, the dogs rose to their feet and slowly moved off the porch. They began trotting down the sidewalk alongside the street, and she hoped they would be safe.

Her cell phone rang, and she saw the caller was Rachel. She answered her phone and told her friend about the unusual visit of the sociable dogs. Between her phone call and the silver shepherds visit on the porch, Tessa began to relax and feel more herself. After ending the phone call, she went inside and made her way to the kitchen, deciding to eat her healthy salad.

After reading her book for a while and her stomach being fed and content, Tessa started to doze off while sitting in her comfy chair. An hour later, she startled awake thinking she heard an odd noise. She wiped her chin of a bit of drool and placed her book on the end table by the dragonfly chair. Walking to her front door, she noticed through the windows the evening's darkness outside. She opened the door, and much to her surprise, the three silver dogs had returned. They lay in front of the door as though they were guarding it.

"Oh, my gosh! You guys are back… and you must have your humans worried. Who do y'all belong to? I'm worried you're going to end up in doggy jail." She spoke to them and petted their silky heads, noticing they didn't wear collars. She almost decided to give them something to eat. Tessa was a nurturer and healer by nature and enjoyed caring for others, but she decided they might not leave if she fed them. She thought they must belong to a neighbor who was probably worried about them and decided she would ask around the neighborhood the next day. She bid the dogs good night, yawned, and went back inside the house.

She got ready for bed and crawled beneath the thick covers. Not five minutes had passed before she had dropped off to sleep. Although she rested well for several hours, the nightmare returned.

Tossing and turning, she woke feeling terrified, and her whole body was trembling. Her eyes glanced at the glowing green numbers on her alarm clock. Once again, the time was four o'clock in the morning, and she had dreamed of the woman from the black water again. She grabbed her dream journal and, with shaking hands, began writing before the details of the dream faded. Although she hoped she would be able to forget the vivid, disturbing details at some point. The nightmare had been one of the worst night terrors she had ever experienced, and she had to keep reminding herself it was only a bad dream.

Not often, but sometimes, Tessa would experience in her dreams as though she were not herself, but instead she became the people she dreamed of. She would experience their feelings as though she were them. She seemed to look from their eyes, hear from their ears, and feel their emotions. She felt as though she were them and not herself at all. During her latest nightmare of the woman from the water, she had seen through the victim's eyes. This caused her to feel disoriented when she woke, and she had a hard time comprehending where she was. A minute had passed before she recognized she was in her own soft bed in her own home. Awakening from the terror of the dark dream, she touched the right side of her head expecting to find an injury.

She opened her dream journal and began sketching a picture of a car key. Remembering how the key was striped with red, white, and blue and had *Pinto* inscribed on the white stripe, she did her best to draw it as she'd seen the key in her dream. She remembered the blue key fob, and there was a silver letter "M" keychain attached as well. After sketching and writing the frightening details from her dream in the journal, she climbed out of bed. Her chest hurt. Standing under her showers hot, pulsating water, Tessa couldn't seem to get warm, and she shivered under the shower's steamy hot spray. She quietly sobbed and slid onto the white ceramic tiled floor of the shower and flashed back to being in the frigidly cold lake in her dream.

Tessa realized she now knew the victim's first name. In the horrifying dream, she heard the murderer's deep taunting voice. He called her Marcy. He told Marcy how he hated her, because she was blonde and reminded him of his wife. There was a loathing hostility in his raging face as he called her a gold digger. Tessa could hear through Marcy's ears and see through her eyes. She felt her fear and felt the brutal blow to Marcy's head. She referred to the malicious man as Daniel, and Marcy begged Daniel not to hurt her anymore. Instead, the vile man slapped her so hard, she fell to the frozen ground.

They were outside, surrounded by an inky, black night. She could see her breath fog in front of her from the cold night air. Marcy saw her attacker silhouetted by a campfire which was near the dark waters. Beer cans were tossed about, and she could feel the brutal temperature seep into her bones. Lying on the hard ground, Marcy looked up to see Daniel glaring down at her, and she felt terrified. He pulled her warm coat from her shoulders and threw it into the campfire. A shadowy figure of a man behind the flames seemed to be observing them. Daniel continued raging at her. As she stared at the silhouette of the man, she thought for a moment she was seeing double and felt confused. She wasn't sure if the blow to her head had caused her to see double, or perhaps there were a second man. That's when Tessa had noticed through Marcy's eyes, the man named Daniel was holding a ring of car keys in his hand. She kept seeing one of the keys that was painted red, white, and blue that said *Pinto.* He stuffed the car keys into his front jeans pocket as the campfire blazed brighter in the background, devouring her warm puffer coat. In minutes, the coat was burned, completely gone. Tessa felt thankful she hadn't seen or felt whatever had happened next to Marcy, but she remembered feeling the frigid lake water. There had seemed to be a heaviness pulling on her ankles and feet, and she had felt her body spiraling downward in the watery grave.

Shaking the terror from her mind, Tessa grabbed a soft bath towel, dried her long hair, and groaned. On the left side of her chest, she continued feeling a sharp ache and looked at her body in the mirror to see if she had a bruise. She wondered if Marcy had perhaps had a heart attack all those years ago. Feeling the warning signs of a migraine, she reached into her medicine cabinet. As she swallowed the prescription pill, she rubbed her aching right temple.

After dressing for work and drinking her morning caffeine, Tessa walked into her home office. Since she had some time before leaving for work, she sat at her antique rolltop desk and opened her laptop. Expecting to find news reports about the discovery of the body in Morrigan, she began typing, hoping to find information. Within a few minutes, there were several links on the screen. After looking through most of them, she was disappointed to find there were no new details other than those she had already heard from the TV news reports the last few days, as well as what Walt Kramer had informed her at the diner.

She decided to check for missing persons in Oklahoma with the first name of Marcy. Before long, she found and opened a news link reporting a missing woman named Marcy Phillips. The news article was dated the eleventh of April in 1992. The missing woman was from a small town near Tulsa. She was twenty-nine years old, single, and had been reported missing by her roommate, Sandra Dawson. The report stated Marcy had worked at Molly's Shamrock Pub which was located near a truck stop and a Peterbilt Truck dealership. The report said Marcy had locked up the bar at one o'clock Wednesday morning, the eighth of April 1992. She had phoned her roommate that she was on her way home, but she never came home and was never seen again. Her car had been found parked in the pub's parking lot the next day. Tessa felt overwhelmed after reading the news article, and she thought it was an odd coincidence that her birthday was the same day Marcy had gone missing twenty-six years ago, the eighth of April.

Noticing the time was getting late, she closed her laptop and gathered her purse and Mabel's keys. She walked through the kitchen and into the garage. As she'd been doing for two years since moving into her cottage home, she pressed the garage door opener, backed her car into the street, and glanced at the front of her house as she made sure the garage door closed behind her.

This was the first morning she had slammed on her brakes, however, and her mouth fell open when she saw the three silver dogs sitting on her front porch. She noticed all three of them seemed to be wearing grins. She had never seen dogs seem to smile like these three. They bounded off the porch and once again trotted down the street's sidewalk away from her. Tessa shook her head, started laughing, and shifted from reverse into first gear.

Even though she was tired from one of the worst nightmares she'd ever experienced, she felt her spirits lifting from the dog's comical antics. She thought they were like angels, helping her through difficult days, so from that point onward she called them the *Angel Dogs*. She looked up into the cloudless, blue spring sky and thanked God for blessing her with the funny, silver German shepherds.

Chapter Six

Tessa's work days during the rest of the week were busy with a steady flow of patients coming to see Dr. Redman. Since the nightmare when Tessa saw the woman, Marcy, being assaulted by the man named Daniel, her week had fortunately been rather uneventful. She was grateful for peaceful, dreamless nights and restful sleep.

The Angel Dogs were consistent with their visits guarding her front door at night and were gone early the next morning. She asked several neighbors if they owned German shepherds or were missing any. She checked with the dog pound, the veterinarian clinics, and newspapers, but no one had reported missing German shepherds. Oddly enough, none of her neighbors had even seen the beautiful dogs. She bought a box of dog treats and left three on the doorstep each night. Other than the treats, she didn't feed the dogs, yet they always seemed well nourished and cared for. She had no idea to whom they belonged, but she enjoyed their company and often sat outside petting them. They seemed to soothe her nerves and lift her spirits.

With no alarm to wake her Saturday morning, she slept in, felt refreshed, and she looked forward to a pleasant weekend. Making her bed, she remembered one of her mother's sayings when she was a child: *Messy bed, messy head*, and she smoothed out all the wrinkles of her bedspread. Thinking of her mother, she decided to drive to her parent's farm the next day.

Instead of coffee, she opted for a cup of hot, herbal lavender tea. She carried the cup of tea and her laptop to the black wrought iron table and chairs sitting on the open wood deck which was built off the enclosed back porch. There were dozens of colorful songbirds in her backyard. Many of them flitted through the trees along the back of her property's lot, singing and taking dips in the bird bath in the flower garden. She enjoyed the serenade of their bright, metallic chirps and whistles. Watching several red cardinals, she remembered her mother once telling her the red birds were symbols of loved ones visiting from heaven.

She sipped her lavender tea and checked her email and messages while listening to country tunes on a small radio which sat on a shelf next to her. As Blake Shelton crooned his song, *I'll Name the Dogs,* she tapped her foot in rhythm. After visiting online with some friends, she decided to check if there were a *Sandra Dawson* on Facebook. Tessa had been thinking of the roommate who had reported her missing friend, Marcy Phillips, back in 1992. She typed in the name and hit enter. Not surprising, there were over a dozen Sandra Dawson's, but only one caught her eye. She was listed as Sandra Dawson-O'Brien, from Tulsa, Oklahoma.

Looking further into the woman's page, she noted Sandra was married and worked as a restaurant manager according to her profile information. Guessing her age, Tessa thought the woman might be in her mid-fifties. In her profile photo, she had dark, auburn hair and was sitting at a white tablecloth-covered dining table with elegant china and fragile looking champagne flutes. She was dressed in a black, long sleeved dress and was smiling at whoever was taking the photo. Just as she was going to click on the photos on Sandra's page, she overheard men's voices near her garage and the gate which led to her backyard.

"Miss Ryan?" she heard a man's deep voice say. "Are you here, Miss Ryan? No one answered your front door, but we could hear your music back here. Are you in the backyard? Are you home?"

Totally startled, Tessa jumped from her perch, closed her laptop, and with bare feet, quickly scampered across the back deck to the wooden gate, where she had heard the man's voice. She wondered who was asking for her on a Saturday morning. Feeling slightly perturbed at having her peaceful morning interrupted, she was also curious. Maybe someone was inquiring about the German shepherds that she'd been asking about.

Opening the back gate, she was even more startled when she recognized one of the men was Detective Craig Taylor. The voice asking if she was home was not from him, but from his partner. The dark-haired man wore sunglasses and introduced himself as Detective Jack Parker.

Before he could introduce his partner, Tessa said, "Nice to meet you, Detective, and how are you feeling, Detective Taylor?"

She invited them both into her tranquil garden as bluish green dragonflies circled and danced around the trio. The detectives followed her onto the wooden deck and sat at the black wrought iron table. Tessa noticed Detective Taylor still sported a slight limp. Jason Aldean was singing *You Make It Easy* on her little radio, and she turned down the volume.

Detective Taylor seemed slightly uncomfortable as he said, "We're sorry to disturb you on your day off, Tessa, but we have some questions for you. I haven't been able to forget what you mentioned to me at Doc Redman's office. Do you mind if we ask how you seemed to know the body found last week was a female? You commented that the body was a woman, yet no one had been informed anything about the body at that time. The medical examiner hadn't even gotten back to the M.E.'s office when you made that comment. You also mentioned hearing about a woman being a victim from the 1990's. I can't help but feel that was more than just an offhand comment. Do you recall when you heard about a woman involved in a crime or disappearance from the '80s or '90s?"

"Of course, I don't mind answering any questions, but may I ask how you knew where I live?" Tessa felt nervous and hoped her words didn't reflect her uneasiness.

"Well, we are detectives, Tessa," Detective Parker said and took off his Ray Ban sunglasses. His brown eyes twinkled as he flashed her a dimpled smile, and Tessa's heart skipped a beat.

Flashbacks from watching the movie *Miss Congeniality* dozens of times with her sister, Trisha, when they were young girls splayed across her mind. Detective Parker had an uncanny resemblance to Benjamin Bratt's character in the movie, FBI Agent Eric Matthews. Feeling tongue-tied, she realized she was staring at him and hoped her cheeks weren't blushing too bright. She nervously coughed, and Detective Taylor rolled his eyes.

"Yes, you are, and I guess we don't exactly live in a huge metropolis," she replied. She turned toward Detective Taylor and hoped she wouldn't sound like an idiot. She silently prayed for the right words.

"When I mentioned I had heard of a similar situation about a woman being a victim of a crime, possibly in the 1990's, I had no sound knowledge if the body discovered from the lake was a woman. It was just a feeling I had. Was the body that was found… a woman who had been killed in the '90s?"

"Yes, the body was a female," answered the younger partner. "She hasn't been identified yet, but the medical examiner reported she was in her twenties and was Caucasian. She was around five-feet three-inches tall and had blonde hair. Does that sound familiar in any way to you?"

Tessa sighed and felt resigned to be totally honest with the detectives. She knew what she had to do and invited the men inside her house. She told them she had something she needed to show them. With widened eyes, the detectives anxiously followed her onto the back porch, then via the kitchen, and into the living room.

"Please wait here while I go to my bedroom to get it." Tessa twisted her hands together trying to stop their shaking as she picked up her dream journal, a spiral notebook with a purple cover. Anxiety clutched at her chest, squeezing her lungs. She had never shown it to anyone, and here she was… going to hand over her private dream journal to two men she barely knew. Yet, her instincts told her it was the right thing to do. She slowly walked back to the living room.

"Please have a seat," she said motioning them towards the brown leather sofa. She sat opposite them in a matching leather chair and continued to speak in a trembling voice. "What I'm holding is a journal… a dream journal."

Both detectives suddenly looked deflated and disappointed. They were clearly not expecting to hear about her dreams or a journal, but they politely listened to Tessa as she explained.

"All my life, I've had dreams that are unique… unconventional. I rarely even mention them to anyone, so my confiding to you both is a big deal to me. Please don't think I'm an insane lunatic, because I most definitely am not. Hours before the body was found by the fishermen, I had a horrible, frightening dream. I journaled it. Open it to the marked pages."

She handed the dream journal to them, and Detective Parker reached for it. She had a hard time releasing it from her shaking hands. They both tugged on the journal at the same time…Tessa not wanting to let it go. He opened the spiral notebook and began reading about the night terror when she'd first dreamed of Marcy

Phillips in the dark water. He held the journal, so his partner could also read it. They both looked stunned after reading the details she had written of both the first nightmare and the one where she sketched the car keys and heard the man named Daniel call his victim by the name of Marcy as he assaulted her.

They were speechless when Tessa commented, "Now, you see why I was hesitant in answering your questions and showing my dream journal. I haven't told anyone about this because I didn't think I'd be taken seriously."

"May we keep this, Tessa?" Detective Parker asked in a soft voice.

"No, because there are other dreams that I've journaled about which aren't relevant to your case, but I will be glad to make copies of the last two dreams for you. I have a copier in my office."

She stood up, reached for her journal, and walked through glass-paned French doors into her office located off the living room to make copies. Both detectives followed her. They seemed solemn and pensive as she asked, "Will this help you with the case? Does it get me into any kind of trouble? What happens next?"

"Are you aware or have any other knowledge that your dreams are connected with our case?" asked Detective Taylor. He seemed uncertain and skeptical. He wondered if she'd written in the journal after the body had been discovered instead of beforehand.

"Well, I did a little research of missing women in Oklahoma with the first name of Marcy from the 1990's. I found a news article about a Marcy Phillips who was reported missing by her roommate, Sandra Dawson, in 1992. Seems Marcy left her work at a bar called Molly's Shamrock Pub near Tulsa at one o'clock that morning after calling her roommate telling her she was on her way home. Only, she never made it home."

The detectives appeared bewildered, as they processed all that Tessa told them. They seemed appreciative and a bit unconvinced at the same time. She could tell Detective Taylor had strong reservations, yet she was quite relieved they had not laughed at her or thought she was deranged.

She handed the copied pages to Detective Parker. As her hand touched the young detective's hand, their eyes met. She wondered if she imagined the sympathy she saw in his eyes. The handsome man obviously shared Native American Indian heritage, just as she did, and his warm brown eyes felt comforting. She liked the way the tall detective carried himself.

"We'll be contacting you soon, Tessa. Thank you for your assistance. Personally, I feel like I'm in uncharted waters. I've never encountered a situation quite like this," Detective Taylor admitted. Both he and his partner handed her their business cards.

She escorted them back through the living room and toward the front door, wondering what kind of fallout was headed her way. She tried to appear calm on the outside, but inside, her emotions were bouncing all over. Clamoring thoughts ricocheted off each other leaving her completely unsettled.

Walking back outside to her laptop, she sat down feeling reflective and sipped her now cold lavender tea. She decided to continue her research on Sandra Dawson-O'Brien's Facebook page. She opened the laptop feeling determined to find more information. As she clicked on Sandra's photos, she noticed many of them seemed work related. Her profile photo and several others were taken inside a refined, stylish restaurant. Sandra was a tall woman, a bit plump, and had a kind smile.

Among her posted photos, there were also a few family photos that looked as though they'd been taken on a vacation. As Tessa clicked on a photo of Sandra standing by a man with dark brown hair peppered with gray, she choked on her lavender tea, gasped and jumped to her feet. It was him! The man in her dream named Daniel, and he had his arm draped around Sandra and was smiling. He was much older than the Daniel she'd seen in her dream, and he was much heavier with a large, paunch of a stomach. His face was fuller, and he had not aged gracefully. On the photo's description, Sandra had typed, "Me and my husband, Daniel."

"No, no, no, no!" Tessa cried out loud, as she backed away from the wrought iron table and laptop. She felt lightheaded, couldn't breathe, and she tore her gaze from the cold steel-blue eyes of the man in the photo. They were the same evil eyes she had seen in her dream. Stumbling into her house, she looked for her cell phone and the business cards of the detectives. Holding Detective Taylor's card in her shaking hand and her phone in the other, she sat on the sofa trying to digest what she had discovered. How was she to tell him? Her anxiety level was high.

She tried calling him, but the call went straight to his voicemail. She decided to try calling Detective Parker and tapped his number into her phone. She heard it ringing and realized she could also hear the phone's ringtone nearby. The melody was loud and sounded like her own phones Marimba ringtone. Realizing it was coming from her front porch, she opened the door to find Detective Parker standing there, looking at his phone in his hand, and then to her with his mouth hanging open and surprise written on his face.

"I didn't even have time to ring your doorbell. I… left my Ray Bans here," he said. His brown eyes were wide, and he asked if he could come inside.

"Yes, please do! I found something very upsetting on Sandra's Facebook page!" She was anxious to inform him of the photo she had seen of Daniel O'Brien, aka Marcy's murderer. "By the way, has anyone ever told you how much you look like Benjamin Bratt? I must have watched *Miss Congeniality* twenty times with my sister, but you've got cuter dimples than Agent Matthews."

Feeling extremely embarrassed and horrified, she felt her face flame, and she glanced away, muttering, "Oh Lord, did I just say that out loud? Um… My laptop is on the deck," Tessa hurried, almost running, to the back of the house and outside.

Detective Parker was shaking his head and grinning as he picked up his sunglasses from the coffee table where he'd left them earlier. He followed her to the backyard. She tapped the screen on the computer. Sandra's photo of her and her husband, Daniel, popped up. Tessa couldn't help but gasp again, as she looked at the killer's face.

"That's him!" she told the young detective. "He's a lot older, of course… twenty-six years older, in fact. But I have no doubt that it's him… the man I saw who hurt Marcy in my dream."

Detective Parker grimaced, "He looks like he fell out of an ugly tree and hit every branch on the way down." The detective seemed uncertain as he continued, "I'm not sure how we'd be able to present this in court, or even to the police chief for that matter. We need to investigate and gather evidence. Can we print this, so I can take it with me? Or maybe send the pic to my phone or Messenger?"

She carried her laptop back to her office where she printed copies of several of Sandra's Facebook photos. Then she noticed on her own Facebook page that she'd received a Friend Request. It was from a Jack Parker, and she recognized his smiling profile photo as Detective Parker. She smiled up at the handsome man who stood beside her. He flashed her another dimpled smile as he held his cell phone which he'd just used to send her the request. She tapped *Confirm*. She was now connected to the detective, in more ways than one. She also felt connected to him as they sought justice for Marcy and having her murderer held responsible for her brutal death.

Chapter Seven

The next day, Tessa made a visit to her parent's home. The drive took almost thirty minutes for her to reach the small farm. The weather was beautiful, and spring was in the air. Enjoying the pleasant ride with the windows rolled down, she turned up the red Mustang's radio and sang along with Chris Stapleton singing *Broken Halos*. Tessa loved to sing, but, as her father used to tease her, she couldn't carry a tune in a bucket. Singing off-key at the top of her lungs, she drove through the rolling Oklahoma hillside. Red bud trees were full blown; their lavender-pink blossoms stunning and bright. Luscious green wheat fields grew alongside the highway looking like gigantic, dark green shag carpets, and the bright, neon yellow canola fields looked magical. She loved this time of the year in Oklahoma when everything came in bloom.

Carol and James Ryan lived in the country on an eighty-acre spread, east of Mineral Springs, which was where Tessa and her siblings had grown up. The ranch-style home sat off a black-top road with a long, winding gravel driveway. Tessa pulled up beside her father's brown Ford pickup truck, shifted her car into neutral, and pulled on the parking brake. She lovingly looked upon her parent's one-story, white painted frame house with its black shutters and tidy yard. The grass was extra green from the spring shower with which they'd been blessed earlier that morning. Sweet smelling lilac bushes, dark purple irises, and pink tulips wore thriving blooms. She turned off the car's engine and walked up the red brick sidewalk to the front porch, carrying a round cake pan holding her contribution to their luncheon meal.

Before she could reach the handle on the exterior screen door, her smiling mother greeted her. Carol Ryan gently grabbed her beautiful daughter in a warm hug and ushered her inside as the screen door sprung back with a loud clack.

James greeted his youngest daughter with a quick hug, and she said, "Dad, I'm enjoying driving Mabel so much. Thank you again for the cool wheels."

"I can't believe a whole week has gone by since your birthday, Tessa," Carol commented.

"Well, you knew I'd be back for more of your home cooking, Mom." Tessa grinned, as she removed the chocolate torte loaded with sliced strawberries from the round cake pan.

"Daughter, your cooking beats mine. Look at that luscious goodness." Carol remarked, as she pulled whipped cream from the freezer to later top the dessert.

Tessa and her parents gathered around the table where her father said grace and thanked God for blessing their family. They enjoyed a wholesome meal of fried chicken, mashed potatoes, and buttery corn on the cob. As they finished the meal with the chocolate and strawberry torte, Carol looked at her daughter, squinted, and tipped her head to one side, studying her.

"Are you feeling troubled or overworked? You seem quiet, Daughter, and you've got dark circles under your eyes. Are you okay?" *How does my mother pick up on my vibes so easily?* Tessa wore a pink cotton blouse, and she felt her cheeks blush, suspecting they were the same shade of pink as her sleeveless top.

Tessa was always amazed when her mother seemed to sense her underlying emotions so well. Growing up, she could never hide anything from her, but she had learned to confide in her mother because of her strong maternal insight. They had a strong relationship where communication was seldom a problem. She wanted to talk to her mother about the murder case, but she held her tongue. Instead, she changed the subject and asked about her brother and sister and their families.

After dinner, she and her mother cleared the dishes from the old, pine wood dining table while her father went outside to the barn to work on his John Deere tractor. Rinsing the dishes and loading the dishwasher, Tessa decided to mention her dreams to her mother.

"Mom, you know I sometimes have dreams... vivid dreams, and I remember you telling me that Grandma Lucy used to have unusual dreams, too. Did Grandma ever talk to you about them?"

"Yes, sometimes, but she mostly kept them to herself. I remember when I was a little girl, I would hear her cry out in her sleep some nights. She would wake up scared and shaky. You remind me of your grandmother, Tessa."

They moved back to the dining room and sat at the pine table again, sipping on fresh glasses of iced tea. As they continued talking about her grandmother, Tessa wondered if she had inherited her gift - or curse - from her late Grandma Lucy. Considering her family roots, she decided to later research her family's genealogy.

Her mother told Tessa how she also had more than the average occurrences with hyper-sensitive intuition. Carol said to have unexpected thoughts pop into her mind for no apparent reason was not unusual for her, which would later prove to be significant.

"Just this morning, I had a lady call, asking if she could buy some eggs and drop by this morning to pick them up. I didn't know her... and had to give her directions to the farm three times before she got it," Carol stated. She and James owned fifteen laying hens which provided more fresh eggs than she and her husband needed, so she advertised in the *Mineral Springs Daily News*: *Fresh Eggs for Sale.*

Carol continued, "As soon as I hung up the phone with that lady, I suddenly pictured a red extended-cab Chevrolet pickup pulling into our driveway. Sure enough, when they came to buy the eggs, guess what they were driving? Yep, a red extended-cab Chevy truck. Tessa, I'm not sure why we seem to have extra sensitive antennas, but we do. I don't have the dreams like you and your grandmother had, but my intuition is almost always accurate."

The long talk with her mother lessened Tessa's worries and stress, but then she suddenly remembered a painful bad dream. She sighed as she recalled the summer of her ninth year.

~~~~~~~~~~~~~~~~~~

She had an adorable black and white paint pony named Dolly. One morning, young nine-year-old Tessa woke up in tears, mourning her little horse because she had dreamed Dolly had died.
~~~~~~~~~~~~~~~~~~

She went into the kitchen with red rimmed eyes, sat at the breakfast table, and her mother asked her what was wrong.

"I dreamed Dolly died!" and the waterworks started back. Tears streaming down her face, she told her parents about the awful dream she had.

Her mother tried reassuring her, "I'm sure Dolly is fine." Handing her a couple of red apples, Carol told her to go feed her pony.

As she traipsed outside toward the pasture where Dolly was kept, her feet felt heavy as lead. She dreaded checking on her little horse because in her gut she knew it was going to be bad. She spotted Dolly by the lean-to shed in the pasture. With fresh tears, she burst out crying and ran to her beloved horse lying in the grass.

Dolly's breathing was rapid, and her stomach was distended. Tessa could feel Dolly's pain as she hugged her neck and kissed the top of the black and white paint's head. She ran back to the house to tell her father and asked him what could be done to help her horse. She remembered her father had mentioned the day before that their veterinarian, a friend of their family, was in Colorado on vacation. Tessa felt panic that her bad dream was coming true.

After informing her father of Dolly's condition, he instructed her to go back to the horse and try to make her stand up. She wasn't to allow the little paint mare to lie down. She grabbed a halter and rope from the lean-to shed and ran back to her precious pony. Once the halter was on, she pulled and tugged on the rope, struggling to get the horse to her feet. Fifteen minutes later, she was slowly leading the pony to the backyard of the house where she could hear her father talking to someone on the phone. Tessa saw her father's concerned face as he stood in the kitchen near the open back door. He hung up the harvest-gold colored phone that was mounted to the kitchen wall and walked outside where Dolly was standing beside Tessa. In pain, Dolly stomped and pawed at the dirt with her right front hoof. Her father ran his hand over the little mare's back, trying to soothe her distress.

"Looks like she's got colic, Tess," he looked at his daughter, wearing her scuffed, worn out cowboy boots and cut-off jean shorts. Her long hair was in two braids reaching her waist, and big sorrowful blue eyes stared back at him. It killed him to see his little girl so frightened and forlorn.

"I just got off the phone with Vernon. He has some medicine he got at the Vet's from when his mule got sick with colic, and he's going to bring it to us." Vernon was their neighbor who lived on a neighboring farm half a mile west of them. Her father instructed her to walk Dolly, hopefully to give the pony relief, and not to let her lie down.

~~~~~~~~~~~~~~~~~~~~

Even with the medicine and Tessa and her father's diligent efforts of tending to and walking Dolly, her cherished paint pony passed away before nightfall. She remembered watching the magnificent sunset that evening. The sky looked like an elegant painting with coral, pink, and blue-violet clouds hovering over the bright, reddish-orange sun slowly dipping below the horizon.

Tessa stroked her mare's neck as she lay beside her in the backyard behind the white frame farmhouse. Dolly no longer struggled in pain, and that thought brought Tessa a little comfort. Her sad eyes were dry, completely cried out with no more tears falling. She looked at the setting sun and said a prayer for Dolly, asking God to take care of her precious friend.
~~~~~~~~~~~~~~~~~~~~

Chapter Eight

Genetics had always interested Tessa, so when she returned to her home after visiting her parents, she snagged her laptop from her oak desk and made her way to the brown leather sofa in her living room. She propped the laptop on the turquoise coffee table in front of the sofa to do some research. The painted coffee table brought out the turquoise blues and greens from the large area rug on which it sat. She discovered several DNA testing sites on the internet, and she decided on one and ordered a kit to be mailed to her house.

Thinking of her grandparents, Tessa wished her Grandma Lucy were still alive. She had so many questions about her strange ability to dream and predict, plus her intuitions seemed much stronger than most of the people she knew. She had never met her father's parents, but she'd studied their family photos. Her grandmother, Mabel, had been a lovely red-haired woman with blue eyes, and her dark-haired grandfather seemed to be gazing at his wife with adoration in the photographs. They had been killed in a car accident the year before she was born. Could she have inherited traits from them as well, traits that were related to her tenacious instincts and dream proficiency?

Tessa was not ashamed of her hyper-sensitivity, yet she felt extremely uncomfortable discussing her unusual ability with anyone. As a child, she felt like a freak among her friends and classmates. She rarely spoke of her dreams or extra-intuitive thoughts. She remembered being in first grade, and she told her fellow students about one of her dreams for Show-and-Tell. As she nervously stood in front of her class and shared a dream from the night before, her classmates only stared at her with expressions of boredom and disbelief. Embarrassed and mortified, she wanted the floor to swallow her up, away from their disinterested and doubtful faces. Tessa rarely shared her unusual premonitions and dreams of forewarnings after that unpleasant experience.

Besides the dreams and premonitions, Tessa would often have sudden thoughts that seemed to jump out of nowhere. She had come to trust those impromptu thoughts and ideas. They were more than instincts or intuition, and her friends called her empathic and psychic. She didn't put a label on herself, and she tried not to take herself too seriously.

Recently, one of her friends asked her to participate in a raffle to raise funds for an animal rescue organization, and she gladly bought a raffle ticket. Part of the fun was guessing the upcoming birthdate of her friend's horse. Her palomino mare's new foal was expected to be born that spring, and the participant who guessed closest to the birthdate of the foal would win a prize. Tessa didn't hesitate. She told her friend the first date that popped into her mind. The tenth of March was her guess, which was quite a bit earlier compared to the guesses of the other participants. A couple of weeks later, Tessa's friend notified her that the palomino foal had indeed been born on the tenth of March, and she had won a lovely prize of hand painted horseshoes which now adorned her back porch and patio.

Her cell phone rang interrupting her notions on genealogy and family, and she looked down at the phone to see Rachel was calling her. She expected the call was regarding their self-defense class.

"Hi, Rach!" and Tessa asked, "Ready for another class tomorrow night and learning more ninja moves?"

"Yes, I am!" She then asked her friend, "Tessa, have you heard much about that body pulled out of Crampton Lake? This whole thing alarms me."

"Why, Rachel? What all have you heard?" Tessa wondered if there had been new developments from the information that she had given the detectives. Other than Detectives Taylor and Parker, she had not told a soul about her nightmares of Marcy Phillips or her online research.

"I was listening to a bunch of people at the Biscuit Hill Diner, and everyone is wondering if the victim was killed by a local person. What if he or she still lives around here?" Rachel fretted. The worrisome case had her and most of the other local citizens on edge. Morrigan was normally a sleepy little town without a lot of crime.

Rachel went on to inform Tessa of the town's gossip and speculation of the murder case. Apparently, the medical examiner was going to be reporting his findings next week. There had been dental comparisons, DNA samples, and specimens sent to toxicology labs.

Rachel continued, "One lady at the diner said there was a positive identification of the body that'll be reported on Monday or Tuesday. Some are speculating the victim was that runaway girl, Jenny, from ten years ago who was rumored to be caught up in a cult of some kind. And, others are thinking it must be from an older crime because of the body's condition. Poor girl had been in the lake for years, according to the gossips."

"Hopefully, the case will be solved soon, and the woman and her family can finally have closure," commented Tessa.

The girls agreed to meet with their mutual friend, Kyra, early the next evening before their self-defense class. There was a popular coffee shop next door to the gym where the class was taught. Tessa was already looking forward to treating herself to a caramel latte at the Java Hut as they ended their call.

Thinking of treats, she grabbed three dog biscuits from the box on the kitchen counter which she'd recently bought and walked onto the front porch. As expected, the Angel Dogs were making themselves comfortable on some old cushions that Tessa had laid by the wicker chairs. She gave each of the shepherds a bone shaped treat and stroked their silky soft heads. "Good night, Angel Dogs," she said and made her way back inside to prepare for her own bedtime.

After soaking in the clawfoot bathtub for over twenty minutes, with water so hot she called her soaks "lobster baths", she slowly propelled herself over the deep tub's edge. Her Kindle tablet played Maren Morris singing *Mona Lisas and Mad Hatters,* and Tessa hummed along. She took time to apply a new cream she'd recently bought for under her eyes and hoped it would help with the dark circles on which her mother had commented. She lavished her hands and arms with thick peachy smelling lotion, enjoying the light, sweet fragrance.

Praying for a peaceful sleep, she made her way to her old bed. It was a four-poster antique bed from 1930, and there was a matching waterfall style dresser with a huge, rounded mirror. As she pulled back the thick covers and handmade quilt, her cell phone rang again. This time, Detective Parker was the caller. She hesitantly answered, “Hello,” and felt her heart flutter.

“Hi Tessa. It’s Jack.” She immediately noticed he didn’t say Detective Parker.

“Hey there, Jack. How was your weekend?”

“Well, it was productive, and I have some good news for you.” She held her breath, expecting his news pertained to the murder case. He continued, “We followed up on your dreams… your hunches, and you were absolutely right. We interviewed Sandra O’Brien about Marcy on the phone. Evidently, in 1992, they were best friends and roommates. Unfortunately, Sandra’s husband, Daniel, wasn’t home. Seems he’s an over the road truck driver and travels all over the country. He isn’t expected to be back in Oklahoma until tomorrow, but we had a very interesting and informative conversation with Mrs. O’Brien. I asked her if she’d ever noticed or had found keys to Marcy’s car, and she seemed surprised. She remembered what the keys looked like and described them exactly as you’d sketched, but she said they had never been located.”

“That’s interesting. I really believe Daniel held onto those car keys after murdering Marcy. When did Sandra and Daniel marry, did she say?” she asked.

“They were married in June of ‘92, only two months after Marcy went missing. Sandra and Daniel were dating at the time of her disappearance. Craig and I pulled the police report from 1992. The report specifically states the Pinto’s car keys could not be located, and there wasn’t an extra set of keys found, either. Daniel will be back in Oklahoma soon, and I look forward to interviewing him. Thank you again for loaning us your journal entries, Tessa.”

She held her breath, praying Daniel would confess, and the whole thing would be over soon. She’d continued feeling oppressed and worried, even though she tried not to be.

“Jack, will you call me once you’ve finished questioning him? I have a self-defense class tomorrow evening which I’ve been taking with my *amigas*, Rachel and Kyra. I should be home by eight o'clock." She couldn't help but feel nervous and cringed, wondering why she'd called her friends *amigas* to him. *He must think I'm one weird chick.*

Jack chuckled and promised to give her a call to inform her of the outcome of the interview. Then he hesitantly said, "I also wanted to tell you, and I know you'll be discreet. There was a missing person from Wichita, Kansas who fit the description of the body found in the lake, as well as a reported teen runaway from ten years ago. The M.E. has been working overtime trying to find a match and ID. Tessa, the dental records from the body of the victim matches the dental records for Marcy Phillips. The results confirm your visions in your nightmares. I can't explain how you were able to dream all that you did, especially the same morning she was discovered in the lake. You seem to have a gift, my friend. We had very few leads on the case until we talked with you. At this time, only Detective Taylor, Chief Mullins, and I know that you helped us."

She wasn't surprised to hear the body had been identified as Marcy, but she was relieved the detectives now had confirmation. Tessa was glad they were keeping her contribution to the case quiet. She worried how people would react if they knew about her knack as a kind of visionary, or whatever it was she had. She didn't know what to call it... a gift or a curse, and she was thankful the nightmares were rare. She'd experienced dark nightmares before, but never as dark as her recent dreams. Most of her premonition types of dreams weren't violent, nothing like the murderous dreams she had of Marcy and O'Brien.

"This is kind of shocking for our little town, and I've been hearing reports about stolen cattle. Dr. Redman was telling me there's been an increase in drug use and arrests, too." Tessa was concerned about their small community's recent crime escalation.

Jack responded, "It's been alarming, for sure. We've been putting in a lot of overtime at the PD. I just left a meeting where Chief Mullins and Lieutenant Johnson informed us to be more conscientious of our work hours for the PD's budgets sake. No worries though, we'll get to the bottom of everything and return our peaceful town to the way it was."

Tessa thought he sounded tired. She and Jack said their good nights, and she pressed her phone to end the call. Part of her felt relief that the murderer would be interviewed the next day, yet she also felt a strong, nagging instinctive fear. She was uneasy as she crawled into her soft bed, and she prayed for a good outcome of the detective's interview with the brutal Daniel. Little did she know, but she had good reasons to feel fear.

Chapter Nine

Arriving back at her house from a long work day, Tessa changed from her nursing scrubs to her new black leggings and pulled on a bright yellow tank top. She laced up her running shoes and grabbed an orange and gray Oklahoma State University sweatshirt for the chilly night temps after their class. She cheerfully headed to Java Hut to enjoy a latte and her friends' fun company. Afterward, they would amble to the gym next door for their self-defense class.

Settled into a half-circular shaped booth in the roasted-bean aroma-filled coffee shop, the three friends chatted about each of their week's events and enjoyed their delicious, caffeinated drinks. Tessa told them more about her Angel Dogs and how much she enjoyed their company. Kyra filled them in on her latest disaster of a date with a guy she met on another online dating site, which had not gone well. Kyra commented she thought the single life was going to remain her permanent status. Rachel showed off her new, short haircut which made her look years younger than her actual age. She also talked about her new job as a dental hygienist and reminded her friends they needed to make appointments soon to get their teeth cleaned.

In no time, their conversation steered to the town's unfolding murder case. Rachel mentioned she had watched a news report earlier, and the M.E.'s office and police chief had announced the murder victim had been identified as Marcy Phillips, age twenty-nine, and had been missing since 1992. Tessa expected one of her friends would speak of the case, and she listened to them speculate without offering anything to the conversation. She sipped on her creamy, caramel latte with her eyes cast downward and prayed the case was solved quickly.

Amped up on sugar and caffeine, they walked into the gym minutes later, where martial arts, kickboxing, and jiu-jitsu were taught, as well as the self-defense class. The girls watched a group of young kids as they were leaving the mats. The youngsters wore white, loose fitting pants and adorable, Karate *gi's* tops. Most of the kids wore yellow or white belts around their waists, indicating they were new students, and the two teenagers assisting the instructors wore purple belts.

The Three *Amigas* joined the five other women in the class. The group was small, yet diverse, with a variety of ages. The youngest girl was sixteen, and the oldest was sixty-five years old. They always managed to learn new techniques at each class and were supportive of each other. The instructor of the self-defense class called them the Lady Warriors. At exactly six o'clock, the man teaching them how to protect themselves sauntered into the gym and toward their group.

"Hello, Lady Warriors!" his voice boomed. Tony Andrews, standing six-feet two-inches tall, with muscles on top of muscles, smiled at his students. "Ready to get started?"

"Yes, sir!" they responded. All eight women stood up straight in a row, pulling their feet close together, crossing their arms and firmly grasping their left wrist with their right hand. They waited for Tony's instructions as he stood facing them with his absurdly broad shoulders.

"Ladies, you've learned the fundamentals, the basics, and now it's time to practice what you've learned. I want to introduce you to one of my best buddies while I was in the Marines. Please go easy on him. He's here to help with demonstrations and has agreed to let you all kick his tail… and I mean that literally." Tony made a sweeping gesture with his arm and looked to the doorway. "Welcome my best mate, Jack!"

Stumbling awkwardly towards the group, a tall man covered from head to toe in a cumbersome suit of guards and pads all over his body, waved with his gloved hand. He wore a black helmet with a protective mesh piece over the face.

"Hello, everyone!" he greeted the group.

She knew that deep voice. *No way!* Tessa thought to herself. *Is that Detective Jack Parker underneath all those pads?*

As Tony continued telling the group not to be bashful and not to be afraid to hit and kick his friend, she noticed Jack stood beside Tony much the same as the girls had been instructed to stand. Back straight, arms crossed in front, and feet together, but poor Jack had so much protective gear on, he couldn't quite get his feet together even though she could tell he was trying. Much to her horror, she giggled out loud. She felt her cheeks flush pink, and for the millionth time thought how she hated that she blushed so easily.

The rest of the night was a blur as they followed Tony's instructions. They practiced defensive moves on Jack, gouging at his eyes, twisting his fingers and thumbs, pushing pressure points, and kicking him in the groin. They were taught to use their arms and elbows to guard themselves, stomp on the hypothetical attacker's toes, feet and insteps. They learned how to twist themselves out of an attacker's embrace if he grabbed them from behind. They tried flipping Jack over their shoulders, but they weren't very successful with that move.

By seven-thirty, they were all exhausted, and poor Jack lay on the thick red mats, unable to move. Tony excused them for the night, and Kyra strolled over to Jack and offered him her hand. She seductively leaned down and reached out to the padded man, and he accepted her help to get to his feet. Tessa and Rachel glanced at each other.

They both recognized their friend's flirting voice as she said, "Come on, Marine… My name is Kyra." She flipped her blonde ponytail over her shoulder.

Jack seemed unaffected. He said, "If you're Kyra, then you must be Rachel." He smiled at Rachel, then he gave Tessa a big grin.

"Tessa told me she was attending the class with you two… her *amigas*." Both of her friends gave her surprised looks, and their mouths fell open.

"Can I speak to you privately, Tessa? After I get out of this ridiculous get up…," Jack asked.

"Sure, I just need to grab my gym bag." She waved goodbye to Kyra and Rachel and helped Jack shuffle toward the door. Her friends continued watching them leave together, completely confused by Jack's knowing Tessa. Their brunette friend had clearly been holding out on them.

Tessa hoped Jack was going to give her a good report of the interview with Daniel O'Brien. Her nerves were taut, and she was anxious to get Jack alone to find out everything that had happened.

A half hour later, Tessa and Jack were relaxing in her backyard on the deck lying on two outdoor chaise lounges. They were both physically wiped out from the class and workout. Sipping from a large glass of iced green tea, Tessa could sense Jack wasn't thrilled about informing her of the interview with the O'Briens earlier in the day.

"The citrus flavor really makes this tea amazing. Thanks, Tessa."

"Stop hedging, Jack, and tell me what happened. I take it the interview with the O'Briens did not go well." Discouragement tinged her voice.

"No, it was not as gratifying as we had hoped. Craig and I drove to their house and knocked on their door around nine o'clock this morning. They live in a very nice, expensive condo in a new residential area. I noticed the wife, Sandra, drives a new Lexus. Observing their apparent lifestyle, they live kind of lavishly. Either Sandra earns a lot of money as a restaurant manager, or truck drivers make some big bucks. We were able to interview her, but the husband, Daniel, had supposedly received orders from the trucking company he works for to pick up extra shipments. We called the trucking company and spoke with one of the dispatchers. Daniel had requested the extra orders, and now he won't be back to his house until tomorrow."

Jack looked aggravated and continued, "Craig spoke with Daniel's supervisor and told him to make sure and notify us as soon as O'Brien was scheduled to arrive at the trucking company's yard. He brings in the truck before taking his days off. We've decided to have officers waiting on him who will escort him back to the station. Maybe, he'll be more forthcoming being questioned there, but the good news is, we now have a matching description of the Pinto's car keys. After Sandra described Marcy's keys, we showed her your sketches and asked if they looked similar. She said they weren't similar. They were exact."

Tessa tried encouraging Jack and buoyed his spirits by the time he left an hour later. Their conversation had become lighthearted, and they both felt at ease.

She looked at his dark red, hooded sweatshirt with white OU letters emblazoned across the left shoulder. With a grimace, Tessa poked him in the side, and said, "What's with the Sooners sweatshirt, Jack? OSU rocks! Go Pokes!" She was referring to the state's universities rivalry between OU, Oklahoma University, and OSU, Oklahoma State University.

"Well, answer me this: Why did the Oklahoma State Cowboys football team cross the road?" asked Jack, and Tessa shrugged her shoulders. Grinning, he laughed and teased, "Because it was easier than crossing the goal line! Boomer Sooners!"

Tessa groaned at his corny joke and jab at OSU's football team and walked outside with him, onto her front porch and down the short sidewalk in front of her house. Jack assured her he'd let her know how the interrogation went the next day with Daniel O'Brien. He slowly backed his work vehicle, a silver Charger, out of her driveway and drove down the quiet tree-lined street.

Walking up the three steps to the porch, she noticed the Angel Dogs watching her. They were quietly, but observantly, sitting near the white wicker chairs. She wished she'd noticed them while Jack had been there, so he could see how sweet and beautiful they were. Thinking of the recipe she'd read earlier in Pinterest, she made a mental note of items she'd need to buy at the store. She knelt next to them and gave all three of the dog's big hugs around their necks and spoke softly to them.

"Sweet pups, I'm baking you some tasty treats tomorrow. Good night, precious Angels."

Chapter Ten

Sandra Dawson-O'Brien was trembling after the detectives left her home. Their questions of her missing roommate from 1992 left her feeling troubled and agitated. They were vague with their answers to her when she asked about the reopening of the cold case. She hoped there would soon be answers to her many questions of what had happened to her dearest friend all those years ago.

Reminiscing to the spring of '92, Sandra could almost see Marcy with her long curly blonde hair and bright green eyes. When Marcy didn't arrive home from work that fateful night, Sandra was frantic. Her best friend wasn't at all thoughtless or irresponsible. She would have called her if she didn't plan on coming home, and the fact she had called her when closing the bar, to say she was headed home to their townhouse after closing, made Sandra even more alarmed.

She remembered talking to Daniel on the phone around eight-thirty that same night. He had said he wasn't going to be able to make their date, because he'd had a flat tire on his rig. He said he was waiting on the side of the road for a guy from the truck stop to help him change the tire. She had told him not to worry about it. She would just watch TV until he was finished, and she mentioned her favorite show, *Roseanne*, would be on that night. She recalled him telling her that the service truck was pulling up behind his rig on the highway, and he had to hang up. She asked him to call her later, once the tire was fixed. Waiting up for both Marcy and Daniel, she had finally drifted off to sleep in the early hours of the morning.

Sandra remembered she hadn't awakened until almost noon the next day, and she'd hastened down the hallway to her roommate's bedroom to check on her. Knocking on Marcy's door, she heard nothing but quiet. She'd gently opened the door and peeked inside. Her bed, with its seafoam green, floral comforter, was still made, and she didn't see Marcy's purse or coat. Sandra had quickly opened the drapes and looked out the window. Usually, she could see Marcy's little blue car parked in one of the carports parking spaces in the back of their townhouse; however, the only car she'd seen was her own.

She had picked up the framed photo of her and Marcy from her friend's bedside table. Smiling at the memory of their fun trip to Puerto Vallarta, one of three different vacations they'd shared in Mexico, she'd ran her fingertips over the sombreros they wore in the photo and Marcy's broad smile. Rubbing pebbly goose bumps from her arms, Sandra had felt a dark foreboding gloom.

She'd looked for her new Motorola cellular phone. Flipping the little flap open that covered the buttons, she punched in the number to Molly's Shamrock Pub. No one answered, so she decided to drive to the pub and look around.

Sandra remembered she had called Daniel before leaving the townhouse, but he didn't answer. She'd quickly dressed, pulled on a heavy jacket and shoes, grabbed her purse and ran out the door. Arriving at the Pub fifteen minutes later, she had spotted Marcy's blue Pinto in the parking lot. No one appeared to be inside the car, so she parked beside it. At that moment, Sandra saw another vehicle. The car parked in front of the pub, and she realized it belonged to Molly Brennan, the owner of the bar. Molly waved to Sandra as she unlocked the front door of the pub and went inside. Sandra had returned the wave and decided to have a closer look at the blue Pinto.

The door was unlocked, and she'd leaned inside to look in the back seat. She thought it was odd that the car was so clean. Marcy didn't have a lot of faults but keeping her vehicle tidy was one of them. Her car tended to be on the messy side. Not that day, though… no, it was spotless and even smelled like strong cleaner had recently been used to wipe down the car's interior. Even the worn, carpeted floorboards had been vacuumed. She didn't see any car keys and suddenly felt baffled. *Where was Marcy?*

With growing concern, Sandra had nervously walked into the pub and saw Molly pulling receipts from the register.

"Hi, Sandra. Is Marcy with you?" Molly was used to seeing the friends together.

"No, and I can't find her. Have you spoken to Marcy today? She called me when she was leaving last night, but I haven't seen or heard from her since." Sandra's voice had risen an octave with her building apprehension.

~~~~~~~~~~~~~~~~~~

"I'll call Janice, the other bartender on duty last night," said Molly. She'd dialed numbers on the rotary phone calling her employee and spoke to the bartender, "What? You know that's against my rules. I'll speak to you about it later. Right now, we need to locate Marcy."

After her phone call, Molly had been angry that Janice had left early and left Marcy alone to close the bar. She never wanted an employee to go outside or leave the pub by themselves at night. Drumming her fingers on the bar's counter and in deep thought, Molly had then dialed another number. Her friend, Ben, worked at the police department. He had only been on the job a few months.

"Ben Reed," he had said, answering his phone. For the next five minutes, he spoke with his friend Molly from the Shamrock Pub and listened as she relayed her concerns about her missing bartender. He'd told her that he would drive to the pub immediately and get a statement from her and the worried roommate.

~~~~~~~~~~~~~~~~~~

The red Volvo semi-truck and its driver traveled southbound down Highway-75 toward Topeka, Kansas. The driver was in deep thought and popped three antacids in his mouth. His stomach was burning.

Remembering his conversation with his wife a couple of days ago, he had assumed that the police wanted to speak to her that following Monday morning regarding the missing items from her restaurant's storeroom which she'd complained about to him. Or, maybe it was something else related to her precious restaurant. Seems like that's all she cared about. He'd felt neglected by Sandra for years and resented the long hours she spent at her job. After his conversation with his wife, he'd decided to call dispatch and see if there was any freight he could pick up, so he could avoid going home until Tuesday. He didn't want to hear about Sandra's stinking restaurant, or hear her whine about the incompetent, ungrateful employees. He certainly did not want to be around any cops, so he'd decided to make sure he wasn't home when they got there.

Now, at midday that Monday, Daniel felt his blood boil as he hung up the call with Sandra. He'd been feeling good about the extra money he'd earned on the shipments he'd delivered that morning, but she was a killjoy, as usual. She was obviously very upset from the visit with the detectives. He almost choked on the Coca-Cola he was drinking when she mentioned her missing friend, Marcy. As Sandra informed him about the detectives coming to their house asking questions about Marcy, he felt the familiar, always simmering rage begin to spill over. He could literally feel his blood pressure rising as he squeezed the aluminum Coke can he held within his hairy fist. In frustration, he volleyed the crushed can which bounced off the dashboard back onto him, staining his red uniform shirt with dredges of Coke left in the bottom of the can. He cursed and spluttered.

How dare the cops go to my house, and how dare they get in my business! What did my swine of a wife tell them? Why are they asking about Marcy now? Dozens of questions bombarded his angry mind.

Daniel pulled into a rest area at the next exit and changed his shirt. His temper and anger were off the charts. He'd had a rough day. Earlier that morning, he'd gotten another disturbing phone call. His girlfriend, Cindy, from Florida was always on FaceBook and all kinds of social media; so was her father. Somehow, Cindy's protective father had discovered Daniel was married from reading his wife, Sandra's, FaceBook page. Apparently, the father had called his daughter and clued her in to Daniel's married status which resulted in a ferocious argument between him and the furious girlfriend. Daniel told her that there had to be a mistake; he wasn't married. Cindy hung up on him. Five minutes later, the angry father called Daniel. In no uncertain terms, he instructed Daniel to never darken his or his daughter's doorsteps again.

He'd been caught in his web of lies. Cindy would never forgive him. He didn't love her, so he didn't really care. She was one of several girlfriends, but having her father defend her and threaten Daniel was more than he could tolerate. As Cindy's livid father had ended the call, slamming the phone in his ear, Daniel began smacking himself in the head with his mobile phone. He was sitting in his truck's sleeper at the time, and with an enraged reflex, he threw the cell phone to the other end of the sleeper. *Crack!* Daniel's blood pressure rose higher when he saw his new flat-screen television which was bolted over his bunk had taken a direct hit and the phone was in pieces. His new Sony flat screen was ruined, and the expensive iPhone was damaged beyond repair.

Pulling out of the rest area, he cursed and pressed down on the gas pedal, angrily pushing the Volvo-semi down the highway. A mile down the road, he was suddenly forced to brake and downshift to a lower gear. He loudly yelled at the slower moving car in the lane in front of him.

"Get outta the way, four-wheeler! You freakin' idiot!" he bellowed and hissed.

He flipped the lever on the Jake-brake to one, and the engine brake noisily began slowing the rig. Creating even more noise, he pulled the cord on the air horn hanging on his left. The elderly couple, in the old four door sedan, became flustered and panic-stricken from the booming blare from the air horn that had been designed to sound like an oncoming train. The elderly man driving the rusty, four door sedan almost lost control of his vehicle as the Volvo moved dangerously close to the old car's back bumper. Swerving back and forth in both lanes, the poor man eventually pulled onto the shoulder of the highway and came to a screeching, sudden halt. Daniel found the old man's terror as hilarious. He roared with laughter, yanked up and down on the air horn again, and shifted gears propelling the rig faster down the highway. He was in his element bullying cars, and even other trucks on the road. He gave the term "Road Rage" a whole new meaning.

Chapter Eleven

Early Tuesday morning, Daniel called Randy, the dispatcher at Thomas Trucking, and told him he'd be dropping off his rig at the yard and going home for his days off. He estimated his time of arrival as nine o'clock, and the dispatcher informed their supervisor, Robert. The supervisor immediately called the Morrigan Police Department asking for Detective Taylor. He left a message on the detective's voicemail of the expected time of arrival for the truck driver.

~~~~~~~~~~~~~~~~~~~~

Right on schedule, Daniel swung the red Volvo truck onto the paved blacktop parking lot. The company truck drivers and owner-operators referred to the area as the yard. Once the rig was parked and the air brakes set, he opened the truck's driver-side door and climbed down, clutching his black duffle bag which held his dirty uniforms, travel toiletries, and porn magazines. As he sauntered to his ten-year-old Chevrolet Impala which he kept parked at the yard to get him back and forth from his home to work, he remembered he needed to pick up the Impala's keys that were kept inside the building. He also recalled an error he had made a few days before on his logs. Changing direction, he walked toward the entrance of the building, so he could ask one of the bookkeeping
~~~~~~~~~~~~~~~~~~~~

ladies about the mistake he'd made on his driver's log. He didn't want the twenty-dollar fine deducted from his paycheck. Daniel knew many thought he was cheap. He considered himself thrifty, even though he'd been accused of squeezing quarters so tight that the eagles screamed. The truth was he needed money for his extra-curricular activities.

Gloria, one of the accountants, informed Daniel the supervisor asked to see him in his office right away, so he hesitantly walked down the hallway and entered the opened door to his boss's office. Standing beside his angry looking supervisor, a uniformed police officer also awaited him. A second officer walked into the room directly behind Daniel and shut the door to the supervisor's office.

Whispering among themselves, the other employees in the trucking company were inquisitive of what was happening, yet they weren't surprised their co-worker was in trouble. They had seen Daniel's dark temper firsthand, and it wasn't pretty. He was not pleasant to be around, although he mistakenly thought he was well liked by everyone.

"What's going on, Robert?" Daniel asked his supervisor. He dropped his travel bag, glared at the officer, and crossed his hairy arms across his barrel chest.

"Daniel, these officers are going to take you to the police station to answer some of their questions." Robert informed the menacing looking employee. Daniel seemed annoyed and confused.

The officer informed him he was a person of interest in a case and guided him out the door, then led Daniel toward the driver's entrance. The other officer picked up the black duffel bag that Daniel had dropped to the floor.

"You've got some heavy uniforms in here, Daniel." Commented the officer carrying the black bag.

The three of them made their way outside to a waiting police cruiser. As the officer steered Daniel toward the back door of the car, he pressed his head down so he wouldn't hit the roof.

As he leaned into the backseat, Daniel asked him, "What the heck is going on here, Ben?" Daniel had known Officer Ben Reed for years. The officer had worked for the same trucking company in Topeka before joining the police force and had been Daniel's co-driver at one time.

"Don't say a word to them, Daniel. Not one word!" Ben muttered.

He quickly took his place behind the steering wheel of the police cruiser. The other officer, who Ben referred to as Officer Warren, climbed into the front passenger seat, and they drove to the police station with a fuming passenger, glowering daggers at them from the backseat. Daniel's eyes had darkened with rage, but he decided to take his old friend's advice and remained silent.

~~~~~~~~~~~~~~~~~~~

Looking through the two-way mirrored glass, Detective Taylor asked his partner, "How's our guest of honor doing? Man, that dude looks like ten miles of bad road."

Jack had been observing Daniel. The fifty-seven-year-old man sitting in the interrogation room looked older than his years. His craggy face, with its heavy jowls and large bulbous nose, had been expressionless during most of Jack's analyzing of him. He noticed two different times when the large man had glanced at the mirrored glass to the observation room with absolute fury and hatred. Jack wasn't sure he had ever seen such dark evil in anyone's eyes before. His pupils appeared almost dilated.

His brown hair was heavily sprinkled with gray, and he kept it cut short, almost military style. Brows that desperately needed trimmed pinched together over his steely dark-blue eyes which went almost black when glaring at the mirrored side of the two-way glass. He was a big man, weighing at least three-hundred pounds and had a large, spare tire looking stomach.

As Jack studied O'Brien, he remembered one of his Psychology courses where they discussed the Dark Triad which was in reference to personality traits of narcissism, Machiavellianism, and psychopathy. Research and many studies on individuals with the dark traits indicated they have no empathy for others. They're socially inept and often are inclined to commit crimes. They're known for their giant egos, and grandiose ideas. They have absolutely no conscience, and they'll often manipulate others to benefit themselves. They have zero remorse and totally disregard morality. When Jack looked at the truck driver, he saw the Dark Triad enshrouded around the sadistic man like a cloak of malevolent depravity.
~~~~~~~~~~~~~~~~~~~

Moments later, Detectives Taylor and Parker strolled into the interrogation room and seated themselves across from the menacing Daniel. After introducing themselves, Detective Taylor calmly lay two photos in front of their suspect on the metal table. They were both of Marcy. One of them was a photo of Marcy which had been taken a few days before she went missing. Her green eyes were bright as she laughed with her co-workers inside Molly's Shamrock Pub. She wore a dark green uniform top and high-waisted *Rocky Mountain* brand jeans. Her honey blonde hair was long, reaching well below her shoulders, with lighter blonde highlights streaking through her curls.

The second photo was taken with Sandra on one of their vacations in Mexico. The young girls wore sundresses and were smiling. They sat at a table on a white sandy beach near aqua blue waters, raising frosty glasses of piná-coladas topped with pineapple and tiny, decorative umbrellas. Floating in smooth waters behind the pretty girls were large cruise-liners loaded with tourists. Bright blue skies with puffy white cumulus clouds dotted the sky in the background.

Jack placed more photos on the table. The third photo was clear and high quality compared to the older photos, but this one showed no smiles. There was a grassy embankment, much different from the white sandy beach, and the nearby water was dark. There was a seventeen-foot aluminum boat with an outboard trolling motor with two, black cushioned swiveling fishing chairs bolted on the deck of the small vessel. It was the same boat on which the two fishermen sat when they came upon Marcy's body. The boat was shown moored to a small wooden deck situated over a shallow part of water near the edge of Crampton Lake. On the packed dirt embankment, a rolled up, muddied sheet of brittle plastic, wrapped with what was once silver-colored duct tape held the body of Marcy Phillips.

The fourth photo revealed the skeletal remains of Marcy. The decomposition of the body and the effects of the water had been harsh for the two and a half decades it had lain on the bottom of the lake. Her blouse was muddy and tattered, barely recognizable as being green, and her once stylish, expensive *Rocky Mountain* jeans only consisted of a waistband and strips of denim covering the front of her femur bones like a pair of grisly chaps.

Jack carefully watched Daniel's face as he was shown the photos. The monster tried concealing any expression, but his eyes told another story. Obviously, the first two photos of Marcy, in her days of youth and beauty, brought fury to the scowling man's eyes. Jack wondered why their suspect had such contempt for the girl. The other photos shown to him of the decomposed body lying beside the lake seemed to sober and calm Daniel. He tried to wear a blank expression, but his eyes became dark again.

Daniel looked up at the detectives with his beady eyes, and with a deep, gruff voice, he uttered one word, "Lawyer."

It was pretty much the reaction Jack had expected, and he and Craig stood to their feet. Jack spoke to Daniel, "Thanks for wrapping Marcy so well with the plastic, Danny. We found a lot of interesting evidence and DNA wrapped inside. Almost like you tied her up special to leave for us. Only thing missing was a big red bow."

When Jack called him *Danny*, the detectives saw an even more vile reflection simmer in Daniel's dark eyes. Jack surprised the scowling man when he pulled an evidence bag holding a set of keys from his jacket pocket. The young detective noisily dropped them onto the metal table, and the jangling clank of the keys pulled Daniel's attention from the photos of Marcy to the unique red, white, and blue striped key and blue key fob saying *Pinto* attached to a letter "M" keychain. His reptilian eyes squinted as he recognized the heavy key ring holding Marcy's car keys, the memento from his kill twenty-six years ago. His nostrils flared, and dark outrage ignited behind his squinting gaze.

Jack slightly bent over the table, leaned toward Daniel, and looked directly into the murderer's hooded eyes. He began reading the repulsive man his rights as a burly, uniformed officer walked into the room.

As Jack picked up the evidence bag holding the keys and placed them back into his pocket, he then gathered the photos of Marcy and said, "Do you understand your rights, Mr. O'Brien?"

Daniel glared at him and grunted.

Craig informed Daniel, "We found Marcy's car keys in your travel bag. Not very bright of you, Danny… to carry stolen car keys on you."

The Ford Pinto keys were discovered inside his black travel bag, along with a hidden cell phone tucked inside a false bottom of the luggage brought into the police station with him earlier. The damning evidence convinced the detectives they had their man. Daniel was now officially considered a suspect in the murder of Marcy Phillips and was under arrest.

The young officer hauled Daniel to his feet, pulled his meaty wrists behind his back and handcuffed him. Daniel stretched to his full six-feet three-inches with an intimidating stance. Craig and Jack ignored his aggressive posture and casually walked out of the interrogation room, leaving a seething Daniel being led away to be processed. The brawny, muscled officer steering him was not easily rattled. He'd purposely tightened the handcuffs on the offensive murder suspect, and none too gently pushed him through the interrogation room's doorway.

Chapter Twelve

On Tessa's lunch break, she multi-tasked eating a cup of blueberry yogurt and scanned through Sandra Dawson-O'Brien's social media. Clicking on the woman's Facebook page, she noticed there were several groups which Sandra had joined. Tessa also noticed that most of those groups had *Sociopath* and *Narcissist* within the group's titles. Tessa wondered if Sandra was studying personality disorders, or perhaps researching the negative effects after being exposed to a sociopath's behavior.

One of Sandra's groups, named *Recovering Survivors of Sociopaths*, seemed interesting to Tessa. The founder was a pretty lady named Karen from Seattle, with long thick hair and kind green eyes. There were tons of informative discussions and posts from the group's fifteen thousand members. Tessa noticed Karen, and other administrative members, would kindly offer encouragement and words of wisdom to the many members of the group. They would often refer to themselves as *their sisterhood* and *their tribe.*

Numerous posts written by the members, who shared their personal stories of pain and abuse made Tessa want to cry. Some had sad, dysfunctional childhoods with sociopath parents and siblings. There were posts about narcissistic co-workers, neighbors, friends, and spouses who made life difficult for all those around them. The toxic relationships resulted in devastation and horrific damage. Tessa could feel the victim's anger, hurt, and confusion written within their words. The replies to these posts, from other members of the group and its admins, were full of advice and supportive, loving comments. The tragic posts made Tessa feel heartbroken for the victims who had been abused, yet she also felt inspired from the empathy and support offered by others who had gone through similar experiences of being with a sociopath, and the survivors had lived to tell their tales.

There were many stories with online links, articles, and studies about personality disorders, especially narcissism and sociopathy. Reading some of the stories grabbed Tessa's attention further, and she observed a post shared with the group written by Sandra Dawson-O'Brien.

Sandra had written: "I can't get it out of my mind. A couple of weeks ago, my husband and I were driving down our street heading to one of our favorite restaurants for brunch. There's a lot of trees and a pretty park in our neighborhood, and cute little squirrels are always running around. When suddenly, we saw two little red squirrels in the middle of the street. One was lying there; evidently, it had been hit by a car and was dead. The other little squirrel was trying to get its mate to stand up and pull it out of the middle of the street. It broke my heart! Then, my cruel husband pointed to them and started roaring, laughing. He thought it was hilarious. I was absolutely mortified and started to cry. Is his reaction a typical response from a narcissist or sociopath? Honestly, I've often thought my husband has traits of a psychopath, but then, I question myself, and think I've overreacted, or maybe I'm imagining things."

There were a dozen replies directed to Sandra's post from others in the group. They were all nonjudgmental and offered encouragement, sharing their opinions and similar experiences from their own narcissistic relationships.

Tessa leaned back in her office chair with her heart pounding. She could visualize in her mind the cruelty from O'Brien and the poor squirrels. *Poor Sandra*, she thought. This wasn't the first time Tessa had felt sympathy for the auburn-haired woman.

She hoped to share the Facebook information with Jack later that day and wondered how the interview was going with the disgusting Daniel at the police station. She had received a text from Jack that morning saying Daniel had been picked up at the trucking company where he worked and was being hauled to the station for questioning.

Tessa checked her watch and saw it was time to get back to work. She logged off her Facebook account and felt preoccupied. She knew the suspect sitting at the MPD was a dangerous man, a psychopath with no soul. The man was a repugnant, heartless spawn of Satan, as far as she was concerned.

She felt irritable for the next hour, until she received a message from Jack. He asked if she'd like to have dinner that evening at a local Italian restaurant named *Marco's Italian Cuisine*, and she'd gladly accepted the invitation. Tessa felt grateful he had come into her life, although she wished the circumstances had been different. They both felt the strong chemistry attraction between them, and she looked forward to spending more time with the young detective.

Once she finished her shift and arrived home, she felt excited about her dinner date with Jack. After taking a shower but feeling a bit tired from her long workday, Tessa pulled a black and pink floral print dress from her walk-in closet and lay it on her bed. A wide black belt, and matching sandals with three-inch heels, completed the ensemble.

She had just finished dressing when she heard her doorbell ring. Expecting it was Jack, her fatigue was quickly forgotten. Tessa opened her front door, and she thought the young detective looked extra attractive. He wore pressed jeans and a white, long sleeve shirt. The white of the shirt contrasted nicely with his tan complexion and black hair.

He looked well put together, and Tessa was embarrassed when she realized she had spoken out loud, "My goodness... tall, dark, and handsome."

"Well, you clean up nicely, too, Tessa. You're beautiful." Gazing at her, he took in her long, loose dark curls reaching the middle of her back and the flowing dress she wore with its hemline striking just above her knees. Even with her three-inch heeled sandals, he stood half a foot taller than her. They made a striking looking couple.

Jack drove a new, dark blue pickup truck, with chrome accents that made it shine. He opened the passenger door for Tessa, and she told him "Nice ride!" as she climbed inside and settled onto the gray leather passenger seat. As they backed out of her driveway, she commented how she liked the backup camera feature.

"It's a great truck," he replied and smiled, "and the four-wheel drive came in handy in the February ice storm. Wish it had better gas mileage, but overall, I love it."

He had chosen *Marco's* to take Tessa for their dinner, because he'd remembered her mentioning how she loved pasta in one of their previous conversations.

"Oh, I love this place!" she exclaimed as they pulled into the restaurant's parking area. Jack was ever the gentleman, as he jumped out of the truck and opened Tessa's door.

"Thank you," she told him, "Chivalry is most refreshing. Gentlemen being mannerly isn't something I see a lot of these days."

"Well, my aunt raised me right," he said and continued speaking of his Aunt Elizabeth Parker who had raised Jack from the age of three. Obviously, he loved his aunt who was more like a mother to him.

Seated in a quiet corner of the restaurant, Tessa and Jack ordered their meals. She chose a linguine dish, and he ordered lasagna. She noticed how at ease she felt with Jack and asked him more about his Aunt Elizabeth.

He told Tessa, "My mother divorced my father right after my first birthday. Then, my father immediately vacated our lives and relinquished his parental rights. I was an only child, and my mother struggled taking care of me by herself. She made a lot of bad choices. Eventually, she was diagnosed as having bipolar disorder, but she tried self-medicating with alcohol and drugs instead of getting professional help. When she'd disappear with one of her loser boyfriends, she often left me with Aunt Elizabeth for weeks at a time." With a troubled expression, he commented, "Things went from bad to worse, and circumstances resulted in the necessity for my aunt to raise me, right after my third birthday."

The waitress arrived and placed their steaming meals on the table. After asking if they needed anything else, she left the handsome couple to enjoy their meals. Jack gently took Tessa's hand and bowed his head. With a gracious blessing spoken over their dinner, Jack also thanked God for blessing him by introducing Tessa to his life.

At the same time, they both said "Amen" and looked at each other with mutual appreciation.

"Dig in," Jack said and grinned at his date with his dimpled smile that Tessa loved.

After enjoying their meal and sharing small talk, Tessa told him, "At lunch today, I found some interesting information on Facebook about Sandra O'Brien. I'd like to share with you what I found."

"I'd love to tell you about the interview with Daniel from earlier at the PD, too, but I don't feel comfortable discussing it in this busy restaurant. Shall we finish discussing things at my place?"

Tessa nodded her head. She was curious about where Jack lived. He had seen her cottage home, and she was anxious to see his house and to learn more about the young detective.

As they arrived at his house, which looked more like a large, two-story log cabin, Jack took Tessa's hand and led her inside. The impressive home sat on an acreage a couple of miles on the northwest side of town. The night was too dark to see much outside, but as he unlocked and opened the front door, she was pleasantly surprised at the rustic, ranch style interior. Cedar log walls lined the entrance, and Jack dropped his truck keys in a wooden dish on a small table holding a stain glass lamp which gave the entranceway a warm, yellow glow.

"This is lovely, Jack!" She admired the large cabin's open design.

Along the far wall in the living area, a tall fireplace covered in large river rock was featured, flanked by two tall shelving units made from cedar wood. She could see into the kitchen with its terracotta tiled floors and dark green painted cabinets. The vaulted ceiling with its rustic log rafters gave an airy feel. A decorative staircase made of peeled logs and branches led upwards to an open loft area, built over the kitchen.

They sat on a black leather sofa with pillows in a Native Indian design of rich earthy red, green, and brown colors. Interesting paintings hung on the walls of Native American Indians sitting bareback on horses loping across prairie fields. Over the dining table, there was a large painting of the face of a buffalo, hanging on a log wall. She was impressed at how put together and neat his home was, and she told him so.

"It actually belongs to my Aunt Elizabeth," he informed her. "I had been renting an apartment in town when her health started failing about six months ago. When she told me that she was moving to an assisted living center, she asked that I move in and take care of the place." His aunt had generously signed over the house and property to her nephew whom she loved like a son.

Tessa had thought there was a woman's touch to the place, and she hoped to meet his loving Aunt Elizabeth someday. He asked Tessa if she would like something to drink, but she abstained.

"I'm too stuffed from dinner, but thank you," she faced him on the sofa and asked him to tell her about the interview from earlier that day.

"Daniel O'Brien is a slippery bugger, Tessa. He never admitted to knowing Marcy Phillips, and he immediately asked for a lawyer when Craig and I showed him pictures of Marcy. There were both before and after photos of her. The photos when she was alive and happy seemed to tick him off… like the fury from his eyes was intense. Then, when he looked at the crime scene photos of the body, he got calm. Anybody else who would look at horrific, gruesome photos of a decomposed body would be sickened, but not him. He's a cold-blooded murderer; I have no doubt."

"What's going to happen now, Jack? How long can they hold him in jail? My dreams won't exactly be considered eyewitness accounts according to a judge."

"No, but there's evidence still being processed from the body and crime scene. Even though it's been twenty-six years since he killed her, the M.E.s might be able to find something. Now, for some extra good news. When O'Brien was brought in for questioning, he was carrying his travel bag. Inside, we discovered there was a hidden compartment at the bottom of the luggage. He had two cell phones and a set of car keys tucked away. The car keys match the exact description of Marcy's Pinto car which, as you know, have been missing all these years. Evidently, the hidden cell phones were used to contact girlfriends and bookies. It's going to take a long time to put a case together, but I hope and pray he isn't released. We need to figure out why he wanted to kill Marcy. We know he had the opportunity and means, but we need to figure out his motive."

Jack had taken a photo of the Pinto's car keys and showed the photo to Tessa on his cell phone. "Does this set of keys look like what you saw in your dream? They definitely look like your sketch."

"Yes, those are the keys." She looked haunted for a moment and became quiet.

The possibility of the monster being released worried Tessa, and she immediately felt a shiver crawl up her spine. She suddenly felt the need to speak to his wife. Somehow, she felt O'Brien's spouse would be his Achilles' heel, and she couldn't ignore the worry and concern she'd been feeling for Sandra. Tessa told Jack of Sandra's Facebook post in the online support group for recovering victims and survivors of sociopath relationships. She pulled up the page on her cell phone and showed Jack the post Sandra had written describing Daniel's sick sense of humor. He read the post and became disgusted by the horrible man's behavior.

Glancing at the clock hanging on the cedar log wall, Tessa groaned. She told Jack she needed to go home and wished tomorrow wasn't a workday. They slowly rose to their feet from his couch, reluctant for the night to end. He pulled Tessa into a gentle embrace and softly kissed her. As she relished his strong arms around her, she smiled and pressed her face into his neck and breathed in his spicy, woodsy scent. *Everything about this man pleases me, even his musky cologne.*

They walked to the front door where he picked up the truck keys, and they headed back to her bungalow home in town. They were both rather quiet on the quick ride back to her house as they silently reflected on the O'Brien case. As she unlocked her home's front door, Jack told her how much he'd enjoyed their evening and hoped they could go out again sometime.

"Me too," Tessa told him. "I had a wonderful time, and Jack… I'm so impressed with you. I haven't had a lot of luck in the romance department. I don't know where this is headed, but I enjoyed spending time with you. I especially felt *connected* when you said grace over our meal. I'm glad you're a Christian."

He kissed her on the forehead and wished her a good night. She turned and walked inside her home. After a minute, she heard his truck back out of her driveway. Suddenly, she yanked the front door open looking worried. Glancing onto the front porch, she looked left, then right, and left again. She saw the three Angel Dogs stand up next to the wicker chairs. Relief flooded her, and she quickly rushed to them. Giving each of the silver dogs a big hug, she told them, "Good night Angels… I love you."

Chapter Thirteen

Sandra O'Brien sat on her white, overstuffed couch in a state of shock. She took a long sip of Chardonnay from the crystal wine glass she held. Her husband was being detained, arrested as a suspect in the murder of her best friend from twenty-six years ago. She was overwhelmed with grief since learning her roommate and best friend, Marcy, had been murdered and left at the bottom of a lake never expected to be found. Yet, she had been found… by two fishermen. If that wasn't bad enough in itself, she was doubly mortified the police suspected her husband, Daniel, was the one who had killed her. The whole scenario didn't make sense to Sandra, yet in her gut, she knew he was capable of murder. Her knight in shining armor, in April of 1992, had quickly turned into a jerk in tin foil within the first year of their marriage.

Sandra recalled an argument she'd had with her husband before he left on his last trip on the truck. She was used to walking on eggshells around him, but he'd been extra irritable the last few months. Anything she said or did seemed to set him off on a petulant tantrum. The smallest slights, even those only he perceived, would draw out the monster within him. Sandra loved to bake, and she'd handed him a Tupperware container holding two dozen freshly baked cookies.

"Here you go. Some chocolate chip cookies for the road." Her smile instantly faded when she saw the fury on his face.

"Chocolate chip? I asked for oatmeal raisin cookies. You can't get anything right!" Daniel spewed in his gravelly voice.

Sandra tried pacifying him, "Sorry, I thought you asked for chocolate chip. I'll bake oatmeal cookies when you get home."

His eyes darkened, piercing her with a look of disgust. She felt anxiety bubble and fizz in her throat. Daniel began raging and screaming profanities as Sandra quietly slipped into the kitchen. Trying not to make a peep, she felt her innards tremble. Hearing a loud crash and the front door slamming, she peeked into the dining area to see the cookies she'd baked with love strewn across the expensive oriental rug. Hurrying to the front door, she turned the deadbolt lock with shaking hands and heard her angry husband's car tires screech out of the driveway.

He was nothing like the man she first met. She remembered how kind and considerate Daniel had been to her after Marcy had gone missing. During the weeks following Marcy's disappearance, she had been inconsolable. He became the shoulder on which she could lean, and there had been dozens of times that she'd cried herself to sleep, being held by her considerate boyfriend. By June, the police, and everyone else for that matter, had given up hope that Marcy would be found, at least not found alive.

All signs pointed to foul play. The fact she'd called Sandra to say she was heading home after closing the bar and never showing up, plus her little Pinto car had been found with absolutely no fingerprints on or inside it. The car had been found unlocked, no keys, and in a pristinely clean condition in the pub's parking lot. There was no activity on her credit card or checking accounts. All the factors pointed to the probability Marcy was gone forever. Sandra had been crushed.

She closed her eyes and flashed back to her 1992 memories of Daniel packing away the photos of Marcy and herself from their vacations and fun times. The many framed photos had sat on tables, dressers, and the fireplace mantle. At that time, he told her to remove them was for the best, to help her heal from her grief, but she also remembered him looking at the photos with an angry scowl. She asked him several times why he was bothered by them, and as always, he had an answer for everything.

"It just makes me mad to know how your friend has hurt you by going missing. She's probably down in Mexico right now, living the good life and drinking margaritas." He made the situation sound as though everything was Marcy's fault.

Sandra knew her well. She felt more like a sister to her than a friend, and she knew there was no way Marcy would do that to her family. Marcy's mother and father were at their wits end and continued searching for their daughter.

~~~~~~~~~~~~~~~~~~~~

Sandra recoiled as her memories from the past haunted her. She pulled her white, fleece robe tighter around her generous form and decided to get dressed and check on the restaurant. Her assistant manager, Wanda, was a tremendous help, and she had encouraged Sandra to stay home for a few days since discovering her best friend had been murdered. Staying busy and keeping her mind occupied was more appealing to Sandra, so she sat down at her vanity to apply her makeup. Then, she would go check on the restaurant.

Looking into the lighted mirror, Sandra cringed at the dark, baggy circles under her sad, hazel-green eyes. She frowned at the image in the mirror. Sandra was extremely self-conscious of the ample freckles that speckled across her face and shoulders. She suddenly recalled how Daniel had told her the freckles were adorable in the first months of their relationship and marriage.

Several months after their wedding, he had started making negative comments about other women they would see in public who were freckled. She was devastated on one occasion when they'd been at a shopping mall, and a lovely red-haired girl with a light dusting of freckles on her milky white complexion walked by them. She was a pretty girl, but Daniel seemed repulsed, called her pasty-faced, and told Sandra what an ugly troll the girl looked like to him. From that day forward, Sandra wore heavy makeup to cover her freckles.

She suddenly felt tired, exhausted to the depths of her soul. Tears rolled down her face, and she decided to stay home after all. She walked into her kitchen and opened the refrigerator door. Finding comfort in the form of food had been Sandra's way to cope with the years of insecurities Daniel had planted in her mind. She had been conditioned to feel ugly, inadequate, and even repugnant for decades. He had manipulated and controlled her for so many years, she had begun to feel that she wanted to escape… forever. She
~~~~~~~~~~~~~~~~~~~~

pulled a quart container of strawberry ice cream from the freezer, got a spoon from the silverware drawer, and returned to her bed. As she polished off the ice cream, she thought she must be the most loathsome woman alive. The thought of suicide crept into her tired mind.

Dragging her lethargic body to her computer, she opened her Facebook page and clicked on her favorite group, *Recovering Survivors of Sociopaths*. Scrolling down the many posts from other members, Sandra read a woman's story which sounded much the same as hers. The woman spoke of a long, sordid marriage and how miserable she had become. She wrote how she was glad she had two children for which to care; otherwise, she would be tempted to end it all. The woman commented that having her family to consider, she would never harm herself, because she loved them too much.

There were many responses to the woman's sad post, but the response that caught Sandra's attention said: "I've considered suicide before, but then I realized if I did it, that makes my narcissistic sociopath the winner. He's been pushing me towards the edge for years. No, not today, Satan, not today."

For decades, Daniel had been pushing Sandra closer and closer to the edge. He was continually throwing raging fits, playing the poor victim in every scenario, and his years of tirades had taken a toll on her. She remembered the early days of their marriage when he went out of his way to be considerate and loving. According to articles and studies she'd recently read about narcissists and sociopaths, those early days of a relationship with personality disordered individuals are called the *Honeymoon Phase*. The narcissists use this phase to get their prey to trust them. They commence *love-bombing* their victims.

She remembered when Daniel had put her on the proverbial pedestal, making her feel like the most gorgeous woman alive. He made her crave him and want to spend every moment she could with him. She'd loved and trusted him with everything in her heart and soul. Looking back, she realized it was all a manipulative act on his part; it was only the typical disgusting behavior of a narcissist. None of his love was real because a narcissist cannot genuinely feel love. They simply are incapable of real love, but they're good at mimicking other's emotions.

Earlier in the Facebook group, she had read one of the founder's posts that made a lot of sense to her. Karen had written:

"Not all narcissists are sociopaths, but all sociopaths are narcissists." She comprehended there were different levels of the personality disorders; a wide spectrum of the abusers. Sandra knew her husband was worse than a narcissist or a sociopath. He had never been physically violent with her, but the emotional abuse she'd withstood made her feel battered.

Sandra felt as though blinders were falling from her eyes, and she could see clearly now. All the articles she had read and studied the last couple of months were making more sense to her. She profoundly believed her husband was a psychopath, with the ability to do harm to others without batting an eye. She had read numerous articles describing a psychopath, and all the pieces of the puzzle were starting to fit together giving her a clear picture of the truth.

Throughout their whole marriage, she had been in denial of the extent of his mental disorder. He had manipulated her into thinking she was the problem. Suddenly, memories of Daniel talking down to her, belittling her with his condescending tone and his cruel remarks came crashing down on her. She also now realized, he'd been making insidious comments for years that undermined her confidence and self-esteem. Sandra felt her heart racing, and she became angry. She was angry at him for the miserable, undeserved persecution and pain he'd inflicted, and she was angry with herself for believing all his lies and tolerating the many years of emotional abuse.

Years ago, she had figured out he had a problem telling the truth, that he loved to exaggerate, but now she realized the man was a pathological liar. As the informative articles stated, many people with these personality disorders are addicts. They can be addicted to drugs and alcohol, gambling, porn, and they were usually promiscuous serial cheaters.

She recalled the times she suspected he was being unfaithful to her, but he always covered his tracks. Being an over the road truck driver traveling all over the country, he was able to cheat and get away with his infidelities. There was one time he had tripped up, though. His mistake happened a little over ten years ago, and she had discovered he was having an affair.

She'd never forget that day. Daniel had been at the O'Hare airport in Chicago, waiting for his plane to depart. While sitting in the airport talking to a random stranger in the lounge, he had accidentally pocket dialed Sandra on his cell phone. Sandra answered her phone, not knowing he had unintentionally called her. Within a few seconds, she realized her husband was speaking with what sounded like an elderly lady at the airport. She overheard their conversation which completely befuddled her. Daniel told the lady that he was flying to New Jersey to check on his ailing father. That part of the conversation was true, but what he said next made her sink to her knees on the floor in shock. She listened as he told the lady that he planned on flying home to see his wife after checking on his father. The lady asked him where he lived, and Daniel nonchalantly told her that he and his wife lived in Georgia. He told the lady his *wife* was a branch manager of a bank.

Sandra was confused and dazed. Last time she looked at a map, Georgia was a long way from Oklahoma, and she managed a restaurant not a bank. Daniel continued stringing the lies along, as he told the lady in the airport that he and his *wife* had three teenage children, but Sandra was unable to have children. About that time, the phone line went dead. She was so angry that she tried calling him back, but evidently, he had shut off his phone, probably getting ready to board the plane.

Fuming, she had sat on the floor for a good ten minutes. To think her husband had such audacity to refer to someone else as his wife made her irate. She recalled how she'd decided to check his phone records to find out the identity of the bank manager *wife*.

Nausea had encumbered Sandra as she'd pulled out the last six months of phone statements from a file cabinet in their home office. Carrying a yellow highlighter pen, she took the statements to the dining room table and began searching for phone numbers with Georgia area codes. She discovered dozens of calls to two different Georgia numbers. After Sandra's scrutiny, Daniel's phone records had revealing, yellow highlighted lines on over half of his phone calls. Sandra also noticed the calls he had made to Georgia lasted longer than the calls he had made to her. The specific times the calls were made to one of the Georgia numbers were late in the evenings, much later than a bank's normal office hours. She'd been beyond angry as she looked at the phone numbers, which she had noted started five months earlier.

Even though she had believed their marriage was a decent one, albeit there were troublesome times like everyone seemed to have with marriage, she'd admitted to herself how she had been in total denial as she gazed at the yellow highlighted phone calls. Their marriage was a complete fraud, and she berated herself for not being a better wife. She remembered thinking, if only she'd been prettier, smarter, funnier, more talented, then perhaps her husband would not have strayed. She had placed the blame on herself.

Sandra continued recalling the painful memory and how she'd kept the knowledge of her husband's infidelity to herself. She'd felt shell-shocked by Daniel's betrayal and cried herself to sleep at nights. She had called both Georgia phone numbers. When she called the first number, she got a voicemail which said, "You've reached Melody Lambert at Georgia National Bank. Please leave a message, and I'll return your call. Have a lovely day."

Dialing the second phone number, which was the one she'd noted had been called late in the evenings, she held her breath. On the third ring, a woman's voice with a thick, syrupy sweet southern accent answered and breathlessly said, "Hello." Sandra had hung up the phone, once again sick at her stomach.

When Daniel had arrived home almost a week after his unbeknownst, inadvertent, pocket-dialed cell phone call to his wife, Sandra was waiting for him at the Tulsa International Airport. He seemed happy to see her as he stood on the sidewalk, waiting for her to pull the car to the curb to pick him up. As Sandra drove toward the smiling, big man standing on the sidewalk, she had fantasized about jumping the curb and running him over. With that satisfying mental image, she had slyly smiled at her cheating spouse as he opened the car door and sat inside.

He'd leaned toward his wife to kiss her, and she turned her face to avoid his cheating lips. She pulled into traffic and drove to their house, barely uttering a word. Daniel sensed his wife was upset, so he carried the conversation telling her about his father and his family in New Jersey. Sandra was surprised at her ability to remain so calm and seemingly composed as her deceptive husband rattled on about his trip.

Walking inside their house, he'd asked her what she'd prepared for dinner. He'd been looking forward to one of her delicious meals all day.

"Oh, I was thinking you might like to eat a little crow. Want some extra salt, to help it taste better?" and she'd flung the revealing, incriminating phone statements with their yellow highlighted Georgia numbers at him. "You always told me you would never cheat, but obviously you lied."

~~~~~~~~~~~~~~~~~~~~

Daniel had glanced at the phone statements, realizing he had underestimated his red-haired wife. He chided himself for his stupidity, knowing he had been sloppy with his deceptions. He'd make sure to buy a burner cell phone the next day to use when calling his girlfriends. He quickly decided to admit being a horrible man, and he'd beg his wife for forgiveness. He decided he'd play the role of the pathetic husband who had given in to temptations from a woman who had chased after him. He'd make Melody the bad guy. He had grown tired of the southern girl from Georgia anyways. Maybe he should end their relationship to give him more time to pursue his latest conquest. A girl in Texas was his most recent victim, whom he'd met at an Urgent Care clinic when he'd needed stitches for his hand after cutting it on a wooden packing crate that he'd unloaded earlier that workday.

Daniel had put his *pitiful mask* onto his monstrous, narcissistic face and looked at Sandra with sad eyes. He began telling her, he couldn't live without her. He even managed to squeeze some tears from his beady eyes as he begged Sandra's forgiveness. He told her he would attend marriage counseling or whatever she wanted, but he'd pleaded that she not give up on him… not to give up on them. What a performance!

~~~~~~~~~~~~~~~~~~~~

Of course, Sandra could only hear his pleading to give their marriage another chance. She had no idea the full scenario of deception within the man who she called *husband.*

After a couple of months of attempting to convince his wife that he had changed his deceiving ways, he became bored. The hearts and flowers and marriage counseling sessions came to a halt. Throughout the following ten years, Sandra and Daniel progressively grew apart. They were married in name only. She turned to her career to fulfill her hours, and he continued his cheating ways.

Unbeknownst to his wife, he also enjoyed gambling at casinos and volunteered going to Las Vegas every opportunity he found. There were perverted sex clubs in Vegas where he could unleash his deviant behavior. Over the years, after being confronted of his affair, he started staying away from his wife and home in Oklahoma. Being gone for weeks at a time, while on the road driving his truck, was not unusual. He had considered divorcing Sandra, but she earned a significant salary. There were times when his gambling cost him more than he earned, and he did not want to lose the security of his faithful, hardworking wife. He also thoroughly enjoyed playing mind games on his gullible spouse.

~~~~~~~~~~~~~~~~~~~

Sandra replayed the scenes of their near break up from ten years ago in her tired mind. She felt like an idiot for not divorcing him at that time, and she thought how she had wasted a huge chunk of her life on a repulsive, murdering psychopath. She crawled into her bed and pulled the covers over her head, wishing she could go back in time. She wished she had never met him. Maybe then, her best friend Marcy would still be alive. Trying to dull her pain, she decided she needed a drink. She rolled out of bed and staggered to the kitchen to open another bottle of wine.
~~~~~~~~~~~~~~~~~~~

Chapter Fourteen

The drive was over twenty-five miles from her home in Morrigan to the O'Brien's residence. Tessa had taken a vacation day from her job, so she could meet Sandra O'Brien.

Since her dinner with Jack, she could not stop worrying about the auburn-haired woman, and she was up much of the night concerned about her. She didn't inform Jack about what she was doing and hoped he would understand her need to check on the woman. Tessa could not shake the feeling that Sandra was in imminent danger. Times before, when she had ignored such instinctive urges, she had regretted them. She trusted her hunches and felt drawn to follow her intuition. The compelling need to check on Sandra O'Brien simply would not leave her mind.

She used her cell phone's GPS app and followed its directions to the address she had found for the O'Brien's condominium. Pulling into the driveway, she noticed a black Lexus parked in front of the garage. The condo was a rather new, three-story building with reddish colored brick. Large gray stones edged around the windows and corners of the building. There were six large condos attached to each other, and a beautiful, wooded park was across the tree-lined street. Each of the homes had a covered arched entranceway trimmed with the gray stone, and the landscaping was meticulous with green shrubbery, and yellow and purple pansies adorning large flowerpots. The traditional style looked elegant and modern with a black, iron filigreed fence and gate in front of the small front yard.

Tessa walked through the intricately scrolled iron gate up to the condo's dark walnut front door, which had an ornate door handle and knocker. She pushed the doorbell and heard the chime sound inside. No one answered, but Tessa could feel Sandra's presence. She rang the bell again, then loudly rapped with the knocker. As she was about to try the bell again, the tall door cracked open.

Bloodshot hazel eyes peeked around the edge. "Sandra?" asked Tessa.

"Yes, may I help you?" the lady asked, squinting her eyes as though the sunlight pained her. Her appearance concerned Tessa, and she tried to hide her shock. Sandra was unkempt, with what looked like several days-old mascara heavily smudged around her eyes. She wore a white, fluffy robe with pink stains all over its front. What astonished her the most was the slump of Sandra's shoulders. Pain seemed to envelope the woman, and Tessa sensed her spirit felt broken. Tessa introduced herself and asked if she could speak with her.

"Are you a reporter?" Sandra asked, with suspicion squinting from her red-rimmed eyes.

"No, but I am aware of your husband's situation. I have a… colleague at the police station in Morrigan," Tessa stammered. "I would sincerely appreciate a few minutes of your time."

At first Tessa thought she might have the door slammed in her face. Sandra's sad eyes studied her, but suddenly, the big door swung open for Tessa to enter. She followed Sandra inside, stepping onto dark marble flooring. In the front room, two large, white upholstered couches faced each other with a mahogany and glass table sitting in between them. A huge red, gray, and black oriental rug with tiny swirls of yellow and green in the print covered the floor of the room. The couches sat in front of an ornate fireplace with a dark marble hearth.

There were antique pieces of furniture throughout the refined living area. The room and the furnishings looked expensive, and Tessa had a difficult time picturing the ogre, the cruel monster Daniel O'Brien, living in such a lavish, elegant home.

"What can I do for you?" she asked, pulling her robe tighter around her. "I'm sorry for my appearance, but I'm not feeling well."

Tessa studied the despondent woman whose face seemed to be growing paler by the second; her dejected demeanor alarmed Tessa. Before seating herself on the other couch facing Sandra, she noticed a wine glass and two empty wine bottles sitting on the long cherrywood dining table next to the living room. There was also an empty bottle that read Royal Scotch laying on its side, and even the blue bottle looked pricey. She correctly deduced Sandra was not only depressed; she was hung over.

As she sat on the white couch, Tessa moved a large, red patterned pillow to sit more comfortably. Under the pillow, lay an orange plastic prescription bottle. Tessa immediately picked it up and read the label which indicated it held a script of Ambien. She checked to see if the pill bottle was empty, fearing Sandra had used the sleeping pills to make a fatal cocktail with the wine and whiskey.

"I didn't take them," muttered Sandra, "although earlier, the thought crossed my mind before you knocked on my front door. Please, don't lecture me." The auburn-haired woman looked even more despondent.

"We need to get you some help," Tessa quietly said. "I'm an RN. I work as a nurse in Morrigan. Please let me help you."

Sandra slowly began to sob. Tessa went to comfort her and put her arm around her trembling shoulders. She asked her if she had a therapist or a primary care physician who they could call.

"There is a counselor I've gone to before, but it's been a couple of months since I last saw her. Her name is Lily Mathis. I've got her number in my phone." Sandra was shaky as she stood and walked to an antique desk where her cell phone lay. "Honestly, I'm okay now. I was only considering taking the pills. Deep down, I know I don't want to die."

Tessa asked her to call the counselor, and Sandra grudgingly pressed the contact button on her phone. After Sandra spoke with Lily Mathis, she breathed a sigh of relief. She told Tessa that Lily could see her in a couple of hours.

"Okay, I'll go with you. I've got plenty of free time today, so why don't you take a shower and get dressed, and I'll wait for you here." Tessa suggested.

"Why would you do that? You don't even know me, so why would you go out of your way to befriend me like this? Why do you even care? Are you sure we haven't met before?" Sandra squinted her eyes, analyzing Tessa as she peppered her with questions, feeling uncertain; but she didn't feel so desperate with this young woman in her home. She didn't tell Tessa, but she had said a frantic prayer less than a minute before she heard Tessa's persistent knocks on her door. As she'd held the bottle of sleeping pills, she had prayed that God would send her a miracle.

While Sandra showered and freshened her appearance, Tessa picked up and placed the empty liquor bottles sitting on the dining table into the garbage recycling bin in the kitchen. She sat the empty wine glass on a white marble countertop by the sink. Dark mahogany cabinets lined the walls, and Tessa smiled when she looked up to see a large, sparkling crystal chandelier hanging from the ceiling. This kitchen was impressive and would have befitted a chef with its commercial grade appliances. It was very ornate yet also efficient. Seating herself on a thick window cushion in a bay window, she gazed outside at the back yard's manicured garden.

A few minutes later, Sandra emerged from her bedroom. "You're still here, and you aren't a figment of my imagination." She smiled and seemed relieved Tessa had not left.

"Can I fix you something to eat, Sandra? Maybe some toast or scrambled eggs?"

"I might have some toast… and coffee. Lots of black coffee." She started for the kitchen, and Tessa offered to fix her breakfast while she finished getting ready to go see her counselor. Sandra touched her still wet hair and thanked her. She made her way back to her bedroom suite.

Later, as they walked into her counselor's waiting room, Sandra looked like a new person. She wasn't as shaky and seemed revitalized. Lily graciously welcomed her client into her office, and Tessa made herself comfortable in a wing-backed chair in the lobby. Music was piped into the waiting area, and Tessa enjoyed listening to a duet sung by Reba McEntire and Lauren Daigle called *Back to God.*

With a relaxed sigh, she took her cell phone from her pocket and texted Jack: "I'm out and about today… running some interesting errands that I need to discuss with you later. Will you be available, or do you have plans for this evening?"

He replied to her text within minutes: "Sure… be glad to meet up with you later. How about six o'clock?" They agreed to meet at her house and grab a quick dinner afterwards.

She closed her eyes reflecting on her unusual morning. The last thing she expected when she arrived on Sandra's doorstep was the incident that had transpired. More than ever, she was glad she'd listened to her intuition and wondered if God had led her to help Sandra. One of Tessa's daily prayers was that God use her as His instrument to do His will and not her own. Going out of her way to help a stranger was not unusual for Tessa. When she felt compelled to do God's work, she listened. She thanked Him for blessing her and asked that Sandra's troubled spirit be healed.

Chapter Fifteen

Jack arrived at Tessa's house a few minutes before six o'clock. He was glad she'd messaged him and hoped to spend more time with the fascinating blue-eyed nurse. Besides being beautiful, he could sense she had a kind, compassionate heart, and he hoped to get to know her better. Taking in the quaint setting and neat front yard and flower garden of her home, he smiled. The girl obviously had a green thumb. The dark pink roses climbing the trellis over the south window alongside her driveway looked like something out of a *Better Home and Gardens* magazine.

~~~~~~~~~~~~~~~~~~~~

Carefully removing the last pan of dog treats from the oven, Tessa decided to let them cool before removing them from the baking sheet. She'd revised the *Pinterest* recipe for homemade dog biscuits, using peanut butter, oatmeal, milk, molasses, and crunched bacon. She placed her new bone shaped cookie cutter and rolling pin in the sink and took a deep breath. The kitchen smelled amazing, almost the same as when she baked peanut butter cookies for herself and friends. She couldn't wait to give the treats to the silver shepherds that night. Hearing her doorbell chime, she tossed potholders on the kitchen counter and hoped the guest ringing at her door was Jack.

~~~~~~~~~~~~~~~~~~~~

Minutes later, sitting on her brown leather sofa, they began sharing their day's interesting events. With relief, Jack informed her a judge had filed an order that would keep Daniel O'Brien in custody, while they gathered evidence to help the district attorney prepare prosecuting the suspect in an arraignment hearing where he would be formally charged.

"Well, I need to tell you about a visit I had with Sandra O'Brien today." She seemed a bit uneasy, and Jack wondered what she was talking about. "First, I need to explain how I've had Sandra on my mind nonstop, and this foreboding kind of worry wouldn't leave. I prayed about it, Jack. My instincts can lead me to do unexpected things sometimes, but I trust my intuition. So, I decided to drive to the O'Brien's house. I had no idea if Sandra was even home or if she'd slam the door in my face when I got there, but I knew I wouldn't be able to rest until I saw her with my own eyes. My gut told me she was in imminent danger."

Jack felt anger and concern stir within him. *Tessa is a smart girl. Why would she be so careless to go alone to the O'Brien's residence?* She went on to tell him about the dire circumstances she found upon arriving at the elegant condo, and the desperation the woman had been experiencing. Tessa told him everything, and she mentioned Sandra had shown her several photos of Marcy and had confided to Tessa about her fears and guilt.

~~~~~~~~~~~~~~~~~~

"She blames herself for Marcy's death. She kept saying how it was all her fault that Marcy was dead, because she'd allowed Daniel into her life." Tessa shook her head and gazed into Jack's brown eyes, hoping he wouldn't be upset that she had gone to see Sandra.

"Another thing that troubled me was how Sandra described her husband's reaction to the photos of her and Marcy. In the early days of their dating, Daniel would come to her and Marcy's house to pick her up for their dates. The first time he came inside her home, he walked to the fireplace mantle where a framed photo of the girls sat. He picked up the photo and became annoyed. He asked Sandra who the blonde was. She told him it was her best friend and roommate, and he made the remark that Sandra was more beautiful.
~~~~~~~~~~~~~~~~~~

"Sandra told me that she assumed he was only trying to flatter her, but she noticed at other times when they were together in the townhouse that he'd glare at the photos. There were a lot of them, too. Those girls were like sisters. Sandra told me how Daniel insisted all the photos be packed away right after they'd gotten married, and he had moved in with her. His behavior struck her as odd, and she asked him why he looked so mad when he looked at the photos. He gave her a lame excuse… said he suspected Marcy had moved to Mexico without notifying anyone. Sandra said he even told her to forget about Marcy and that she was probably sitting on a beach and drinking margaritas.

"Five years ago, Sandra bought the condo she now lives in, which has two identical master bedroom suites. They don't share a bedroom, and Sandra unpacked her beloved photos of her and Marcy. She has them all placed on a built-in shelving unit in her bedroom. I counted… there are ten of them."

Cringing, Tessa noted the flickering anger spark in Jack's eyes.

~~~~~~~~~~~~~~~~~~~

Jack absorbed all Tessa had just told him, and replied, "Tessa, I wish you would have asked me about going to the O'Brien's house. Until we complete the investigation, we don't know the extent of the danger of these people. I'm sure you have excellent instincts, but I worry about you. Luckily, I don't think your visit there hurt the case, but what if you had come across evidence that could have been compromised? What if that ruined evidence had resulted in that murdering monster being released and free to kill again? We can't be too careful. Next time your instincts can potentially damage my investigation, let me know first."

Jack felt conflicted. He was glad Tessa had helped Sandra O'Brien, but she could have put herself in danger or hurt their case against the murderer. He saw the distress on Tessa's face from the tone of voice he'd used, so he tried to take some of the sting out of his words.

"Tessa, what you've just told me about Daniel's hostility about those photos and his reactions to the ones we showed him in the interrogation room make me question why he seems to have such an aversion to Marcy. So, he and Sandra have separate bedrooms?"
~~~~~~~~~~~~~~~~~~~

~~~~~~~~~~~~~~~~~~~~

Tessa had been afraid Jack would be upset. She didn't mean to step on his or the MPD's toes by going to check on Sandra. She hadn't considered the possibility that she might have endangered the investigation, and she suddenly realized the outcome of the visit could have been devastating for the case against O'Brien. Looking distraught, she answered his question.

"No, and Sandra told me they had grown apart since she discovered he had an affair ten years ago. Jack, do you remember me telling you that in the second dream I had of him and Marcy, he told her she reminded him of his wife? When I asked Sandra about her husband's first marriage, she was surprised and told me he had never been married before. That puzzles me, because in my bad dream, Daniel looked furious at the mere mention of his blonde wife."

~~~~~~~~~~~~~~~~~~~~

Jack shook his head trying to make sense of it all. His stomach growled. Thinking how he was starving, he told her, "Let's grab a bite at Sonny's Drive-In. I'm craving a cheeseburger."

Jack stood up, offered Tessa his hand, and gently pulled her from the couch. He wrapped his strong arms around her and inhaled the sweet scent from her hair. He thought, *I should be more upset with her for going to the O'Briens alone, but how can I be? She's so beautiful, and her intentions to help Sandra were honorable.* Looking down at her sparkling blue eyes, he leaned down and touched his lips to hers. The kiss was deeply moving, and their chemistry sparked like fireworks on the fourth of July.

"I need to grab my purse and put some shoes on. I'll just be a minute. Do you mind closing and locking my back door? I left it open to air the kitchen. Be right back." Tessa made her way to her bedroom.

On his way back to the front room after locking the kitchen door, his stomach growled again. Noticing the cookie sheet filled with what he assumed were peanut butter cookies from the kitchen's aroma, he decided to give one a try. Just as Tessa walked into the front room, Jack walked out of the kitchen, taking a big bite of the treat.

"Oh Jack, no! Those aren't people cookies." Tessa tried to warn him, but she wasn't in time.

His smiling face quickly appeared confused as he slowly chewed the large bite of the dog treat. With effort, he swallowed, choked, and told her, "Um, Tess, I think you forgot the sugar in your batch of cookies you just baked. Did you use parsley in your recipe?"

She couldn't stop her giggle and led him back into the kitchen.

"So, Detective, take a closer look at the treats for a clue and tell me what you deduce. By the way, parsley is healthy, packed with vitamins."

"Ugh… they're shaped like bones. Dog biscuits, right? For your Angel Dogs?" he groaned. "Some detective I am."

As Tessa looked at the half-eaten dog treat sitting on the counter, she grinned and asked, "Want to save the rest for later?"

~~~~~~~~~~~~~~~~~~

Parked in front of Sonny's Drive-in, they ordered their burgers, then drove to a public park a few blocks away. They carried their burgers and drinks to a concrete picnic table and sat down as a half dozen runners jogged around the park. There was a strong, deeply alluring attraction between Jack and Tessa. Like magnets, they inched closer to each other on the concrete bench, drawn together until their shoulders bumped into each other.

As she sipped her cherry limeade, she asked Jack if he was sure there weren't any records of a first marriage of Daniel O'Brien. He shook his head and replied, "No, there aren't any records of a previous marriage. I checked myself. I just had an idea, though."

He told Tessa about a young officer at the police station, named Tiffany Connors, who had a petite frame and blonde hair. He hoped they could convince her to help them in the next interview with Daniel. A plan started forming in his mind. He needed to talk to the chief and Craig.

They said grace over their burgers, finished their meals, and drove back to Tessa's home. He walked her to her front door and told her he'd let her know how the interview went the following day. He kissed her again and was grinning all the way back to his car. There was an endearing quality to his sudden energy concerning his
~~~~~~~~~~~~~~~~~~

plan for the interview. She watched him back his Charger out of the driveway as he waved at her, and she was smiling as she walked into her house.

As he drove back to the police station and called his partner, Jack was on Cloud Nine. Tessa was different from the other girls he'd dated. He loved how she had an altruistic heart, was genuine and real, and his frustration with her earlier for going to the O'Briens residence had clearly dissipated. More than anything, he had been concerned for Tessa's safety.

Speaking to Craig about his idea of having the blonde-haired officer, Tiffany Connors, sit in on their scheduled interview with O'Brien and his lawyer the next morning, Craig agreed it couldn't hurt.

He told Jack, "Tiffany's on duty this evening, if you want to approach her about your idea. She sure is a hardworking, young officer. I have a hard time understanding her youngster verbiage sometimes, but she connects with the younger crowd well. Our best informants seem to trust her cause she speaks their lingo and acts almost like a liaison for them."

As soon as Jack arrived at the station, he called Tiffany to meet him in his and Craig's office. A few minutes later, the young officer walked into the room looking curious, wondering why she was being called in. He motioned her to have a seat in the chair across from his desk, and then he asked her how long her hair was. She always wore it pulled back in a bun on her head.

She looked puzzled and asked him, "Umm… Detective, why do you want to know?"

"Well, Officer Connors, we're hoping to startle some information out of Daniel O'Brien in the morning. Seems he has a strong predilection for women with long blonde hair, especially petite blonde women with green eyes." He handed her a photo of Marcy Phillips with her smiling face and head full of long, blonde curls. "Want to sit in the next interview with me and Detective Taylor when we question him tomorrow?"

Officer Connors gave Jack a broad grin and said, "I like your way of thinking, Detective. On the *down low*…I'm game." Tiffany was already thinking she'd need to borrow her mother's hairspray to create the '90s big hair look.

Chapter Sixteen

Jack wished there had been a way to have Tessa observe the interview which was about to start, but he didn't think Dr. Redman would appreciate another unexpected PTO request from her. He hoped he'd be able to share encouraging news with his pretty Tessa later that day. Through the two-way mirrored glass, he watched O'Brien lower his large frame in a chair next to the metal table in the interrogation room. Daniel's attorney was a much shorter and younger man than his client, with closely trimmed dark hair and a beard. He took a seat next to the glowering O'Brien.

Detectives Taylor and Parker, along with Officer Connors, calmly strolled into the room. Craig sat down. Tiffany Connors walked in next, and Jack took the other seat beside Tiffany who was situated directly in front of O'Brien. Tiffany wore plain clothes instead of her uniform. Her dark green blouse matched her green eyes, and she wore her long blonde hair styled with loose curls. Her bangs were curled and teased with the reminiscent *big hair* look from the eighties and early nineties.

Jack's plan had a profound effect on Daniel. He couldn't take his eyes off Tiffany Connors. Blinking rapidly, Daniel's eyes widened in surprise. His face began to contort and redden with anger and hatred. He glanced at the detectives with dark fury in his eyes.

"Hello, Danny," Jack said and smiled.

"Why did you bring her in here?" Daniel loudly grumbled, not taking his eyes off Tiffany.

His attorney told Daniel to be quiet, and he quickly informed the detectives his client would need to be released soon, since they hadn't formally charged him with a crime. Daniel's face continued to darken.

Before the detectives could respond to the attorney, Daniel stood up, wearing his orange jumpsuit provided by the county jail. He pointed to Officer Connors, looked at the detectives and gruffly asked them with his lisping voice, "Where did you find her? Where did you find Teresa?"

Without warning, he lunged across the metal table toward the blonde officer. He was met with a ferocious quick jab to his double chin from Officer Connors. For a small woman, she had a wicked right hook. Daniel had grabbed her hair with both of his large pudgy hands, and he stumbled backwards from her unexpected powerful punch.

"Cuff him, Jack!" bellowed Detective Taylor. Metal chairs flew around the room as both detectives pounced on O'Brien and pushed him to the floor. His bearded attorney stood watching them with his mouth hanging open.

"Your client just assaulted an officer. He won't be released anytime soon," said Detective Taylor as he pushed Daniel out the door of the interrogation room. The shocked attorney followed them. Jack rushed over to Tiffany and asked her if she was all right. He was horrified that Daniel put his hands on the young officer.

"I'm fine. My mom was right. This Aqua Net hairspray is amazing. He didn't even mess up my hairdo. Bangs are still *on fleek*." She fluffed her stiff hair and laughed.

Jack nervously laughed along with her, feeling extremely impressed with his coworker and her brave demeanor. Her slang for still looking good made him grin. They walked into the breakroom where they each got a strong cup of coffee from the vending machine. From a cabinet in the breakroom, Jack found a towel. He got a cup of ice and brought them to the table.

"Are you sure you're okay? I had hoped for a reaction from O'Brien when he saw you, but I never expected him to become violent in front of us." Jack continued to look at her with concern and made a makeshift icepack and placed it on Tiffany's right hand.

She wrapped the ice pack around her swelling knuckles and commented, "Honestly, I'm okay. I could do with something stronger to drink right now rather than this crummy coffee, but I'm fine. That dude went all *cray cray*. Detective, who is Teresa? He called me Teresa."

Jack had wondered the same thing when Daniel referred to the blonde officer and asked where they'd found someone named Teresa.

"I don't know, but he obviously hates her. He was downright demented. I thought he would possibly be reminded of our murder victim, Marcy, when he saw you, not some other woman."

Detective Taylor walked into the breakroom and joined them at the round table where they were seated. "Officer Connors, are you all right?"

She smiled and assured him, "Really, I'm okay."

"Can you believe that just happened?" Craig asked them. "In my wildest dreams, I never expected anything like that. Looks like we've got some more digging to do in O'Brien's past." He looked at his partner, and they both stood up from the table.

Craig looked worried and commented, "Tiffany, you might have your hand checked out if it gets worse. Young lady, I bet you loosened some fillings with that right hook. Dynamite does indeed come in small packages."

Laughing, they commended the young officer for her boxing ability. The detectives left the breakroom and anxiously began searching for additional information on the mysterious woman named Teresa.

Jack and Craig searched for names of anyone associated with O'Brien with that name, and they tried numerous nicknames and spellings. Without any luck, Jack inspected a list of O'Brien's contacts and family members. Both of his parents were deceased, but there were two siblings. A younger brother named Frank O'Brien and an older sister, Marie Grimaldi, who still lived in New Jersey. He decided to call Daniel's sister, Marie, and hoped she could shine some light on their quest for the mysterious Teresa.

The call was answered on the second ring. "Mrs. Grimaldi?" asked Jack. "My name is Detective Jack Parker from the Morrigan Police Department in Oklahoma. Could I please take a few moments of your time?"

"Are you calling about Daniel? Is he okay?" Marie inquired.

"Yes, he's fine. I'm hoping to get some contact information from you about a woman named Teresa, who Mr. O'Brien asked us about."

You could have heard crickets, it was so quiet on the line. Finally, Marie replied, "I'm sure this is all a big misunderstanding with my brother and the woman they found in that lake. The only Teresa I can think of that my brother would be talking about is Teresa D'Angelo. Unless there's another Teresa I'm not aware of. When we were teenagers, the D'Angelo family lived next to us in Roseburg. Oh, she was a lovely girl, and I'm sure Daniel had a big crush on her. Hey, get away from the macaroons! Sorry I yelled in your ear, Detective. I'm baking with my grandkids today."

"That's okay, ma'am. I appreciate your visiting with me. One last question… would you say your brother is an easy-going guy, kind of mellow?" asked Jack, as he scribbled the name Teresa D'Angelo on a notepad.

She snickered, "My brother? No, he's always had anger management issues. Even as a kid, he would get so mad at Frank, our younger brother. One time, he set Frank's train set on fire in the basement. I could tell you lots of other stories about Daniel, but no… he's anything but mellow." Jack heard a child's voice in the background asking *Nonna* for a cookie.

He thanked Marie for her time and hung up the phone. Looking across the office at his partner, Jack grinned and yelled, "Boom!"

He filled Craig in on the information he'd acquired from Marie Grimaldi, turned back to his computer, and immediately began searching for a Teresa D'Angelo from Roseburg, New Jersey.

Chapter Seventeen

Sandra felt calm and collected after her recent session with Lily. However, she was still mortified she had let her depression and drinking bring her so close to the edge, especially on the morning Tessa had stepped into her life and later escorted her to see Lily for her impromptu appointment. The last few days, Sandra felt she was awakening from the terror of being married to a murderer, and she felt extremely overwhelmed.

Her counselor was a kind, Christian woman who genuinely cared about her clients. Lily Mathis was in her mid-sixties, with a slim, athletic build and short silver hair. She was also the marriage counselor to whom she and Daniel had gone to when she'd caught him in an affair ten years ago. Since then, Sandra would schedule a session with her every few months.

Sandra cringed as she recalled the embarrassing session, which was the last session she and her husband had attended together with the counselor. When Lily had informed Daniel that he would benefit from reading about sex addiction, he became irate. He stormed out of Lily's office and vowed to never return, but Sandra returned… by herself. She had very slowly started rebuilding herself and began focusing on her career and taking her counselor's advice to move forward.

She learned about co-dependence and how she needed to work on having better boundaries in her relationships with others. She had recently learned and comprehended how co-dependent people are givers, while narcissists and sociopaths are takers. Sandra also admitted to herself that she was a fixer, which explained why she had always been a magnet to men who took advantage of her giving nature all her life. She didn't realize at those times, but she had been trying to fix them and help them. Yet, they would cheat and lie to her. One guy even stole some of her cash and her antique typewriter which he took to a pawn shop. She never saw her typewriter again, nor did she ever see the deadbeat boyfriend again. As Sandra reflected on her life, she felt ashamed, foolish, and used.

A couple of months ago, when Sandra had started suspecting her husband's behavior was growing progressively worse, she had typed in the search bar on her computer: liar, cheater, manipulator. Tapping the *Enter* button on the keyboard, she was stunned to see dozens of links pop up, and most of them referred to *Narcissist Personality Disorder*. She began educating herself, with a thirst for knowledge and truth, and she bought several books about mental disorders. On Facebook, she looked for online support groups of other victims of emotional abuse.

There were several groups with informative posts, but the group where she felt most comfortable was called *Recovering Survivors of Sociopaths*. Karen, who had started the group five years prior, was a strong woman with a heart of gold. She listened to thousands of women describe their traumatic relationships with narcissists, sociopaths, and psychopaths. Karen was also tough and didn't allow any bullying or judgmental behavior towards the fellow members. Being a victim of a sociopath herself, she promoted healing and growing, from being a victim to become a survivor. With time and a lot of effort to continue healing, the survivor was inspired to become a *thriver*. That's what Sandra wanted to be… a *thriver*. Sandra wanted to enjoy life to its fullest. When she read the many posts of other members recounting their personal dilemmas, she realized she wasn't alone. There were many women in the group who were, or had been, emotionally and physically abused.

Shifting her thoughts, she felt her stomach drop when she once again contemplated Daniel had murdered her best friend. Sandra was horrified that her husband was suspected to be the one responsible for Marcy's murder. She was still trying to wrap her mind around the whole sordid situation. Thinking of her demented husband, she felt relief that she didn't have to look at Daniel's ugly, evil face anymore. She took comfort knowing he would never be allowed to step foot in her home ever again, and she had an appointment with her lawyer the next week to start divorce proceedings. Sandra looked forward to the day she was no longer tethered to the monster.

She curled up on her white couch holding her tablet and opened a link she had been reading earlier which Karen had posted in her group. It described *Gaslighting* which is one of the many forms of narcissistic abuse. The article went on to say gaslighting is a form of manipulation and control. The article explained how, especially after long periods of time, the victims become brainwashed into doubting themselves and begin feeling inept and sometimes even insane. The abuser dominates their victim that way. The manipulation is insidious, and the mind games are usually covert and sinister. The victims are duped into thinking there was something wrong with themselves.

Sandra suddenly remembered the many times that she couldn't find her car keys when she knew she had left them on her dresser, and other times when pieces of her jewelry would disappear yet reappear in her jewelry chest the next day. One time, sitting at her desk in the living room, she was working on an inventory report for the restaurant. She walked out of the room to turn off the oven timer and remove a dish she was baking in the kitchen. Less than twenty minutes later, after she'd cleaned the dirty dishes in the sink, she returned to her desk to finish the report. She looked under the desk and all over the living room and dining area, but her inventory report was gone. She felt flustered, because she needed to turn the report in the next day. She was already exhausted from working fifty hours that week and burst into tears.

A few minutes later, Daniel found her sitting on the floor beside the antique desk sobbing, and he asked her what was wrong. After telling him how exasperated she was that she couldn't find her report and that she felt overworked, he simply shrugged his shoulders and mumbled, "I'm sure it'll turn up somewhere."

She dragged herself to her bathroom for a cold washcloth to place over her puffy eyes and to lie down for a minute on her bed. When she flipped on the bathroom light, there it was; her report lay on the marble-topped vanity. Sandra picked up the papers as Daniel walked in and asked her when dinner would be ready. He looked at the report which she held and said, "See… I told you it would turn up. So, what time is dinner?"

For a few minutes, she had thought she must be losing her mind. She wondered if she was developing Alzheimer's disease or dementia, yet she knew she hadn't even been in her bedroom suite since arriving home from work. She shook her head and walked to the kitchen to finish their dinner.

As Sandra finished reading the article about gaslighting, it suddenly dawned on her that the times the incidents, such as the missing inventory report, occurred only when Daniel was home. When he was traveling on the road, sometimes for over two and three weeks, she didn't have things disappear, but as soon as he got home, she seemed to become forgetful.

Comprehending her husband had been playing mind games and gaslighting her for decades, her anger flared. She had seen Daniel's mask fall and completely believed he was a monster. She'd been made the fool so many times by her perverse husband. No more, though. Now, she hoped he'd rot in jail.

Chapter Eighteen

Tessa and the other lady warriors were feeling melancholy that their self-defense class was coming to an end. Meetings at the *Java Hut* for coffee beforehand were always fun, and she loved her spunky friends. They were meeting for their last class that evening. While they were reluctant for its end, they were also proud of all they'd learned. The next couple of hours with their instructor and their classmates went quickly, and Tony applauded their accomplishments. Tessa watched the women in their group and thought how they all walked a little straighter and were more observant and mindful of their surroundings. Their confidence levels had certainly been boosted. Taking the class had been an empowering experience, and she would miss their meetings and the comradery.

Carrying her gym bag to her red Mustang, she was pleasantly surprised to see Jack pull into the gym's parking lot. Both Rachel and Kyra gave Tessa teasing, sly smiles and told their friend to have a nice evening.

Jack rolled down his window, grinned from ear to ear and asked her, "Hey Ninja-girl, care to hear some great news?"

His eyes sparkled, and his enthusiasm was infectious. She eagerly replied, "Yes, of course! Meet me at my house. I want to take a quick shower, but I can't wait to hear what's going on."

A half hour later, they were relaxing on the chaise lounges in her backyard, and she sipped from a syrupy, cherry limeade that Jack had thoughtfully brought her from Sonny's Drive-In.

"Okay, buddy… spill it. I can tell you're about to burst at the seams. What awesome thing happened today?" She grinned and speculated that the interview with O'Brien and his attorney must have gone well.

"I'll start from the beginning. O'Brien and his attorney were sitting in the interrogation room, and Craig, me, and Officer Connors walked in and sat across from them. You won't believe what happened!" Jack grinned and took a long sip from his icy Dr. Pepper slush from Sonny's and suddenly looked in pain.

"Oh, I hate it when that happens! Brain-freeze!" They both laughed, and Jack continued informing Tessa about the intense reaction they got from O'Brien in the interrogation room and how he was charged with assaulting an officer.

"I was mortified that creep laid hands on Tiffany, but she handled herself well. She rung his bell good. And now, since he's been charged with a crime, he won't be released soon like we'd feared. We've got time to investigate properly and put together the evidence needed for an arraignment."

"That's such a relief. I've been worried that time was running out on how long he could be held. I'm so proud of you and Craig and Tiffany. Go, Tiffany! Bet O'Brien didn't see that coming. Ha!" Tessa pictured the big, ugly bully getting a taste of his own medicine from the fearless, young officer. She laughed so hard, she snorted, which caused them both to laugh.

"Well, that's not all that happened. O'Brien unwittingly gave us a lead. When he referred to Tiffany as *Teresa*, we began searching. I spoke with his sister, Marie, in Jersey, and she mentioned a neighbor named Teresa that her brother used to date. Her name is Teresa D'Angelo, but she's now Teresa Carter. She married and moved to Puget Sound. After speaking with Teresa on the phone, it was obvious she has a ton of information about O'Brien. To get the full scoop from her, Craig and I are flying to Washington tomorrow to further interview her. I've got a good feeling about this meeting. On the phone, she was very cooperative, but I got the impression she has something important she needs to share. Seemed like I even heard relief in her voice when I called her back with confirmation that we'd meet her. So, I'd better go home and pack, Tessa." Jack rose to his feet, feeling ambitious and enthusiastic.

Tessa slowly stood up from the chaise, and he gave her a tight hug. He thought he smelled peaches and smiled.

"Hmmm... you smell amazing, Ninja-girl." He leaned back and gazed into her blue eyes and kissed her.

"I'll miss you while you're gone. Please be careful... and enjoy your flight," she told him, and realized she truly would miss him.

Instead of walking back through her house, Jack left the backyard through the wooden gate by the garage with an energetic stride and pep in his step.

~~~~~~~~~~~~~~~~~~~

Tessa settled back onto her chaise, adjusting the thick cushioned chair to an almost lying position. She gazed in awe at the overhead brilliant lights in the clear skies and watched a falling star streak across the celestial heavens. She spotted the Little Dipper, and the bright Polaris star glowed from the end of the dipper's long handle.

She silently thanked God for blessing her life with Jack. She wondered where their futures were headed. She lay there for another half hour, watching the shimmering night sky and reflected on everything Jack had told her about the latest developments in the murder case. She prayed for Jack and Craig's safety as they traveled to and from Washington, and she also prayed they would discover useful information from Teresa Carter.

She walked inside, locked the doors, and stopped in her kitchen to refill her coffee maker for her morning caffeine fix. Grabbing three peanut butter dog treats, she walked onto her front porch. The Angel Dogs were patiently waiting for her. She gave them their biscuits, said good night and slowly went back inside to her soft warm bed. She slept better that night than she had in months.

~~~~~~~~~~~~~~~~~~~

Departing from the Tulsa International Airport to the Dallas Ft. Worth Airport for their connecting flight to Seattle, Jack and Craig discussed their scheduled meeting with Teresa D'Angelo-Carter. They were anxious to hear all she knew about O'Brien. The background check they did on Teresa verified she had lived in

Roseburg, New Jersey, and had married a man named Brent Carter. They had moved to Puget Sound, Washington the year after they wed, due to her husband's promotion and job transfer. They had two sons, named Alex and Gregory, within the first five years of their marriage.

Jack had observed the couple's joint Facebook account and studied their family photos. They seemed to be the typical all-American family, complete with a billowing American flag planted in their front yard. Craig and Jack were scheduled to meet the Carters that evening and would return to Morrigan the following day. The flight schedule would undoubtedly be exhausting for the detectives, but more economical for the department's budget.

Sitting cramped in the small, economy coach seats in Row 15 of the 737, Craig mentioned how O'Brien's stay the last few weeks at the county jail was already taking a toll on the man.

"His cheese has done fallen off his cracker," Craig said, in his Oklahoma drawl.

"Yes, it has," replied Jack. "His soon to be ex-wife, told Tessa he seemed to be coming unraveled. Sandra mentioned he's gotten progressively more unstable in the last year. When she went to have him sign divorce papers last week, he went totally ballistic."

Jack continued, "According to what Tessa told me, Sandra says she's feeling better than she has in years. She's receiving therapy and getting the help she needs. Can you imagine the effect on someone who's had a guy like O'Brien as a spouse for over twenty-five years? I'm glad the poor lady is starting to recover."

Craig smiled and said, "Makes me realize how lucky I am. Tina has been supportive of me and this crazy job we have, and Jack... that's a rare thing. I don't know what I would have done without her the last ten years we've been married."

"You are blessed, my friend." Jack nodded and said, "When I got back from Afghanistan, we went through a transition assistance program, and there was mandatory counseling. They also strongly advised psychological exams later, once we were more settled. PTSD is almost always one of the things we deal with, especially when we first come back to the states. My first year back, it was hard. I'd jump three feet high if a car backfired within a block of me. From what Sandra's therapist told her, she and other people who've been severely, emotionally abused, suffer from PTSD like a lot of the soldiers in the military. There's violent combat-trauma versus noncombat-PTSD. The war zone she experienced was psychological. She's been traumatized by O'Brien. It's going to take a long while before she's completely recovered."

Jack suddenly got that haunted look in his eyes when discussing anything to do with his tour in Afghanistan. Craig noticed his partner's momentary dark expression. He always recognized the sad look the young man got when he spoke of his days in the military. He rarely mentioned his time in the Marines. From one of their mutual friends, he'd heard that Jack had seen a lot of action during his tour of duty. That kind of trauma had to do a number on him.

~~~~~~~~~~~~~~~~~~

Once they arrived at the Seattle-Tacoma airport, they rented a car and drove to the designated address where they'd agreed to meet the Carters. Traffic was heavy, but once they traveled north of Seattle on Highway 90, it became less congested. Within two hours, they were awaiting Teresa and Brent Carter at a seafood restaurant, with its walls wrapped in floor to ceiling windows offering an exquisite, panoramic view of Puget Sound.

Jack walked outside onto the boardwalk and realized he was facing southwest. Mt. Rainier could be seen with its majestic, snow-peaked mountaintop in the distance. A breathtaking sunset with coral-pinks and shades of violet bounced off the snow-covered peak. Calm waters in the harbor seemed to take on a dark purple hue, reflecting the sunset's magical ambience. The young detective felt spellbound as he gazed across the vast landscape.

Seattle's unique skyline, with the six-hundred feet in the air Space Needle, beckoned Jack as lights began twinkling in the early dusk. An incoming, slow moving evening fog seemed to float leisurely among the sailboats with their lowered masts, as they began docking in the marina. He wished there were more time to go sightseeing while they were in Washington, and he wished gorgeous Tessa was with him to share the magic.

Craig walked up and stood beside Jack, sighed and quietly said, "Impressive."

"Yes, it's stunning. I would have paid my own travel costs for this view alone. Don't tell the Chief that." Jack softly chuckled,
~~~~~~~~~~~~~~~~~~

yet he was being sincere. He planned a return trip to Seattle when there was adequate time to enjoy the city.

The men turned to go inside to wait for the Carters. Inhaling the spicy, pungent fragrance of the enticing seafood, they took their seats at a corner table and continued absorbing the skyscape. Minutes later both men stood as the hostess led the Carters, a handsome couple, to their table, and she told the diners their server would be with them momentarily.

After shaking hands and introductions, the foursome sat down together at the table, and a server immediately began taking their drink orders. Teresa and Brent Carter both ordered red merlot, while the detectives ordered coffees.

Teresa was barely five-feet two-inches tall, very petite, and wore her blond hair in a chin length, stylish bobbed cut. At fifty-five, she appeared many years younger. Her sparkling, green eyes looked up at her husband with ardent love. Brent was around five-feet nine-inches tall, with a slim build, and he gazed at his wife, of almost three decades, with obvious devotion and adoration.

Brent Carter was an engineer for an environmental company based in Tacoma, and he'd been with the same company for thirty years. Teresa worked for a nonprofit group which helped numerous people in their area. The nonprofit provided shelters for the homeless, and she was an advocate for abused women and children.

Between watching the happy couple in front of him, and thinking of Craig, and his successful marriage, Jack thought maybe the idea of wedlock could be a happy venture. Based on his mother's short, but tragic marriage with his father, plus some of the dreadful marriages of his military buddies, Jack had been skeptical, almost cynical, of having a successful relationship or marriage. He'd had a few serious relationships in his life, and he'd dated several girls, but none of the relationships ever lasted. Now that he'd met Tessa, he wondered if the tide was turning for him. Between his military career and being in law enforcement, he'd devoted his time and energy to his careers. *Maybe it was time to change things... if it was God's Will.*

He directed his attention back to the conversation at the dinner table. In a soft voice, Teresa spoke of her family's love for Washington.

"We've never regretted moving here. The sights and views are magnificent, and the people are refreshing. The pace of living here compared to New Jersey is different, stimulating without the aggression."

Brent added, "Lots of other people have fallen in love with Seattle, too. We've noticed the last ten years or so, there's been a surge of new residents. Unfortunately, the cost of living has significantly risen, and traffic can be hellacious. We love it here though, and I doubt we'll ever leave."

"Yes, we've also seen a rise in homelessness since the population growth. My nonprofit group is involved in assisting a lot of people who seem to have fallen through the cracks. Anyways, gentlemen, what can we do to help you with your investigation?" asked Teresa.

"We're hoping you can help us learn some things about Daniel O'Brien. What makes him tick? What's his history? May I turn on my recorder, so we don't miss anything in our conversation?" Craig pulled a recorder from his pocket.

"No problem, Detective. By the way, if you've never tried smoked trout, it's excellent here. Oh, and save room for bread pudding." Teresa suggested.

The server walked to their table, served their drinks, and took their dinner order. Jack's mouth watered as he saw the table next to them being served steaming plates of blackened salmon. Jack had ordered the pan seared Alaskan halibut.

After the server left, Teresa began her story. "I met Daniel in my junior year of high school. He was a senior, and our families lived next door to each other. The O'Brien's seemed like a decent family. My folks and I even attended the same Methodist Church in our neighborhood with the O'Briens. I liked Frank and Marie... Daniel's brother and sister. His parents were nice, too, but his grandfather who lived with Daniel's family was a holy terror. He seemed to resent Daniel and was actually mean to him."

Jack curiously asked, "What did the grandfather do to him that made you feel that way?"

"It felt like he used Daniel as a kind of whipping post... not physically, but he was always putting him down verbally. I heard him being berated and belittled by his grandfather many times, and I'm sure his grandfather was an alcoholic, even though he tried hiding it. Maybe that's one reason he had such a mean spirit. Anyways, the grandfather would hide liquor around the house. He even hid whiskey in his mouthwash bottle in his bathroom's medicine cabinet, and Daniel told me he'd caught his grandfather taking swigs from the bottle hidden in the bathroom throughout the day and even at night. I remember one time his grandfather had been especially cruel to Daniel about his report cards. His grades were average, and his grandfather was always comparing him to Daniel's brother. Frank got straight A's, but I think Daniel was more intelligent than Frank. School just didn't interest him, so he didn't try very hard."

Jack asked, "Teresa, do you recall what the grandfather's name was?"

"Yes, it was Daniel O'Brien, Sr., and Daniel had been named after Grandpa O'Brien. The grandfather was originally from Brooklyn… I remember him saying he was from Hell's Kitchen. Grandpa O'Brien used to call Daniel, *Danny*, when he'd torment him. I learned quickly not to ever call him Danny. Made him furious. So, after Grandpa O'Brien cruelly criticized Daniel about his average grades, in front of all his family, Daniel told me he'd decided to get even with his grandpa that night.

"He knew that his grandpa wouldn't turn on the bathroom light when he'd sneak swigs from his *mouthwash* late at night, because he was drinking on the sly and didn't want to wake up anyone. That night, Grandpa O'Brien snuck into his bathroom, took a huge swig from the mouthwash bottle, and spewed it out… all over the room! When he switched on the light, he saw he'd spit black stuff all over the shower curtain and mirror. He had black stains around his mouth and dripping down his chin. It permanently stained and ruined his white beard. Later, he had to shave it off. Daniel had poured out half of the whiskey and replaced it with black shoe polish. His grandfather was sick the rest of that night from the toxic black whiskey. He knew Daniel was the one who did it and started screaming at him. It was 2:00am, and he woke up the whole household. Daniel said he played totally innocent and got away with his vengeance. What a mess."

They all shook their heads thinking about the grandson giving his abusive grandfather a taste of his own medicine, quite literally. The server approached their table with a large oval platter, laden with dishes of the eagerly anticipated seafood. After enjoying their meals for a few minutes, Teresa continued her story. Jack noticed she'd only picked at her meal. She sipped her merlot, and her voice took on a sad tone.

"In my senior year of high school, I started dating Daniel. I think I kind of felt sorry for him, but he also had a way of making me feel extremely special. I was just a kid, and his flattery stroked my ego. After a while, his attention became obsessive, and he'd call me a dozen times a day… always checking to see where I was, what I was doing, and who I was with. When I realized he was following me when I was with my girlfriends… going to the mall and shopping, or eating out, I started getting annoyed. I felt like he was stalking me, smothering me."

She stopped and took another long sip of her wine, looked at the detectives and her husband, and sighed. She seemed uncertain about continuing, and Brent, began speaking for her.

"That's when Daniel's dark side started coming out. It's hard for Teresa to talk about. Are you up to it, darling?" he gently asked his wife.

"Yes, I need to do this. When I started distancing myself from Daniel, he really started to pour on the charm. He was back to acting the sweet, attentive Daniel. He apologized for being 'overprotective' of me and changed his attitude back to the good Daniel. He knew I enjoyed playing golf, so he learned how to play golf. Then, for my birthday, he surprised me with a new set of golf clubs. They were an expensive set of Wilsons, and Daniel even had a designer golf bag with my name embroidered on it in purple… which he knew was my favorite color. He also had bought himself a nice set of clubs."

Teresa stopped for a moment and took a breath, "When I sought therapy a short while after the fiasco with Daniel, my therapist informed me that Daniel's behavior was called *mirroring*. It's a control tactic used by sociopaths to make their victims think they've found their soulmate… thinking they're so much alike. They suddenly take on their victim's interests, likes, and dislikes, mirroring their prey's behavior to gain their trust; pure manipulation. And, I was his prey.

"After he gave me the generous present, we went the next day to play a round of golf at the country club. At one point, I noticed I was beating the socks off him. It surprised me that he became more and more angry, because I was playing better than him, and I reminded him that I'd been playing golf for a couple years longer. Anyways, I was putting one of my wedges back in the golf bag and pulled out a putter to make a short shot. I could see out of the corner of my eye, Daniel pulling out one of his irons from his bag. I leaned over placing my feet just right, getting the feel of the club… and suddenly, he swung his iron and purposely hit me over my back and shoulders. It hurt so bad! I fell to my knees… and asked him why he'd do such a thing. I started crying, and he started laughing. I mean, who does that?"

Brent seemed saddened and interrupted, "This is upsetting Teresa… Are you sure you want to go on?"

Teresa wiped tears from her cheeks as she slowly nodded her head and continued.

"It gets worse. I staggered to the golf cart, took off, and left him on the greens. Back at the clubhouse, I called one of my girlfriends and asked her to please come get me. She said she and her big brother were on their way. Shortly after that, Daniel pushed his way into the ladies' restroom where I was waiting for my girlfriend, Connie. He was sweating bullets. Evidently, he'd run all the way from the greens and was searching for me. I told him he could shove his golf clubs and to never call or even look at me again. He slapped me… hard, knocked me backwards, and my head hit the porcelain sink along the wall. It felt like every one of my teeth were loosened. He hit me again. This time with his fist, and I saw black… totally knocked me out."

Teresa's face had paled to an ashen white. Her husband looked concerned, but she shook her head at him and said she needed to tell everything.

"When I became conscious, I was in the back seat of his car. I'm not sure how he got me out of the country club and to his car without being seen. My head hurt so bad… it was splitting, and my shoulders and back hurt. The pain was ungodly. He had pulled onto a side road in the woods about a half of a mile from the club, parked the car and got in the back seat with me. He ripped my blouse. His hands were all over. I was screaming as loud as I could, trying to push him off. Then both the car doors were suddenly yanked open, and I could hear people yelling. It was my girlfriend, Connie, and her brother. They'd seen Daniel take the side road and followed. Connie had recognized his black Monte Carlo… it had dark tinted windows. They saved me."

A quiet sob escaped from Teresa, and she tenderly smiled at Brent and said, "Connie's big brother pulled Daniel off me and yanked him out of the car. He smacked him over the head with a big stick laying on the side of the road. It was the first time I'd ever met her big brother. I instantly fell in love with him and knew I wanted to marry that man. Connie's amazing big brother is my husband."

She looked at her husband, her hero, and they obviously had a strong bond, as they laced their fingers together and smiled into each other's eyes.

Brent squeezed her hand and interjected, "My main thought at the time was to get Teresa to the hospital. He'd beat her up badly. I carried her to my car, and Connie and I rushed her out of there. Daniel was still lying on the ground by his car."

Teresa continued, "We stopped at the clubhouse, and Brent called an ambulance and the police. They got there fast and took me to the hospital. Connie rode with me in the ambulance. Brent stayed at the club and told the police what happened and showed them where he'd left Daniel, but he and his car were long gone.

"After I filed a police report and wanted to press charges, no one could find Daniel. His family obviously covered for him and wouldn't tell where he was. There was a warrant out for him, but it was like he disappeared off the face of the earth. It was years later, we had already moved to Washington, and I heard Daniel had moved somewhere in the Midwest. The police tried finding him, but he had been using a different social security number. Ironically, it was his grandfathers, and he had been loading and unloading trucks for cash, so he kept a low profile. By the time we knew exactly where he was, the statute of limitations had run out. That monster got away with it." She took a deep breath.

Jack and Craig glanced at each other. Craig told Teresa and Brent how much they appreciated all they'd informed them about their traumatic past experiences with Daniel O'Brien.

Brent looked uncertain and said, "Something else that I worry about is what O'Brien *might* have done. We don't have proof, and I know it sounds like I'm only speculating. A girl was reported missing a couple of days before Daniel attacked Teresa. The girl was from the next town east of Roseburg. She was blonde, too, and looked quite a bit like my wife. We brought photos, although I'm not sure it will help. The thing is, O'Brien was obsessed with Teresa, more than an infatuation. It was a sick, violent, delusional fantasy."

Teresa pulled a manila envelope from her purse, handed it to Craig and said, "There's some copies of old photos of me from my senior year in here, and some old newspaper clippings about the missing girl who was later found murdered. She looked a lot like me."

Craig opened the envelope and his eyes widened in surprise. He handed the photos to Jack and said, "Remind you of anyone?"

There was most certainly a strong resemblance between her and the missing girl who was found murdered in New Jersey. Looking at the photo of Teresa in her senior picture, both detectives thought Tiffany Connors could be Teresa's twin sister when she'd been a high school senior. No wonder O'Brien had wigged out when he saw her in the interrogation room.

Marcy was unfortunate that she favored Teresa as well. The murdered woman near Roseburg, Tiffany Connors, and Marcy Phillips all had an uncanny resemblance to Teresa Carter. The detectives now had their motive for their case. The chief should be happy with the new information, which would hopefully help him justify the cost of the trip to Seattle, which put a big dent in the department's budget.

After leaving the Carters and traveling in the rental car to their hotel near the airport, rain began to softly fall on the green, lush landscape along the roadway. Jack and Craig began mentally processing everything they'd just learned. They were glad they'd made the trip. It had been enlightening, and the interview wasn't one to have been made over the phone. They didn't think the protective Brent Carter would have agreed to anything less than meeting face to face, for the sake of his wife. There had been three major factors to the murder case thus far: the keys to the Ford Pinto found in the hidden compartment of O'Brien's luggage, the extreme physical likeness of the green-eyed blondes, and O'Brien's sick obsession with Teresa, not to mention Tessa's dream journal and nightmares.

Jack looked forward to returning home to tell Tessa about their productive interview with Teresa. He texted her that he'd like to see her the next day after she finished her shift. Within two minutes, she replied to him that she'd been thinking about him. She looked forward to seeing him. Wearing a content, satisfied smile, he listened to the refreshing rain patter against the hotel's window and closed his eyes. Back in Morrigan in her bungalow house, Tessa was smiling, too.

Chapter Nineteen

Inmate O'Brien sat sulking in his cell. His attorney advised him to sign the divorce papers that Sandra had served him. He had read the papers, which basically said he would get nothing from the condo or Sandra's things, but all his clothing, his Impala, his Volvo truck, and the money in his bank accounts and retirement fund would be his. She didn't want anything of his, not even his last name. That made him furious, but just about everything seemed to make him furious anymore.

Thoughtfully pondering, he could not believe the mess into which he'd gotten himself. The shock of the last few weeks was wearing off. He wanted to know how the cops were able to connect him with Marcy's rotting body. Just because he was dating Sandra at the time her roommate went missing, should not have been enough evidence for the police to come after him as a person of interest. That he'd been carrying his duffle bag when the cops picked him up was just his bad luck, and they found his memento of Marcy's car keys. That smart-aleck Detective Parker said they'd found DNA and evidence from the plastic in which he'd wrapped her, but he wasn't convinced. The kid was probably just trying to rattle him into saying something incriminating.

He remembered the night well that he had partied with Marcy in 1992. She acted like she didn't want him, but all women were like that. They played hard to get, but they were all a bunch of gold diggers. Daniel wondered if his old buddy had betrayed him, and maybe he'd ratted him out. There were only two people who knew about his propensity for green eyed blondes and the hobby he'd been enjoying for years. One was himself, and the other was his old friend who used to be his co-driver. His old friend had even joined him on his late night "hunts" a couple of times and had showed up the night he was with Marcy at the lake. He chuckled as he reminisced about his co-driver's excitement during the hunting expeditions. His fellow hunter had recently promised O'Brien that he'd pull some strings for him in jail, but so far, he wasn't impressed with his old friend's efforts.

"If he knows what's good for him, he'd better help me out of this quagmire." Daniel said aloud. The demented inmate had been carrying on conversations with himself for the last few days.

He thought of the woman with which the cops had tricked him in the interrogation room. She was the spitting image of his Teresa. Seeing her had thrown him off balance, and his violent reaction of grabbing the blonde even surprised himself.

"Stupid, stupid, stupid!" he kept muttering and began punching himself in the side of his head.

He couldn't stop thinking of Teresa. His mind went back to his high school sweetheart, and how deeply he had become infatuated with his petite blonde neighbor. He tried everything he could think of to make her love him, and it worked for a while, too. He blamed her witch of a best friend and her jerk brother. He despised Connie and Brent for messing up his relationship with Teresa. It was all their fault things got so screwed up.

He remembered how he tried to convince himself he had a chance to get things right with her and even imagined Teresa was his wife. Instead, she married Brent Carter. His eyes became dark as he thought of them. Daniel stayed in touch with his family, and he remembered when he heard the Carters had moved from Jersey to Washington.

While working in Kansas, and being hired by drivers at truck stops, Daniel helped the truck drivers load and unload freight, furniture, electronics… all kinds of things. The name, or job title of him and the other men who hung out at the truck stops looking to find work, was "lumper." Daniel loathed that name, but he was paid in cash, so he worked as a lumper and stayed under the radar.

A year later, when working directly for a trucking company based out of Topeka, he'd sometimes ride with the drivers to the cargo's destinations and help the truckers unload the shipments; then they'd go to another company or agent and reload the truck with more tonnage to haul back to the Topeka agent. They drove all over the country, from coast to coast. Their goal was to never drive the truck without freight in the trailer. If they didn't have *loaded miles* with cargo on board, the trip would cost them money because of the high expense of diesel fuel. Sometimes, that meant waiting for the outgoing freight to be shipped.

One time, he rode with a driver to deliver a load of office furniture to Puget Sound, Washington, and he looked up Teresa and Brent's address. He and the truck driver had two days to wait until the returning freight to Topeka would be ready, so they rented a room at a cheap motel.

Narcissists can usually talk people into doing what they want, and Daniel had befriended the motel's desk clerk. He talked her into loaning him her car. Sitting in the clerk's old ratty Chevy that smelled like dirty socks, he parked across the street from the Carter's home. He watched Teresa and Brent Carter pull into their house's driveway in a new looking minivan. Brent opened the car's side door and removed a grocery bag. Then, he opened the passenger door and helped Teresa out. She was huge! Enormous and pregnant, she waddled into their big house with her sissy husband panting along after her. The sight made Daniel sick. He could see fat Teresa walking in the living room through a large window.

He sat in the clerk's old car, angrily fumed, and fantasized about driving through the large plate glass window of the house and mowing Teresa down. A moment later, another car drove into their driveway. A young couple with a little boy that looked around three or four years old knocked on their door and went inside. Too many witnesses, he thought, and he drove the sour smelling car back to the cheap motel.

As the years progressed, O'Brien worked up the ranks and became a driver for the Topeka trucking company. He even became a recruiter and trainer for new drivers. The late 1980's was an exciting time for the predator.

~~~~~~~~~~~~~~~~~~~~

Inmate O'Brien stretched out on the cell bunk's thin mattress and let his mind wander to the first hunt. It was his senior year, and he had been out drinking with some of his friends. At the end of the
~~~~~~~~~~~~~~~~~~~~

night, they dropped him off a block from his house. He knew he'd better sneak in the back way, so his mother didn't catch him.

As he prowled down the dark alley near his home, he saw a young teenage girl walk out the back door of her house carrying a bag of garbage. He had noticed the young, blonde neighbor a few days before and thought the gods of opportunity were shining down on him that night. He focused on her alabaster neck, luminous from the light of her home's kitchen window, and he wondered how that slender neck would feel under his strong hands. Practically holding his breath, he watched her casually walk to the narrow alley to a big, black trash can. She lifted the lid, plopped the bag of garbage inside and put the lid back on. In that short amount of time, Daniel decided he couldn't pass up the chance to overtake her. His hands trembled, and the urge couldn't be tamed. His long, athletic legs easily jumped over the yard's chain link fence, and he crept up behind her. He was stealthy, a natural born hunter. Quickly placing his hand over her mouth, he lifted her small frame and ran out the back gate.

The girl was wiry and stronger than she looked. She kicked and struggled and surprisingly managed to get away from him. He was glad the alley had no lights; it was pitch dark. She had no idea that her attacker was him as she ran screaming back to her house, and he dove further into the alley's long shadows. The next day, concerned neighbors were talking about the near abduction of the girl and warned everyone to be extra careful and to lock their doors. He learned something that night. He learned to hunt away from his home turf, to be prepared and always have rope and duct tape ready for the next time. He knew there would be a next time because the rush of adrenaline had been exhilarating for him.

The next hunt, he drove to a town east of Roseburg. He cruised around, looking for a target… his prey. After a couple hours of scoping the area, he saw a blonde girl who reminded him of his girlfriend, Teresa. She was a little taller than Teresa, but the likeness was very close. Their hairstyle was identical. The teenager jogged along the edge of the residential street onto which he'd turned. He drove a black Monte Carlo with very dark tinted windows. Carefully observing the neighborhood, he checked if anyone could see him. He rolled down the passenger side window and pulled up beside the blonde jogger.

Noticing her eyes were green, he slyly smiled and said, "Excuse me, Miss… have you seen this dog around here, by any chance? She's very small and answers to the name Sugar."

He held out a photo of a small, chocolate brown poodle wearing a pink collar with rhinestones. The little dog happened to belong to his brother Frank's girlfriend, and Daniel had swiped the photo from his brother's dresser. The blonde jogger tried to look at the photo more closely, but Daniel covertly pulled the photo further into the car towards him. As she approached his car and leaned toward him to have a better look, he yanked her inside and rolled up the dark tinted window. Daniel was quite strong, and he was able to overtake her easily.

"Hello, Sugar," he growled into her left ear and nibbled on the pierced lobe. Daniel knew his obsession to control and have Teresa was amplifying into something he'd only fantasized. Since he couldn't dominate the love of his life, he felt momentary satisfaction by pretending blonde women who favored her likeness were her. In minutes, he'd assaulted and kidnapped his first prey. Less than an hour later, the hapless blonde jogger was dead and dumped off a bridge into a stream several miles from her neighborhood. She wasn't located for days. When she was discovered, she was missing her wallet, house keys, and her left ear. The police didn't add the detail of her ear being carved off to the publicized report, and many mistakenly regarded the crime as a typical mugging.

Daniel was hooked. His addiction for stalking and hunting blonde, green-eyed women who reminded him of Teresa became his hobby, his demented obsession. Driving all over the country in a truck enabled him to hunt easily. The prostitutes or "lot lizards", who he often saw at truck stops and in Las Vegas, made the killing hunts too easy. He preferred a challenge, so he didn't hunt as often as he would have liked. Over the last thirty years, he had claimed the ill-fated lives of eight green-eyed, blonde women, including Marcy Phillips, and he had beaten and used dozens of prostitutes. In order to entertain himself the last couple of weeks, he had been reliving every single hunt in his warped mind. Remembering his past helped his time behind bars feel more bearable.

Dominating women and causing them to feel fear and pain was his passion. Being in jail prevented him from barely looking at a woman, not to mention being able to hunt and stalk them. His anxiety level had exceeded its limit, and he was itching to cause a woman to feel pain. He needed a hunt. He was going through withdrawal of his perverse addiction, and he didn't know if he'd survive.

Chapter Twenty

Enjoying the company of her big sister Trisha and her four-year old niece Sophia, Tessa paid for her purchases at the register of their favorite boutique, *Chantelle's Chic Boutique*, which was one of several quaint stores they often frequented on Main Street in Morrigan. They had been shopping and found some excellent sales that morning. Tessa was excited to wear the new running outfits she'd bought.

Trisha and Sophia had surprised her with a Saturday morning visit, and Tessa was ecstatic. She hadn't seen them since her birthday party and had missed her big sister and adorable niece. After shopping, they went to their favorite ice cream store with its fifty different flavors of ice cream and ordered chocolate fudge sundaes. Sliding onto the pink and purple vinyl-covered booths, anxious to devour her dessert, Sophia clapped her hands and grinned. Minutes later, they celebrated their bargain shopping with whipped cream-covered, chocolate goodness.

"It's a good thing I'll be running with the *amigas* starting tomorrow," Tessa said. She closed her eyes and savored her first bite of ice cream. "I'm afraid there's a thousand calories here! Did I tell you they've extended the running trail at the park? I can't wait to check it out."

Since the self-defense class was concluded, the Three *Amigas* had decided to start running together at Cedar Trails, the local walking path, and meet before the crack of dawn. Since the Oklahoma temperatures were warming and the early springtime winds had begun to calm, the weather wasn't as big a hindrance. The girls looked forward to their runs and being outdoors.

Trisha smiled and squinted at her little sister. "Well, you need to spill the beans and tell me what exactly has you in such a good mood, Sis. I don't think it's the ice cream or the new running trail that's put that twinkle in your eyes. Maybe I should ask, *who* has put the twinkle in your eyes?"

"Well, I've met a wonderful guy. His name is Jack Parker," Tessa answered, feeling her cheeks flush pink. "I met him through his work partner at Dr. Redman's. He's a detective at the police department, and what I really love is that he seems to be a strong Christian. However, what *you* will like about him is how much he looks like FBI Agent, Eric Matthews, from the *Miss Congeniality* movie."

"What? Are you serious? I love that old movie. We must have watched it thirty times when we were kids, and ooh-la-la, a Benjamin Bratt look-alike? Um, he's not as old as Benjamin Bratt, is he?"

Tessa laughed, "No, he's young… twenty-nine. I really think you'll like him."

"That makes me happy, Tessa. You deserve the best guy out there. I look forward to meeting him. How about you invite him to Mom's birthday party? I promise not to give him the third degree."

"Sure, I'll invite him. I can't wait to have another family gathering. We're so lucky, Trisha. We have a big loving family, and I'm starting to be more appreciative of that blessing. I recently met a lady who doesn't have children. Her parents passed away almost thirty years ago, and she was an only child. She has cousins that are scattered across the country, but she isn't close to any of them. It makes me grateful to have you all and be a part of a tight-knit family."

Trisha beamed, and tears gathered in her big brown eyes. She looked at her little sister, sniffed, and said, "I'm sorry, Tessa. For some reason, I've been extra emotional lately."

"Have you checked yet? Maybe you should stop by the pharmacy and pick up a pregnancy test." Tessa said and winked at her sister. Trisha looked alarmed.

"Don't say it, Tessa! At least not in front of this one," she glanced at her daughter and asked Tessa, "How did you know? I haven't even mentioned it to my husband yet."

"Let's just call it a feeling…and um, you might want to buy some blue paint." Tessa laughed, and Trisha giggled.

With chocolate syrup dripping off her chin, Sophia looked at them both, and asked, "What's so funny?" Her innocent question made them laugh more.

Trisha promised to pick up the kit at the pharmacy after she dropped off Tessa at her house. They picked up their empty plastic ice cream bowls, placed them in the trash can, and walked to Trisha's car.

Back at her home, Tessa waved to her sister and niece as they drove away from her house. She was grinning from ear to ear, feeling wonderful joy. Appreciating her loved ones, she wished Sandra could experience how elated she was feeling, being a part of a loving family.

Tessa had grown closer to Sandra. There had been several phone conversations, messages, and texts between the two. She didn't have the frightening worries any longer about Sandra's wellbeing, and Tessa could feel her new friend was healing. They'd discussed their first meeting when Tessa showed up unannounced on her doorstep. They both were in awe of how God had brought them together. Sandra confessed she'd been on the brink of darkness, and Tessa had pulled her away from the edge.

~~~~~~~~~~~~~~~~~~~

Unlike most people Sandra met, she felt complete trust with her new friend. Sandra had confided to Tessa about her parents, who had unexpectedly passed away in 1990. They had left her with a large inheritance, and she'd never had to struggle financially. Her soon to be ex-husband knew her parents were deceased, but she had never told him about her trust fund, growing investment portfolio, and large bank accounts. While Daniel knew she owned their condominium, he didn't know she owned the whole block, all six of the condos. Since Sandra had filed divorce proceedings on him recently, she was glad she had kept that information to herself. She was also looking forward to restoring her last name to Dawson. She didn't want to be associated with him in any way.

When they'd first met in 1992, Sandra needed to believe Daniel wanted her for being herself and not for her money. That factor, and her instincts, kept her from disclosing her wealth to him.
~~~~~~~~~~~~~~~~~~~

Besides Tessa, only Sandra's accountant and banker knew of her assets and fortune. She had lived well below her means since receiving her inheritance, and she had an excellent investment agent who had helped her with wise advice and had significantly grown her money over the years. She hadn't needed to work, but she enjoyed being at the restaurant. The owner was a high school friend of hers, and Sandra had invested a lot of money in the business with him. The employees had become like family to her, especially since she didn't have many relatives.

Since Daniel's arrest, it had become increasingly difficult for her to work at the restaurant. There had been harassing reporters, and some of the customers had been rude to her. She decided to work behind the scenes as only an investor in the restaurant. She had recommended that her business partner promote Wanda, the assistant manager, to her position. The girl had been supportive and gracious to Sandra, and she was more than capable of performing the job duties. Wanda was the only one of the employees who had been concerned and kind to her the last few weeks, and Sandra was quite disappointed because she thought the relationships with the other employees at the restaurant had been closer. The time had come for her to move on. Sandra had several future projects in the works and needed more time for them, anyway.

She'd been messaging Karen, the founder of the Facebook support group. She had an idea about a new venture in which she wanted to invest and had sought advice from Karen. They'd also been discussing how to form websites and blogs to help the public become more aware of personality disorders and domestic abuse. They wanted to help people gain knowledge and become educated about narcissists and sociopaths. Awareness of the personality disorders was crucial in helping the victims. Sandra also acknowledged she might still be blaming herself for Daniel's atrocious behavior, if she hadn't stumbled onto Karen's group. She spent several hours each day visiting among the other members. Sandra had grown to love the women in their tight-knit sisterhood. She had bonded with dozens of the women and had a ton of respect for her *sisters*. They were intelligent, funny, beautiful brave souls, and she hoped to one day meet them in person.

Another undertaking she was contemplating was assisting those in her local area. She planned to build a type of sanctuary, a safehouse, where those escaping from the abuse of the monsters like

Daniel, could have a means to regain their footing after the victims ended their relationships from their abusers. From the extensive research she'd been doing the last few months, she greatly sympathized with those who were feeling desperate and alone, needing a safe place to go while they healed and began their new lives.

In the support group, she'd noticed many of the members had commented how they felt hopeless and stuck in their deplorable situations, because they had no support from family and were penniless. Sandra had ambitious plans to become part of the solution to the problem of those less fortunate than herself, and she was excited to break ground for the sanctuary of peace and recovery for those wounded from narcissistic monsters. She had also met with Lily Mathis about providing counseling for the victims, and Lily had graciously told her she'd be glad to provide *pro bono* therapy to those who couldn't afford treatment.

Sandra also wanted to take a trip to Mexico where she could properly mourn her friend, Marcy. She needed to return to their old stomping grounds and celebrate the good memories. The time had come for Sandra to travel more, enjoy herself, and continue her own recovery. The time had arrived for her to begin a new chapter and embark on her exciting, new adventure.

Chapter Twenty-One

That same Saturday morning, Jack had awakened from his own bad dream. He'd felt sympathy, as well as empathy, when Tessa had handed him her dream journal a few weeks prior, the first day they'd met. He had an idea of what she went through with the nightmares. His dreams were not prophetic like some of Tessa's, but he experienced frightful anxiety and horror with the recurring nightmares of his time in Afghanistan.

Awakening from the terror of his past, he sat up in bed and combed his fingers through his damp hair. He had terrible night sweats with the cruel dreams. Managing to crawl out from under the blanket, he slowly rose and opened his bedroom window seeking fresh air. He tried shaking the agonizing memories, but he could still hear screams, loud explosions, and bursts of gunfire echo inside his tortured mind.

Jack often dreamed of walking through the cornfields in the Helmand Province in Afghanistan. When he first arrived at the province and saw the vast amount of vegetation there, he had been extremely surprised. Other provinces were dry as a bone with a desert climate. He soon learned of the canals built in the 1950's by the United States to help the local farmers divert water from the Helmand and the Arghandab rivers used to water the crops. Unfortunately, the most profitable crops currently were the drug farms with their many acres and large amounts of opium poppies.

Haunting memories of ambushes from the Taliban, using the tall corn stalks and maise fields as cover to hide, and the deadly occurrences of finding I.E.D.'s, improvised explosive devices, were scarred into his subconscious. Tragically, he'd lost several friends and comrades to the devices. The homemade bombs, costing only ten dollars to make, cost many soldiers their lives.

Bitter memories of the notorious sand fleas, which were more like gnats or small flies, made him flinch. He had the unfortunate experience of being bitten many times, and on one occasion a bite resulted in a terrible, painful boil. The scar on his right calf was his reminder. Jack would always bear the scars, physically and emotionally, but he fully comprehended his scars were minor compared to the fallen and severely wounded troops of his brothers and sisters in arms.

Inhaling a deep breath, he let the cool air drifting from the opened window soothe him. The sun hadn't risen yet, and he noticed the song of a lone whip-poor-will bird not far from his house. He focused on the bird's serenade and began his morning prayer. After his spiritual talk with God, he felt calm and released a long sigh as the whip-poor-will continued singing.

Jack decided to take a long, steamy shower. Afterwards, dressed in jeans and a white t-shirt with USMC in red letters splayed across his chest, he decided to wash his sheets and tackled the huge mound of his dirty clothes, as well. Within a few hours, he'd finished his laundry and remade his bed, vacuumed the area rugs, swept, and mopped the terracotta tiles in the kitchen.

He turned on the outside water sprinkler. He was doing his best to keep his aunt's garden alive. Fragrant hyacinths, purple crocus, and bright yellow daffodils graced the front flower bed. Trying to keep busy to prevent his troubled mind from recalling the dreadful flashbacks, he turned on Aunt Elizabeth's old stereo and cranked up the bass, making the speakers thrum to the music.

He loved her choice of cd's and grinned as one of his aunt's favorite bands began playing. He turned up the volume and sang along with ZZ Top. Thinking of Tessa, he started dancing in the kitchen to *Sharp Dressed Man*. He continued cleaning, placing plates and glasses in the dishwasher and emptied the trash can. The next song, *Cheap Sunglasses*, began to play, and Jack turned up the volume on his vocal cords. As he was dancing and loudly jamming to the southern-boogie tunes, he began to relax, and the nightmare continued to recede. Jack was feeling much better; then he noticed he wasn't alone.

"Don't stop on my account. You're doing great!" Tessa leaned on the front doorjamb wearing a huge grin, and he quickly walked over to the front entrance and pulled her inside the house.

Jack spun her around the living room, dancing to the loud music, and they both were singing and laughing. When *She's Got Legs* began playing, he teasingly eyed Tessa's long legs. Once the song and two more of ZZ Top's hits had stopped playing, they collapsed on the couch, holding each other's hands and feeling pure joy.

They spent the rest of the afternoon and evening talking until they were hoarse. Jack told her more about his beloved aunt, and she told him about her big family. She invited him to her mother's birthday party, and he quickly accepted.

After grilling steaks and baked potatoes outside, they feasted and later decided to watch a movie on his large, seventy-two-inch flat screen television. Getting comfortable on the black leather couch, Tessa settled into Jack's arms. They watched *Stranger Things* on Netflix, which seemed perfect for their unplanned, spontaneous date. The day had turned into a genuinely entertaining and fun time for both Jack and Tessa.

When the time came for her to leave, he walked her outside and opened her Mustang's car door. He held her tight, and they stood beside Mabel for several minutes, swaying to the remembered tunes of the southern-rock music to which they'd danced earlier. Jack hummed, and their feet gently shuffled to the lingering beat.

"Thank you for coming to see me, Tessa. I can't tell you how much I needed this. Call me as soon as you get home, so I'll know you made it safely."

Jack leaned down, and they shared a tender kiss. Tessa sighed, slowly sat down on the mustang's front seat and turned the key in the ignition. Mabel purred to life, and she waved at Jack as she put the car in reverse and backed away. Shifting into first gear, she glanced in her rearview mirror. She could see him standing there, watching her accelerate down the graveled driveway. She hadn't been so ecstatically happy in ages.

~~~~~~~~~~~~~~~~~~~~

Jack was almost skipping when he went back into the big log house. It had been such a simple impromptu evening, but he'd
~~~~~~~~~~~~~~~~~~~~

enjoyed their time immensely. He was completely at ease with Tessa, and he thought she seemed to feel the same about him. They enjoyed each other's company, and he thought his Aunt Elizabeth would like her.

The next morning, he planned on going to the assisted living center where his beloved aunt now lived. She had invited him to join her, to attend church services, and he looked forward to seeing her. He loved his Aunt Elizabeth and knew he could never repay her for taking him in and raising him. She had been his rock, and she'd taught him about all the important things in life. He recalled her saying on many occasions to him, "Treat people how you want to be treated." The Golden Rule.

She'd taught him about God and the importance of being a servant to the Lord. He read the Bible she'd gifted to him, and she'd explained scripture from God's Word. She also instructed him to be a gentleman, to be kind and thoughtful of others. He knew he was lucky he had a loving aunt and the warm home she'd shared with him.

He looked around the clean kitchen and tidy living room and was glad he'd spent his morning taking care of the big old house. He decided to ask his aunt if she'd like to spend tomorrow afternoon in her home after church, and he'd take her back to the assisted living center afterwards. Moving two rib-eye steaks from the freezer to the refrigerator to thaw, he planned on cooking a delicious meal for his dear aunt. By the time he had prepared his clothes for church for the next day, he didn't even realize he'd driven the haunting battles of Afghanistan out of his mind. Promises of a bright future overruled the darkness of his past.

Chapter Twenty-Two

The OSBI, Oklahoma State Bureau of Investigations, was now involved with the investigation of the death of Marcy Phillips. Another body with the same physical description as Marcy had been discovered in a town in southwest Oklahoma in 2014. She had been identified as a cashier who worked at a truck stop. Since the prime suspect, Daniel O'Brien, was a truck driver, whose logbook and fuel card were reported used near the truck stop at the time of the woman's demise, speculation and theories were being discussed that O'Brien may have murdered both Marcy and the woman found in 2014.

Detective Parker had been assigned other cases, but he stayed abreast of the progress of the ongoing O'Brien case. Currently, he and Craig were investigating the increasing reports of thefts in the small town. Most of the thefts seemed related with several details. The thieves had been targeting farms, barns, and houses in rural areas. Evidence so far determined that the robbers were hitting the houses and barns late at night. A wide variety of the reported stolen items included electronic items such as televisions and computer equipment, jewelry and cash… to larger items such as motorcycles, ATV four wheelers, farm equipment, and even large amounts of diesel. Jack was determined to help find the thieves and hopefully have some of the stolen items returned to their rightful owners.

Craig walked into the office and asked Jack how his weekend had gone, and Jack answered him with a big, loopy smile. "So, that grin makes me think you spent some quality time with that blue-eyed nurse, right?" Craig drawled.

"Yes, we hung out together and grilled some steaks on Saturday. Then, I spent all day Sunday with my Aunt Elizabeth. It was a great weekend. How was yours?"

Craig smiled and said, "Tina and I finally finished building our outdoor kitchen and grill in the back yard. We've enjoyed it already and decided we need a big barbeque next weekend to celebrate. Of course, you're invited and more than welcome to bring Tessa. I've got the swimming pool going, so you might want to bring your swim trunks."

"Isn't it a little cool in the evenings to go swimming?"

Craig grinned, "No worries. Mine is a heated pool, and that bad boy feels like a hot tub."

Jack thanked his partner and said he'd be sure to ask Tessa if she'd be available.

The time was only 11:00am, but Jack was hungry. He'd been up since five o'clock working out at the gym with his friend, Tony Andrews. He'd only had a light breakfast consisting of a protein shake, so he decided he'd have an early lunch at the Biscuit Hill Diner and beat the lunch rush. As he walked into the diner, sniffing the fragrant aroma of old-fashioned burgers fried with onions, he saw Robert, the supervisor from Thomas Trucking, and four other employees of the trucking company. They wore red, short sleeved uniform shirts with black stripes on the sleeves, and they were seated in a large corner booth. Robert saw him and waved, and Jack took a seat at a small table next to the booth where the men were finishing their coffee.

"Hey there, Robert. How are you guys doing?" Jack greeted them.

Robert smiled and replied, "All is good. Any new developments in O'Brien's case… that you can talk about?"

When Jack shook his head, Robert continued, "Jack, I want you to know how mortified we all were when everything came out about O'Brien." The other four men in the booth nodded their heads in agreement and looked sorrowful. He continued, "Word around town is that there was an anonymous witness who steered you guys into looking at O'Brien for killing that girl found in the lake. Is that true?"

Jack answered, "I can't really get into any details about the case, Robert, but hopefully the OSBI will have more answers for us soon."

A smiling waitress approached his table, and Jack ordered a chicken fried steak sandwich and a Dr Pepper. As she left to turn in his order, the other men in the booth joined the conversation.

One of the men, with the name tag on his shirt reading *Brian*, said, "Men like Daniel give truckers a bad name. I never did like that guy. I know lots of truck drivers who are outstanding fathers and husbands, family men, who work hard and provide well for their families."

The older man sitting next to Brian, who's name tag read *David* chimed in, "That's true. There's lots of good folks who are drivers. We have several husband and wife teams who drive together. They're law abiding, hard-working people who get a bad rap because of jerks like O'Brien. It isn't right."

The other men sitting with them nodded in agreement. Robert glanced at his watch, asked them if they were ready to head back to the yard, and they rose from the booth and wished Jack good luck with the case.

After they left the diner, the waitress served Jack his sandwich and drink. He bowed his head and silently said Grace over his meal. He refueled his body with the tasty sandwich and asked the waitress if he could get a Dr Pepper to go.

Driving back to the station, he continued contemplating Robert's comment about the town gossip regarding the murder case. He needed to ask Craig about exactly what was being said regarding the *anonymous witness* part of the gossip. Only he, Craig, and Chief Mullins knew the only witness was Tessa, and her witnessing the murder in her nightmare was supposed to have been kept confidential. He and Craig had been careful to work the set of Pinto car keys, found in O'Brien's luggage, into the case evidence using Sandra's confirmation of the keys description and had left out the sketches drawn by Tessa. Maybe the chief had informed the OSBI of information about the dream journals, and someone had slipped up. He prayed Tessa's name wouldn't be associated with the case, and he felt his neck muscles stiffen and tense as he worried.

Back in his office, the old, outdated telephone on his desk rang. There had been another theft from a farmer's barn, and Jack took the call. He wrote down the address and agreed to meet the latest victim of the *Barn Raiders*, as the thieves had become known. Observing the address, he noticed it was between Morrigan and Mineral Springs. Jack thought about Tessa's parents living on a farm not far from there. He needed to remind her to give her parents a heads up and to lock and secure their house, barn and equipment. The thieves seemed to be widening their perimeter.

A half hour later, he pulled into the farmhouse's driveway, and Jack noticed an elderly farmer walking toward him from the barn. He was in his seventies, wearing denim overalls, not quite six feet tall, with white hair and light blue eyes. He reached out to shake his hand, and Jack felt the vise-like grip of the farmer's large calloused handshake. Like many of the farmers and ranchers Jack knew, this man had a ruddy complexion from working too many long hours in Oklahoma's ruthless weather. He had worked hard for what he owned, and Jack's temper flared to think some punk thieves stole from him.

He introduced himself as Marvin Ellison. His eyes were kind, and he smiled at Jack saying, "Glad you could make it all the way out here, Detective. I'll show you what's missing from my barn. I have a list."

After taking Marvin's statement and the long list of stolen items, he dusted the barn's doorknobs and door handles for fingerprints. He walked around the outside of the building, but there weren't any tire tracks on the grass and nothing to indicate anything was amiss.

Marvin commented, "I didn't lock the barn door last night, but the wife and I didn't hear anything unusual either. I did hear Betty barking around 2:00am, but I thought she was barking at coyotes." About that time, a large black Labrador retriever trotted towards them. She warily looked at Jack and wedged herself between him and Marvin, protecting her master.

Jack told Marvin, as he handed him his card, "Give me a call if you think of anything else. We'll do everything possible to try locating your property, Sir."

It was after three o'clock by the time he returned to his desk, and he was feeling concerned about Tessa and any potential problems that might result from the rumor of an anonymous witness. He noticed Craig had just walked in. No one else was in the office, so he asked his partner, "Have you heard about the latest gossip in town? I had lunch at Biscuit Hill, and Robert, from Thomas Trucking, was there. He mentioned there was a rumor of an anonymous witness implicating O'Brien as the murderer of Marcy Phillips."

Craig frowned and answered, “I hadn’t heard about that rumor, Jack. We need to speak to the chief to see what’s going on. By the way, our *Barn Raiders* case just got more complicated. They’ve graduated to stealing cattle… a lot of them. We’ve got cattle rustlers to deal with now.”

Chapter Twenty-Three

The Three *Amigas*, met at the Cedar Trail walking path at six-thirty. The trail had been expanded and runners and walkers had the option of one, or two-mile sections, since the city had purchased and cleared land adjacent to the old park. There were still lots of trees and wild sand-plum bushes surrounding the new trail. Tessa thought how she would be glad when there was more daylight in the early mornings as summer progressed. The shadows in the trees made her uneasy, even knowing the shadows were only of more trees and cottontail rabbits that hopped from the trail into the nearby tree line.

After the first mile, the girls were taking deep breaths. They slowed their pace and commented how there were more rolling terraces with steeper grades on the new mile section. Tessa liked her new running tights and being outside felt exhilarating. They ran the two-mile trail a second time and then stopped at the paved parking area where their cars were parked.

"That was a great four miles, girls!" Tessa told her friends. They stretched their legs and took long swigs from their water bottles. "Provided the weather cooperates with us, want to do this again on Wednesday morning?"

The friends agreed to meet in a couple of days. As Tessa drove to her house which was only a few miles away, she looked in her rearview mirror noticing a burgundy colored, late model sedan following her from Cedar Trails. She observed there were two men in the car, and they turned their heads to look at her house when she pulled into her driveway. They slowly continued driving down the street, and she squinted at the sedans license plate noting it was a New Jersey tag. Tessa chided herself for feeling uneasy and told herself she was being paranoid, yet the slowly moving vehicle made her feel apprehensive. She ran inside, took a quick shower, and hurriedly dressed in her nursing scrubs and slipped on comfortable Nike work shoes. She pulled back her long hair, put on a little mascara, swiped her favorite coral-colored lip gloss on her chapped lips, and was out the door.

Her workday was uneventful, and as she drove Mabel home, she hoped she'd hear from Jack later. Once she changed into her favorite gardening clothes, old jean shorts and a faded tank top, Tessa eagerly went outside to feel the warm sunshine on her face. She pulled weeds and grass from the flower garden in her back yard. After watering the pink and purple petunias and newly sprouted marigolds, she took her weed whacker from the garage and started trimming around the borders of the flower garden and around the wooden deck. She continued edging around the front yard, sidewalk, and the driveway.

After admiring her work, she went inside the house to shower and put on fresh clothes. As she was combing her towel dried hair, she heard her front doorbell chime. Carrying her wide toothed comb with her, she went to the door and was pleasantly surprised to see Jack. Seeing him in person was much better than a text or phone call.

"Hey, there!" She eagerly invited him inside.

"Tess, your flowers are beautiful," he genuinely praised, as he gazed at the peachy orange of the daylilies planted next to the front porch.

She thanked him, and he followed her inside and into the kitchen. She poured tall glasses of iced mint tea, and they sat at her round kitchen table.

"You seem worried, Jack. What's going on?" Tessa had noticed he seemed tense as he rubbed the back of his neck. She continued studying his worry lines between his brows as she finished combing tangles from her freshly washed hair.

"I've just got a lot on my mind, but I wanted to let you know about a case I'm working on right now. Have you heard about the recent thefts around Morrigan?"

"Yes, I was just reading in the newspaper at work today how the thefts seem to be increasing. Is there more to it?"

"I spoke with a farmer today… his name is Marvin, and he lives between Morrigan and Mineral Springs. He and a lot of other farmers have been hit by these punk thieves. They're expanding their area, and I wanted to let you know to give your parents a heads up. I know a lot of people who live in the country and on farms are trusting souls who rarely lock their barns or houses." Thinking of the kind old farmer he'd spoken with earlier renewed his ambition to apprehend the thieves.

"There's something else I wanted to mention to you. I had a guy ask me this morning if there's an anonymous eyewitness to the Marcy Phillip's case. Has anyone said anything to you or asked you about it?"

She looked concerned and answered, "Yes, I've heard that's the latest rumor being told… that there's a witness who implicated Daniel O'Brien as the murderer. Do you think someone found out about me… and my inadvertently seeing him assault Marcy in my dream?"

Jack told her, "I'm not aware of what exactly has been said, but I assure you, Craig and I will get to the bottom of it. Have you heard about the latest robberies in the area? There's been new reports of cattle rustling."

"Cattle rustling? What's going on in our sleepy, little town, Jack?"

They discussed theories that the thefts and the recent cattle rustling were considered the result of increased drug use, especially methamphetamines and heroin within the whole state. The drug users needed more money to buy, and the manufacturers needed more money to make their poison. The vicious circle created destruction and loss to many lives.

"It's getting worse every day. Makes me furious…and sad." Jack shook his head and looked frustrated.

Tessa told him about a patient who had come into the doctor's office earlier that day. Because of HIPPA laws, she couldn't give him the girl's name.

Tessa commented, "I was horrified at the scabs on the girl's skin and even on her scalp. They were infected, and her teeth… the few she had left, were a decaying mess. She was practically skeletal. She was only twenty-four years old but easily looked twice her age. The doctor gave her a prescription for antibiotics, but other than that… there wasn't much he could do."

They sat in Tessa's cozy kitchen and discussed the tragedy of drug addiction and the appalling aftermath resulting from the destructive dependence, including robberies and thefts. Tessa promised to call her parents that evening and warn them to keep everything under lock and key.

"There's one other thing I need to ask you. Craig and his wife, Tina, are having a barbeque next weekend, and we're both invited. Want to go with me, or do you already have plans?" Jack was hoping she'd say yes.

"Yes, I'd love to. Do I need to bring a dish or anything?" Tessa was thrilled he had asked.

Standing and stretching, he said, "I don't think we do, but I'll ask. Craig mentioned he has their swimming pool open and suggested we bring our swimsuits. It's a heated pool, so the water should be plenty warm and comfortable. Well, I'd better get to work on this cattle theft case."

She walked him to the door, and they both were smiling as they looked forward to the weekend. He planted a gentle kiss on her lips and headed back to the station. The night was going to be a long one for Jack and his pursuit of the cattle rustlers.

Chapter Twenty-Four

After Jack left Tessa's house, he decided to drive to the coffee shop and grill in town where quite a few farmers and ranchers often hung out. He wanted to pick their brains, see if they had any information that hadn't been reported. Sometimes, town gossip could be enlightening.

Entering *Ethel's Grill*, Jack took a seat at the counter and ordered a cup of black coffee and a slice of pecan pie. *Ethel's* was a small restaurant with four booths on one wall, four large round tables, and the counter where he sat had eight barstools. The coffee shop was over half full, and as he'd expected, the topic of conversation was the recent cattle rustling.

Several of the men in the restaurant smiled and waved at Jack. Marvin Ellison, the kind farmer he'd met earlier that day, was sitting with a group of elderly farmers. He spotted Jack and waved him over to their table.

"Sit down with us, Jack," he invited.

"Thanks fellas… how's it going?" he smiled and joined the group of men, who were hard working souls, dedicated to their farms and families. He had known several of them all his life.

"We're just sitting here trying to solve all the world's problems. Would be nice if we could start with the thieving meth heads here in our town first," one of the men said.

Another farmer added, "These drug addicts are making it hard on honest people, stealing from us to feed their dang habit. I hear tell heroin and cocaine are on the rise, not just meth."

"Have you guys got any ideas who might be leading this band of thieves?" asked Jack as he took another bite of pecan pie. "We have a few leads, but I appreciate any input you'd like to add."

"I don't know, but they have to be scoping us out. The cattle they stole from Johnny Kendall's place had just been moved to the pasture north of their house, where they easily stole them without being seen. The pasture is situated a fair distance from the house," said Jim, a neighbor who lived south of the Kendall Ranch.

The farmer sitting beside Jim commented, "Ole Ben Reed was seen driving his police cruiser by the Kendall Ranch last week. Not sure what he was looking for." Lines crinkled around his eyes as he grinned and continued, "Officer Reed couldn't find his butt with both hands in his back pockets."

The friends and cronies chuckled. Another of the older fellows held an unlit pipe to his mouth, and chimed in, "Wish they'd make it like the old days and hang cattle rustlers and thieves."

Jack grinned and replied, "Well, Titus, that's illegal." Everyone laughed, and Jack continued, "Actually, hanging horse thieves and cattle rustlers never was legal, but vigilantes would sometimes take the law into their own hands. The bad thing about that is they hung the wrong people a lot of times. We'll catch these thieves, but if you guys hear anything, please give me a holler."

Jack handed out his business cards to everyone in the coffee shop. The customers all knew he was a man of his word and had every intention of catching the thieves. He started to pay for his coffee and pie, but the waitress told him it was on the house. Jack thanked her and waved to everyone as he left.

He drove back to the station to look over the evidence gathered from the Kendall Ranch. He wanted to take a hard look at the list of employees who worked there. Jim had a good point about the herd just being moved to the pasture where no one could see them being loaded and then stolen.

The hour was late when he parked his car in the police station's nearly empty parking lot. In the shadows where there were few security light poles, he noticed Ben Reed was talking to someone in a silver Ford dually pickup. As Ben walked away from the big truck and got in his police cruiser, the driver of the truck was rolling up his window. Jack couldn't see the face of the driver, but he noticed the man wore a red shirt which jogged something in Jack's memory. Both the dually pickup truck and Ben, in his cruiser, drove away with Ben following the loud diesel truck down the street.

Where have I seen a shirt like that? he wondered to himself. Feeling apprehensive, he tried to remember and wished he could have seen the man's face. He got out of his sedan and watched the vehicles drive away for as far as he could see them. Another cruiser pulled into the parking lot, and Sergeant Gary Deevers and K-9 Officer Thor climbed out of the car.

Sergeant Deevers was a stocky built man, sixty-two years old and had been a veteran of the police force for over thirty years. Thor was a four-year old Belgian Malinois, a cousin of German Shepherds, that had been part of the MPD for the last year. The black and tan K-9 had proven himself invaluable as a detection trained dog. Since the recent outbreak of drug activity, he had been instrumental in several drug busts and had also protected his handler when an aggressive addict had been overly stimulated from meth. Sergeant Deevers had been overtaken by the violent addict, but Thor quickly turned the criminal into a chew toy. The fearless K-9 officer had received extra dog treats that day, and Sergeant Deevers had given his notice to the Chief. He was in the process of training the new handler, as well as eagerly planning his golden years. After the one-month bonding process for Thor and his new handler, to establish their relationship was complete, Sergeant Deevers would begin his long-awaited retirement.

Jack greeted the officers, "Hey there Sergeant. How are you doing, Thor?" The keen-eyed K-9 officer wagged his tail in greeting.

"Working late tonight, Parker?" asked the Sergeant.

"Yes sir, guess we're all putting in overtime these days," Jack answered. "Have a good night, Sarge."

Jack waved and walked into the station to his office. Craig was still there, sitting at his cluttered desk, and was going through the evidence from the cattle theft. He told Jack he had double-checked all the livestock auction sites in the area, making sure no one had brought in cattle to sell matching the description of the stolen herd. Jack began looking through the case file and noticed the brand used on the cattle. It was the letter K, and it had a letter R overlapping the K. He took a photo of the brand with his cell phone.

Next, he looked at the list of ranch hands and employees of the Kendall Ranch. Even though the ranch hands had given their statements at the station, Jack and Craig decided to pay each of the employees a visit the next day. The evening was getting late, and both the detectives decided to call it a night.

As Jack was driving out of the parking lot, he hit his brakes as he suddenly remembered where he'd seen the red shirt before worn by the man talking to Ben. Wondering what the connection was to Ben Reed, he vowed to find out the next day after he and Craig questioned the ranch employees.

Chapter Twenty-Five

Tessa immediately called her father after hearing the warnings from Jack about the increase in thefts and burglaries. Her father promised to be extra cautious and to keep his eyes peeled. Tessa smiled when he made that comment, because she knew he'd be carrying binoculars and patrolling the back roads in his area.

Shortly after hanging up her call with her father, she received a call from Sandra Dawson. She was pleased to hear from her and even more happy to hear her good news. Sandra was on a roll with her new venture of the shelter, safehouse which she was building for abused women and children. She was making amazing progress.

She planned on naming it after her slain friend, Marcy, but she hadn't decided what the exact name would be yet. Her plan was to lease her condo and live on the same grounds of the sanctuary. She would have her home on the property as well as sixteen apartments, within eight duplexes. They would be temporary homes for the guests… the abused victims. Once they had found their footing, she would help them find employment and their own home. Her objective was to give them a safe place to heal and find peace.

With counseling and some time, she hoped to help them find their joy and purpose.

Several offices would be located on the grounds. There would be an office for her accountant, one for her lawyer, one for counselor Lily Mathis, one set up with supplies and instruments for minor medical needs, and there would be a conference room. Sandra wanted to make her effort a professional venture and knew she'd be meeting with benefactors, attorneys, church and state officials.

There would also be a clubhouse, where children could play in a safe, protected environment. They would be able to play outside as well, on a gigantic fenced in playground. Sandra's enthusiasm was delightful.

Tessa asked her how she'd been feeling, and Sandra confided to her that she had good days and bad days. She still had moments when the dark memories of Daniel overwhelmed her, and she mentioned she was still researching personality disorders. They discussed how education and becoming informed was the key to recovery. Her online support group was continuing to give her insight and knowledge. She was growing, and she was happier than she'd been in many years. She told her young friend about the group of women, who she called her "Sisterhood". Their love and support for one another was genuine and treasured. She mentioned the founder of the group to Tessa.

"Tessa, this group of survivors have become like family to me. Karen founded the group five years ago, and there are thousands of women who have become educated about narcissism and psychopathy through this FaceBook group. We've healed and grown together. I feel as though my energy, my spirit, is filled to the brim. All these years with Daniel, he must have been draining me. I've heard people refer to sociopaths and narcissists as energy vampires and soul vampires, basically depleting their victims as their supply as they abused and controlled them. Now, I get it… I understand the analogy. I feel like a new person. All those years of being on edge, carefully walking on eggshells to not disturb him, I was a nervous wreck." Sandra sounded more positive and optimistic than Tessa had expected.

When they hung up their call, Tessa felt pleased that her new friend was doing so well. She knelt in front of her dragonfly chair. Closing her eyes, the prayer warrior bowed her head and began praising God for His blessings. She prayed that He would give

Sandra knowledge and guidance with building the sanctuary of peace and healing. She prayed for protection and safety for her family and for Jack.

As she ended her prayer, she stood up and walked onto her front porch. The Angel Dogs were there, as they had been for weeks, guarding her home at night. She sat on the floor of the porch to be near them and felt thankful for the blessing of her sweet-natured furry friends.

She remained with the Angel Dogs for several minutes with their soft silver heads in her lap, and she quietly spoke to them and pet them. She stood and went to fetch the dogs their biscuit treats. Back inside her warm home, she prepared for bed. She was tired and fell asleep right away. After a few hours of fitful sleep, she saw the monster.

In her dream, Daniel O'Brien was young. Tessa was looking through Marcy's eyes again the night she had died. They were at Lake Crampton, and the night's darkness concealed the shadow of someone standing a few feet behind the murderer. The men were standing in front of the campfire beside the lake, and O'Brien seemed drunk as he staggered toward her. The shadow man was motionless, and she couldn't distinguish anything significant about him. He remained a dark silhouette beside the roaring fire as the flames spit red sparks, landing and sputtering into ash on the lakes beach. O'Brien drank from a silver beer can, tipped it back, swigging every drop, then crushed it within his fist and tossed it aside.

The next second, her dream morphed. Looking through her own eyes, not Marcy's, Tessa saw herself running along the Cedar Trails path. She came to a screeching halt when she saw the murderer blocking the trail. He appeared to be in present day, with gray hair and a large paunchy stomach. With wide shoulders hunched forward, he looked dark and sinister. He glared at her with his hooded evil eyes. Wearing a smirk, he crossed his arms across his thick chest, and his viper-eyes suddenly shifted to something or someone behind her. In the dream, she turned to see what he was staring at. She saw two large menacing men. O'Brien's flying monkeys were stalking her. The same as the silhouette of the man standing on the lakes rocky beach by the campfire, she couldn't make out their faces. Her heart pounded against her chest, and panic clutched at her lungs. She felt vulnerable, exposed, and she couldn't breathe. O'Brien laughed at her fear.

She would never forget that horrible, cruel laugh and gravelly voice, as he uttered and hissed with his lisp, "I know it was you… who gave me up to the cops. You ruined my life. I'll be seeing you soon, Tessa Ryan."

With a loud gasp, Tessa woke and opened her eyes wide. Sitting upright in her bed, taking deep breaths, Tessa trembled from her head to her toes. She wondered what the bad dream meant and asked herself who the shadowy men were. Obviously, they were O'Brien's henchmen, but who were they? Both macabre scenarios felt unnerving. Tessa also wondered why her dream patterns seemed to be changing. Until recently, she had never had dreams that seemed to shift gears, changing from the past to the present in the blink of an eye.

Looking at the clock on her nightstand, she saw the green neon numbers saying the time was 4:01am. She slowly crawled out of bed and padded to her front door. She glanced outside, and the three Angel Dogs raised their silver heads and looked at her. She was relieved to see them and closed her front door, quickly turning the lock.

Sitting on her dragonfly chair, she wrapped herself in a velvety fleece blanket and tried to quiet her racing mind. Warning bells and red flags were telling her *Danger! Danger! Danger!* She had no doubt she was in danger from Daniel O'Brien. She knew it with absolute certainty. Somehow, he had discovered she was the one who had identified him and was the anonymous eyewitness. *How is that even possible?*

Trying to calm her nerves, she flipped on her television to try focusing on something else. The fifty-inch flat screen was mounted on the wall over the fireplace; an arched Edwardian hearth which was wrapped in dark green tiles from the 1930's. Realizing she wasn't even watching the program on the screen, she turned off the TV a half hour later. She gazed around her beloved, cozy home and for the first time, she felt unsafe.

Looking at her inadequate old locks on her front door, she stood and strode to her laptop with purpose in her step. Clicking the online Yellow Pages, she searched for locksmiths in her area and wrote down a couple of phone numbers. As soon as their shops opened, she would call and compare prices, then she'd order all new locks for each exterior door. She walked through every room of her house and checked that the windows were locked.

Suddenly, she didn't feel fear; she felt anger. There was no way she would allow the monster to cause her to feel afraid. She would take precautions, but she wouldn't let him intimidate her. She added another phone number beside the locksmiths. She'd hire a carpenter to install motion sensor lights, especially in the back yard and by the garage. She was also considering installing a security system. She would be ready for him and his flying monkeys.

She normally felt a kind of sadness after a bad dream, but this one just made her furious and determined to overcome the evil that emanated from O'Brien. She would not become one of his victims. She wrote in her dream journal, noting everything she could remember of the dark dream with her teeth grinding in determination to overcome the barbaric, hideous brute's attack. With absolute certainty, she knew he was coming for her. When she'd first heard the rumor about an anonymous witness implicating O'Brien, she knew it was a matter of time before she'd be identified. Her question was how and who had named her.

Tessa pondered what the man in the shadows by the firepit at Lake Crampton meant. *Was there more than one person involved in Marcy's death, or were their other victims at that location?* She decided to share the dream and her concerns with Jack.

Chapter Twenty-Six

In the early morning of the shift, Craig and Jack were anxious to get some answers on the cattle rustling case. As they made their way toward their office, Jack saw Ben amble into the breakroom.

He told Craig he'd meet him in the office in a few minutes and followed Ben. Jack got a strong cup of coffee from the vending machine, which he referred to as his *mud,* and watched Ben sit down and make a phone call on his cell. He wandered toward the table where the grumpy looking officer sat and dropped quarters into a vending machine near him. As he bent down to retrieve his granola bar in the bottom of the machine, he overheard Ben speaking with someone, and the annoyance in the tone of his voice spoke volumes.

Jack heard him say, "I wish I'd never met him or even heard his name before. You have to shut him up, hear me?"

Ben hung up his call and stomped out of the breakroom. Jack nonchalantly followed, taking a bite of the granola bar and sipped on his mud. He followed Ben to the front of the station and watched him hurry outside towards the west side of the building. Jack carefully strolled to one of the offices where he could look out a window. He observed Ben speaking to the driver in the silver dually pick-up truck again. Frustrated, Jack couldn't see the driver to verify who he suspected was meeting the crabby officer.

When Ben came back inside, he looked annoyed, piquing Jack's interest further. He saw Ben leave with his co-worker and partner, Officer Warren, and heard him mention they needed to check on a call. As they left the building, Jack noticed Officer Connors entering the station. He took a last swig and threw the paper cup and granola wrapper into a nearby trash can. He waved at Tiffany.

"Buy you a cup of coffee, Connors?" Jack offered.

"I need something stronger, Detective, like a six-pack of mega Red Bull. I worked the late shift and need to do a load of paperwork, and then I can *bounce*." She looked tired, and Jack thought he'd hurry and ask her a couple of quick questions before she clocked out and went home.

"Any news out on the street… about the thefts going on, or anything from any narcs about dope dealers lately?" he hoped she had heard something.

"There's talk about the cattle rustling… mostly it's only people talking, and there's a lot of speculating going on, but people are being more conscientious about locking their doors. There's a couple of guys whose names were mentioned last night. Matt and Jeff Hayes… brothers, and their names came up when a couple of our snitches talked about dealing meth. One of my informants was *throwing shade* on Matt, the older brother. Apparently, he's a real *skeve*." She shrugged her shoulders.

Jack wondered if the Hayes brother being a jerk and disliked by his users and dealers might be helpful for them at some point in the investigation. "Thanks for that info. Hey, do you ever work with Officer Reed? He's been jumpy lately… wondering if he's okay."

"I try to avoid Officer Reed if I can, but now that you mention it, he has been more irritable lately. Of course, he's always ticked off about something. Wish he'd retire."

Jack thanked Tiffany and told her to go home and get some well-deserved rest. He walked down the hall to his and Craig's office. He expected Craig was ready to drive out to Johnny Kendall's ranch.

After interviewing the seven employees and ranch hands on the Kendall Ranch, Craig and Jack narrowed their list down to three employees they suspected could potentially be involved in the cattle rustling. One of the employees had a history of DUI's, and the other two had ties to people with drug arrests, although they themselves hadn't been arrested.

Jack asked, "How do we know if any of these three guys were involved or had any knowledge of the cattle being stolen? Can we request drug tests to be done on them?"

"As a matter of fact, Johnny Kendall did just that. He told the employees that drug tests were going to be mandatory, and there would be random drug tests done in the future. We should have the employee's test results back today."

Walking to his desk, Jack felt his phone vibrate. Pulling the cell from his pocket, he saw it was a call from Tessa. He immediately answered and became concerned from the tone of her voice.

"Jack… I need to tell you about something. It's important. Can you come by my house this evening?"

Suddenly feeling uneasy, he responded, "Has something happened, Tess? When is your lunch break? How about we grab something at Sonny's Drive-In?"

"It was another dream… nightmare. I'll explain later. Yeah, lunch sounds good. I can leave here in fifteen minutes."

Sitting at the drive-in, munching on a cheeseburger, Jack listened to Tessa inform him of her latest bad dream. Her body language indicated she was extremely tense. Having complete confidence in her dreams and their interpretation, he could feel himself become tense as well. He knew she wasn't overreacting or being paranoid. Tessa wasn't the type to be overly dramatic, so if she said she believed she was in potential danger, Jack believed her completely.

"Would you consider staying with your friends, your *amigas*, until we can get to the bottom of this?" When she shook her head no, he suggested, "Then, please consider installing a security system. I'd rather you not take any chances." He felt protective of her and quite worried.

She replied, "I don't want to put them in possible danger, and since I don't know who O'Brien's flying monkeys are… I'm not sure exactly what to do. We're too busy at the doctor's office for me to take vacation days. I think I just need to be extra cautious and install some dead bolt locks. I've already called a locksmith, and I'm waiting on a callback about costs of a security system, too."

Jack felt a sinking feeling in the pit of his stomach. Her dreams like this were always accurate. He wondered who O'Brien's two cronies were, or flying monkeys, as Tessa called them.

"No doubt, this criminal has several thugs in his orbit who are much like him. I'm going to check the visitors log from where O'Brien has been held and find out who all the monster has seen or called from jail. Tessa, I promise to keep you safe, and we will figure out who named you as the anonymous witness."

Only able to eat half his cheeseburger, he held her soft hand. Vigilant, protective feelings for the beautiful sapphire-eyed nurse jangled his nerves. The thought of anyone harming her made his stomach clench, and he tossed the untouched fries and remaining burger in the garbage. The time came to drive her back to Dr. Redman's office, but he only wanted to drive her to his house and lock the doors. He didn't want her out of his sight. *I need to make the Chief and Craig aware there could possibly be a second suspect in the murder of Marcy Phillips.* He also wondered who O'Brien's co-driver or co-workers were in 2014 at the time of the woman's death in western Oklahoma.

He gave an unhappy sigh and said, "Tessa, I know it's time to go back to work, but do you think you can take off early to meet someone about an alarm system? I have a buddy who would do us a favor and take care of the installation right away."

She knew checking into a security system was the prudent thing to do. "Jack, I promise to take off work early. Do you know what time your friend can meet us at my house?"

Three hours later, both Tessa and Jack greeted his friend, Curtis, who owned an alarm and security business. Curtis was ex-military like Jack, and he seemed very knowledgeable of his field. She invited him to have dinner with her and Jack, and he graciously accepted.

She changed out of her nursing scrubs while Jack helped his friend take measurements of the rooms and house. Wearing Levi jeans and a black sleeveless blouse, she went into her kitchen pulling spices from shelves and cooking utensils from drawers. She gathered all the ingredients for her dish and started peeling and chopping potatoes and slicing Polish sausage. Sprinkling the casserole with pepper and salt, she covered the dish with foil and popped it in the oven. Cooking was one of her passions, especially when she was nervous. An hour later, Jack poked his head in the dining room, sniffing loudly as he breathed in the spicy aroma of her dish baking in the cheerful kitchen.

"Ahhhh, what is that amazing aroma?" he asked with a giant, dimpled grin.

"It's just a basic little casserole I learned how to make from my mom. You take Polish sausage and potatoes, cut into thin slices and layer in a casserole dish, then layer with green beans. Pour beef broth over it, cover and bake. I've got homemade biscuits to go with it, too. Oh… and I hope you and Curtis like apple pie."

"Oh, Tess. How much longer till it's done?" He looked and sounded like an impatient little boy. She informed him the meal should be ready in a few minutes. Jack offered to set the table and pour drinks. She removed a pitcher of ice-tea and a six-pack of Dr. Pepper from the refrigerator and handed it to him. Both men sat at the table, salivating for the sausage and potato casserole.

While partaking of generous helpings of the food, Jack and Curtis talked about the days they served together in Afghanistan. They'd been good friends before serving together, but now they were life-long buddies. They had a special kind of brotherhood. After a while, Tessa noticed Curtis was looking at her with an odd, curious expression. She asked him if anything was wrong.

"No, nothing is wrong, but I can't help but worry why you're wanting this security system installed so quickly. Are you okay? Has someone threatened you?" He seemed genuinely concerned.

"Not exactly, but I am uneasy of a… potential situation. Guess I just want to be proactive." Tessa tried to appear nonchalant.

"When you're at home, do you park your car inside your garage at all times? If you don't, please start keeping it there, and lock the garage doors when you walk into the house. Another thing that might be a good idea if you ever think you should become more proactive, take some clear scotch tape and place it towards the bottom of your car doors and the front of the hood after you get home at night, or when you park your car at work. Then, always check the tape to see if it's been disturbed before opening the door. It really isn't that hard to unlock someone's car. If someone has opened a door or tampered with your car, you'll be able to tell." Curtis had some good ideas.

By the end of the evening, Tessa had a more than adequate security system. Curtis would need to return to finish all the wiring and place some cameras outside, which would allow her to monitor her house with her cell phone and laptop. All in all, she felt ten times safer and beholden to both Curtis and Jack. Curtis left to go home, and Jack was double checking a few things on the sensors and indoor cameras. As Jack walked to the front door to leave, he felt distressed leaving Tessa alone.

"Lock up as soon as I leave, okay?" he felt conflicted.

She assured him she would be fine and thanked him for his thoughtfulness. She wrapped her arms around his waist and lay her head on his shoulder, breathing in his woodsy cologne. It was masculine, yet she thought it reminded her of rain in the forest.

She had a flashback of riding her paint pony Dolly through the woods near her childhood home. The gentle rain had washed the air clean that morning, giving the cottonwood trees a fresh, earthy perfume. She remembered looking up into the tall, glistening trees as raindrops plopped onto her cheeks. She'd never forget that special day with her pony and Mother Nature, and Jack's cologne triggered that fond memory.

"I love your necklace, Tess. Such a pretty cross." Jack complimented her turquoise pendant hanging from her neck which had been a gift from her Grandma Lucy. The necklace gave her comfort, and she wore it often.

"Thanks, I don't wear a lot of jewelry, but I seem to wear this pendant a lot. My grandmother gave it to me, so it's pretty special." Tessa smiled and wrapped her arms around Jack again.

"Special jewelry for a special girl." Jack didn't want to leave. He eventually walked out the front door to his pickup truck parked in her driveway. He hadn't been gone a minute when he called. She answered her phone and felt herself droop as he said, "Tessa, please shut your blinds in your windows. I know you've got the drapes pulled shut, but I can see your silhouette."

She closed the blinds, then tightly pulled the drapes shut. She was upset with herself that she hadn't thought of that.

"Is that better, Jack? Can you see anything now?" Her voice had a little tremble, and it was all he could do to leave. He assured her everything was fine and asked her to call him if anything happened, or if she needed him. She did her best to sound brave and confident. She thanked him again and wished him good night.

Chapter Twenty-Seven

Early the next morning, Tessa woke with a splitting headache. She text messaged her *amigas* that she couldn't make their morning run. She rarely called in sick for work, but her eye's blurriness considerably affected her vision. Painfully squinting, she seemed to be looking through a fuzzy tunnel. Sunlight sent searing pain through her temples, especially her right temple. Tessa wasn't confident she'd be able to drive. She called Dr. Redman to let him know she would need the day off, apologized for the unexpected time off request, and took some migraine medicine. She was glad she didn't have the awful headaches very often.

She crawled back into her four-poster bed, praying for relief from the pain. Within minutes, she had drifted back to sleep. When she awoke two hours later, the murderous pain had dulled significantly. The daylight didn't hurt her eyes as badly as when she'd first woke. She checked her phone and saw she'd received a text from Jack. She replied to his message and told him about her horrible headache. He immediately responded saying he hoped she felt better and to let him know if she needed him. Tessa took a long, leisurely bubble bath enjoying not having to rush. Thinking of the dark-haired detective, she hoped she would see Jack later.

~~~~~~~~~~~~~~~~~~~~
~~~~~~~~~~~~~~~~~~~~

Thirty miles away, Sandra was ecstatic her condo had leased so quickly. Ironically, the new tenant was Wanda from the restaurant. Sandra was thrilled the new manager was doing so well and wanted to lease her home. Wanda was ready to move in right away, so Sandra had started calling movers immediately. Her house was now empty, waiting for its new tenant. Sandra was anxious to move from the home she had shared with Daniel. She had decided to move into a hotel suite temporarily which was only a few miles from her new property. She had signed a contract with a local, well recommended carpenter, named Jacob Kiefer, who owned a contractor business with his son, Eric. They were making outstanding progress with the construction of her new home.

They'd prepared the site where the new house would be built, and they were currently installing the plumbing that needed finished before pouring the concrete foundation. She had felt excitement when gazing at the freshly dug dirt of the leveled building site, with pipe sticking up from the ground for future faucets and drains. She thought the construction site was a beautiful thing. Her mind raced as she imagined the rooms with their eclectic, modern ranch style décor. The house design she'd chosen was a large two-story, complete with a wide wrap-around porch. She closed her eyes and envisioned scattered pots of colorful flowers and rocking chairs along the covered veranda. She imagined herself sitting in one of the rockers, sipping from a cup of coffee and gazing at the magnificent view of the wooded, rolling hillside of her property.

Sandra planned on living in her hotel suite while the house was being completed. Her temporary living quarters were spacious and a bit ritzy, but she felt she needed pampering. During her wait for the completion of her new home, she also planned on staying in Cancun, Mexico for at least two weeks. Marcy and she had spent a memorable, fun five days there in 1991. That time had been their last vacation together, before she was brutally taken from her loved ones. She missed her best friend terribly. Even if her loss was so many years ago, the pain still grieved her.

The moving company packed most of her items and furniture. She packed her personal things and decided what she would need to take with her to the hotel and what could be put into storage at the moving company's warehouse until her new home was built. The moving company had also packed Daniel's furniture and clothes from his bedroom. She didn't want to look at or touch anything belonging to the monster. As soon as he'd signed the divorce papers, she had his things placed into a storage unit and paid for six months of storage costs per the terms of the divorce agreement. After that, he would need to take care of his property, even if he was in prison. She felt unburdened to put it behind her.

Within no time, all her belongings had been packed and moved to storage. While some things had been sold, several items she seldom used had been given away. She looked forward to buying new furniture for her new home. The time had come to say goodbye to her old house and her old life.

Walking from one empty room to the next, she realized there were mostly dismal memories in the condo. Even though Daniel had been gone much of the time, his presence darkened her thoughts. She stood in the middle of his old bedroom and visibly cringed thinking how she'd lived with a murderer.

The condo had two identical master bedroom suites. His mirrored hers in size and dimensions exactly. Their bathrooms were also the same size. He had a shelving unit the same as she had, and the large walk-in closets space was the exact same size as hers. As she was turning to leave, she looked at the shelving unit again. The police and OSBI had gone through his room, plus the movers had packed everything and moved out all of Daniel's belongings. So, why did she feel something was wrong, as though something was still here? The shelving unit felt off… different from hers, but they should have been identical.

She walked back into her now empty bedroom and looked closely at the shelving unit. Then, she quickly walked back to his bedroom. Comparing them, she realized the right lower shelves were different, but they shouldn't have been. To be able to examine them closer, she used the flashlight app on her phone and got down on her knees to look at the asymmetrical shelves. She wondered why she'd never noticed it before, but in truth, she rarely came into the room since she'd bought the condos almost six years ago.

Sandra realized she'd need some tools, so she went into the mostly empty garage and searched through the cabinets which were built on the side walls. She found a rusty putty knife about two inches wide and a little jar holding different sizes of screws and nails. She dumped the jar and picked out a nail around three inches long. With her makeshift tools, she hurried back to Daniel's shelving unit.

Prying along the edge of a board which was around three feet in length and about a foot in height, she could barely loosen the board. Daniel had evidently enclosed the lowest shelf. He had done an excellent job on matching the stain on the board compared to the rest of the unit. He had even used a router to round the edges giving the job a professional look. Suddenly, she was afraid of what she'd find. She quickly stood up and backed away from the shelf, goosebumps covering her arms. Shaking, she called Tessa and told her what she thought she may have stumbled upon. If she had found a hiding spot of Daniel's, what was hidden there? Tessa told her she'd call Jack immediately and advised Sandra to call the OSBI agent in charge of the murder case. Sandra told her she had his phone number and would call him as soon as they hung up.

In less than an hour, Sandra was joined by Tessa and Jack, and two agents who had brought tools, plus a video camera to film the investigation. Not being allowed in the room, Tessa and Sandra stood in the hall and curiously looked through the doorway leading into Daniel's old bedroom. They watched the agent who held a mallet, and what looked like some type of flexible joint knife. He gently tapped and began wedging the tool between the board and sides of the shelf unit. In a few minutes, he had pried the board loose. There were interior hinges on the bottom of the board that weren't visible from the outside, and the board flipped open, revealing a box.

The long, metal box was about ten inches tall which fit well inside the shelf space. Tessa looked at Jack and knew there was something horrible and sinister inside. She suggested she and Sandra wait in the front room, and Jack solemnly nodded in agreement. Taking Sandra by the hand, she led her away from whatever sick things Daniel had stashed in the hiding spot.

From the dining room, they could hear Jack and the men talking, but then the room got suspiciously quiet. A few minutes later, Jack walked into the front of the house where the women were waiting, sitting on the cushioned window seat in the dining area. His face was expressionless, but his eyes seemed troubled.

He softly said, "It seems we now have solid evidence tying Daniel to Marcy's death."

Sandra's hands lay in her lap, tight fisted. With her right fist, she pressed against her lips as a quiet sob escaped her throat. Tessa wrapped her arms around her friend, and as Tessa's eyes met Jack's, she knew there was a lot more that he hadn't told them.

She asked her grieving friend, "Would you like to come stay with me awhile, Sandra? Or is there somewhere else we can take you?" She wanted to get Sandra out of the house right away.

Sandra replied, "No, dear girl. It's okay. I have a hotel suite already, and I unpacked there this morning. I'm going to call Lily and see if she can meet me this evening. I think I need a session, or twelve, with my therapist after today. Thank you so much for coming here right away and bringing Jack. I can't imagine going through this horror without you two."

"Can I drive you to your hotel? Are you feeling up to driving?" Tessa noticed her friend's hands wouldn't stop shaking. "Jack and I rode together from Morrigan. How about I drive you in your car to your hotel, and Jack follows us?"

Sandra nodded and wiped her tear-stained cheeks. Once they'd escorted Sandra to her hotel suite, Jack and Tessa drove back to Morrigan. The first ten minutes of the drive were quiet ones.

Finally, Tessa asked him, "What was in that metal box? The dark vibes I felt in his room almost knocked me to the floor. What in heavens name was in it?"

"It was bad, Tessa. I'm not sure you want to know." Jack's somber eyes reflected his anguish. "I've seen some horrible things in my life... in Afghanistan especially, but what I saw in that monster's room, his collection of mementos of his kills... I'm afraid Marcy was not his only victim. The agents called in the crime lab techs to investigate and search the whole house more thoroughly."

Tessa reached across the center console of the car, and he wove his fingers within hers. The silence in the car enveloped them. The new evidence from the hidden shelf confirmed to them what a savage, evil psychopath with which they were dealing. Jack prayed she wouldn't have any more nightmares of the demon. Tears slid down Tessa's face, and her right temple ached. Her headache was back.

Chapter Twenty-Eight

The Daniel O'Brien murder case had graduated from county, then to a state investigated case, and now it was considered a federal case. The discovery of the metal box in the hidden shelf felt as though they'd opened Pandora's Box. The medical examiners and federal investigators were being extremely thorough, uncovering every scrap of evidence they could find. Already, the investigative findings had determined and confirmed victims from all over the United States had been brutally butchered by the hands of O'Brien.

As Jack and Craig read the long list of growing evidence accumulated on O'Brien thus far, they were appalled at the heinous depravity of his crimes. The list of the contents of the metal box was not released to the public.

Jack was greatly troubled by what he and the agents had seen when they'd opened the metal box. Inside were eight, clear plastic containers. Comprehension of what was visible through the plastic had taken a few minutes. Jack remembered the expressions on the two agents faces, which probably mirrored his own look of horror.

He recalled asking, "Are those what I think they are?" Jack had whispered, and the agents had looked at him and grimly nodded.

Inside the clear canisters of death were long handled stiletto-style switchblade knives, one per each clear box. As Jack glimpsed into the second one, he thought he recognized a photo of Marcy. It turned out to be her driver's license, and there appeared to be a rusty looking blade of a partially opened bone-handled knife next to the license in the container. Along with her license and the dried bloody blade, there was a polaroid photo showing the beautiful young girl, deceased, with the knife in her chest. In another of the clear boxes, he saw another switchblade knife with a different driver's license and polaroid photo. All eight had different licenses and ID cards, one had a library card, and one had a student ID. A different stiletto switchblade and polaroid of each victim were his trophies; O'Brien's souvenirs from each of the women he'd slain. Counting Marcy's murder, there were eight cold cases being reopened. The murdered woman's driver's license and a polaroid photo from 2014 was also among the victims. Once all the post-mortem studies were completed, conclusive evidence would confirm the tragic murders by the hands of the heinous O'Brien.

The Feds had subpoenaed Daniel's personal items in the storage unit where Sandra had them moved. Going through his items and clothing, the federal agents had discovered five sets of house and car keys which were suspected to belong to some of his victims. They also found and bagged six t-shirts and several baseball caps into evidence. The t-shirts and caps had numerous logos of "Marine" and "Marine Vet" on the items. There was an orange rubber wristband that read "Marine Vet–Agent Orange". What the investigators found unusual about these pieces of clothing and items was the fact Daniel had never been in the military. Obviously, he had been pretending to be a retired Marine Veteran. They were uncertain if the clothing would become part of the murder investigation, or perhaps the items only confirmed O'Brien was a man of deception. Either way, his lies and fraudulence felt disturbing to the federal agents.

As Jack mused the growing list of evidence, he became more concerned about the latest in the local rumor mill of speculation regarding a witness of Marcy's murder. He made some calls and requested the visitor's log and list of phone calls to and from O'Brien since he'd been held in jail. The list was supposed to be faxed to him later that morning. He intended to find out who had started the rumor of the *anonymous eyewitness* in the case and determine if someone was pointing to Tessa. He prayed it was a false alarm.

Sitting at his desk, Jack unlocked and opened the drawer of his desk and removed the manila file which held Tessa's journal entries. He remembered something she'd written and wanted to verify his memory. To his fright and dismay, the file that held Tessa's information was empty. The copied pages from her dream journal were missing.

~~~~~~~~~~~~~~~~~~~~

Craig glanced up from his computer and gazed across the office to see his partner's ashen face. He became greatly concerned, and slowly said, "Brother, you look like the most pale-faced Indian I've ever seen. What's wrong, son?" Craig thought his partner looked anemic from the loss of color in his face.

Jack stood, looked at Craig and nervously asked him if he still had his copies of Tessa's dream journal. Scowling, Jack held up his manila file. "Mine's empty. They're gone."

Craig quickly unlocked his desk. His copy of the files was still there, and he handed it to his anxious partner. As Jack read Tessa's dream journals, he loudly groaned. Handing back the papers to Craig, Jack told him to read the journals again.

Jack made a call to have his desk and the empty file printed. He didn't think there would be fingerprints left by the thief, but he needed to be cautious. He heard Craig mutter and curse after he'd re-read the dream journals.

Craig quietly commented, "Both entries, of each of her nightmares, mentioned several times about her feeling extreme pain in her chest. Jack, was she feeling pain from Marcy being stabbed by O'Brien?"

Craig stood up and began aimlessly walking around the office in deep thought. He told Jack he needed to speak with Chief Mullins and Lieutenant Johnson. He told Jack to wait for the lab guys to check for prints, and he'd be back in a few minutes.

~~~~~~~~~~~~~~~~~~~~

While impatiently waiting, Jack called Tessa. She had finished her lunch break and was preparing to see the first afternoon patient. Jack told her to be extra careful, and he was going to be there as soon as he could. He would explain when he arrived.

Once prints were lifted from his desk, he left a voicemail on Craig's phone saying he was going to check on Tessa at the doctor's office. He grabbed the fax that had just been transmitted on the fax machine next to his desk and ran out the door. Sprinting to his Charger, he felt a dreadful uneasiness that Tessa was in danger. He was glad the doctor's office was only a few blocks away, but even that seemed too far.

He parked his car several spaces from the front of the office and hastily went inside. Through the glass window where Angie, sat, he asked to speak with Tessa as soon as possible. Looking around the lobby, he noticed a young mother holding a sleeping infant waiting to see the doctor. There was an elderly man reading a magazine also patiently waiting.

Walking into the lobby, a man with sandy colored hair, wearing aviator sunglasses with mirrored lenses came to an abrupt stop. He stood in the doorway, looked at Jack, and didn't say a word. He had recognized Jack immediately, and after a few seconds, Jack recognized him. Sunglasses-man instantly turned around and bolted out of the lobby. Jack took chase and ran after him. He called out, "Halt! Police!"

Jack was younger and more fit than Sunglasses-man. Chasing him outside, Jack easily hurtled over a large sidewalk planter of red geraniums and overtook the fleeing man. He tackled him to the ground and pushed him against the concrete. With effort, Jack quickly hauled him to his feet. The tall, lanky man's wrists were pulled behind him, and Jack had handcuffs on him before he could think straight.

"Where are you headed to in such a rush, Randy?" he asked the dispatcher from Thomas Trucking. Randy's sunglasses were crooked and awry from the brief struggle. He marched him to the Charger and none too gently maneuvered Randy into the back seat. As Jack called Craig to meet him at the doctor's office, Tessa hurried outside looking terrified.

"Are you okay, Jack? What happened? Who is that?" she asked looking at the back window of his car.

"That guy… that guy's name is Randy. He works as a dispatcher for Thomas Trucking Company. Could you please go inside for me and check if he's on your afternoon schedule?" Jack needed to see if Randy had made an appointment with the doctor to gain access to Tessa.

With great effort, Jack did his best to control himself. Part of him desperately wanted to grab Tessa and run, to get her to safety. Another part of him wanted to pull Randy out of the car and beat him to a pulp. Looking around the parking spaces, he confirmed his theory as he noticed a silver Ford dually pickup truck parked in front of the clinic. He'd thought it was Randy when he caught a glimpse of the red uniform shirt with the black striped sleeves, the night he saw Ben Reed talking to him in the MPD's parking lot. Randy had also been with the men drinking coffee with Robert at the Biscuit Hill Diner awhile back wearing the same red shirt. Yesterday, Jack had done some checking on the dispatcher, and today's information confirmed the man sitting in his backseat was in cahoots with O'Brien.

Tessa walked outside to where Jack nervously stood and told him Randy was a new patient for Dr. Redman. He was supposed to see the doctor that afternoon for a wellness checkup. His full name was Randy Dillard.

Craig pulled up in his sedan, looking curious of the situation. He walked up to Jack's car, studied the backseat passenger who wore bent, crooked sunglasses, squinted at him, and asked in his deep voiced drawl, "What have we here, Jack? Bud, your sunglasses are all jacked up." He smiled at his pun.

"It's his fault! I didn't do anything!" yelled Randy.

"Meet Randy Dillard. He conveniently had an appointment to see the doctor... and to see Tessa. Mr. Dillard works as a dispatcher at Thomas Trucking, where O'Brien worked." Jack said as he glared at Sunglasses-man. "As soon as he saw me waiting in the lobby to see Tessa, Randy took off like a streak of lightning... looking quite guilty for some reason." Turning to the backseat passenger, he asked, "I told you to halt, but you only ran faster. So, what are you feeling so guilty about, Randy? Did it have anything to do with your being O'Brien's co-driver for a few years?"

Randy sat in the backseat, looking angry and distressed. Jack rolled up the back window and told Craig and Tessa how he had observed Ben Reed talking to Randy in the parking lot at the station late at night and another occasion in the early morning hours. He explained that Randy worked with O'Brien as his co-driver several years ago before Randy became a dispatcher. Jack looked at Tessa with worry lining his face and asked her if she could leave work.

"No, I've missed too much work lately. We only have three more patients, and then I can clock out. I'll go home as soon as I can. Since you have Randy in custody, I shouldn't be in danger; although I'm not sure if he would harm me anyways. I didn't see him in my dream." Tessa answered.

Craig said, "I'll stay here at the doctor's office and get statements from the witnesses, as well as from Tessa and Angie. Jack, read Randy his rights for fleeing and eluding, and take him to the station. Then drive back and escort Tessa home after her shift."

Jack agreed and then remembered. He leaned into his car and retrieved a piece of paper. The wrinkled paper was the fax he'd grabbed as he ran out of his and Craig's office on his way to Dr. Redman's.

He said, "One minute, I want you guys to see this. Notice any familiar names on O'Brien's visitor log and phone call list from the jail? Tessa, this is one reason I worry about this jerk." Jack glared at Randy again as he pointed to Dillard's name on the list.

Chapter Twenty-Nine

Just before six-thirty the next morning, Jack and Craig were seated across from Randy Dillard in the interrogation room in Morrigan's Police Department. After receiving authorization from the Feds, who would be arriving that afternoon, and an agent on speakerphone, they began interrogating Randy. The detectives coldly stared at the squirming man. He tried to act aloof and unaffected, but the sweat dripping down Randy's back and along his balding hairline said otherwise.

Jack pushed the short list of names of O'Brien's visitor log toward Randy. He pointed to Randy's name and asked him why he'd gone to see O'Brien.

Not making eye contact with the detectives, Randy looked down and studied the paper and muttered, "You guys know I worked with Daniel. What's the big deal? When I went to the jail to see him, they hadn't charged him with murder yet. I didn't know he was a killer."

"Why did you make the appointment at Dr. Redman's?" asked Craig. "No one at Thomas Trucking said anything about required wellness checks or physicals. So, why were you there? If it had been a legitimate reason, why would you have run from Jack... even when he told you to halt?"

Randy Dillard's left eye began to twitch, and he wriggled on the hard metal chair. Jack loudly slammed his fist on the table, causing Randy to jump.

"I want answers now, Dillard!" Jack yelled. Randy looked sheepish and began talking.

"O'Brien and I had a deal… we were working a side job together. It isn't exactly legal, and I wanted to discuss details about our arrangement. I wanted out, but O'Brien said he was going to tell the feds about me. I asked him, what would it take for me to get out of the deal?"

Craig leaned his head sideways, squinted at Randy, and asked, "What kind of deal did you have? Be specific."

Randy sighed in resignation of his fate and quietly said, "O'Brien and I would deliver packages to some guys that live near Mineral Springs. I'm not sure what was in the packages, but I suspect it was cash that had been laundered from drug money. It always came from a bank out of Tulsa. Our contact person there was a gal named Melody, and we delivered it to either Matt or Jeff Hayes. They're brothers, and a bunch of dealers get their dope from them. At least, that was what I heard. I never saw any drug deals go down." Randy leaned back in the chair and appeared relieved to get it off his chest.

Jack calmly looked Randy in the eye and asked, "What did O'Brien want from you in exchange to keep him from turning you in? What exactly was your deal with the devil?"

Randy sighed and answered, "I was supposed to find out everything I could about Tessa Ryan. Daniel had been informed that she had information about the Marcy Phillips murder. It's been rumored that she had documents from an eyewitness from '92. I was supposed to feel her out… see if it was a legitimate witness from back then and find out if the eyewitness was still alive. I figured with her being so young, whatever she had, must have been given to her from someone more O'Brien's age. I'm still confused on the details, but you should know… Daniel holds this Tessa girl responsible for fingering him to you cops. He's been raging about his arrest being all her fault, and I'm sure he plans on getting revenge the first available opportunity."

Craig frowned, and asked Randy, "How long did you drive as O'Brien's co-driver? In 2014, were you with him at the time of the woman's murder? The woman whose death the federal agents are investigating from western Oklahoma?"

"I worked as co-driver for a lot of different drivers at Thomas Trucking before becoming a dispatcher. O'Brien has a reputation for being difficult. Not many of us would work with him, but I did work as his co-driver for a year or so. I don't know a thing about the woman from 2014." Randy replied, looking nervous.

Craig asked him, "How did you and O'Brien get hooked up with the Hayes boys?"

"A friend of a friend asked if I knew anyone wanting to make some easy money hauling a package every week out of Tulsa. It seemed harmless at the time. I approached O'Brien since I knew he had a girlfriend in Tulsa, and he was all for it. Apparently, O'Brien already knew the Hayes brothers. He was friends with their father years ago." Randy began looking skittish.

His response didn't ring true to the detectives. They both thought there was more to Randy's connection to the Hayes brothers.

"Who told O'Brien that Miss Ryan had information regarding an eyewitness, and how do you know Ben Reed?" asked Jack.

Randy began fidgeting. He told Craig and Jack he'd told them enough. He said he wouldn't tell them anything more without a lawyer. They'd gotten more information out of Dillard than they'd expected and had a lot to investigate. Craig informed Randy the federal agents would be visiting with him later that day, and he'd be assigned an attorney.

He and Jack went back to their office where Craig made a phone call. When he hung up, he told Jack, "That slimy weasel, Ben Reed, conveniently called in sick this morning. What do ya' want to bet he and Dillard are both in cahoots with O'Brien? Reed is crooked as a dog's hind leg. I'll call the Chief to start getting warrants issued for the Hayes brothers."

The detectives filled out reports to be given to the federal agents, so they could prepare for their turn to have a crack at the truck dispatcher / money launderer. They felt certain the man had a lot more information to share.

Waiting for the necessary warrants and paperwork, Jack felt glad for the weekend and that Tessa didn't have to work. Craig's barbeque was planned for six o'clock that evening. He and Tina had everything prepared and hoped some good food and a relaxing environment might help with the tense nerves and stress in the air.

"Is there anything I can do to help with the barbeque? Tessa offered to bring a dish, if you'd like. She's a fantastic cook." Jack rubbed his stomach and grinned.

"We've got everything covered. You and Tessa just need to bring your appetites." Craig smiled, and suggested Jack should check on Tessa and take an early lunch.

Craig didn't have to twist his arm, so Jack called Tessa to see if she were home. She seemed glad to hear Jack's voice and invited him over. He looked forward to seeing her with his own two eyes, to feel reassured she was completely safe. He also wanted to inform her of what Randy Dillard had told them. They'd gotten a few answers, but the interview had given them more questions, as well.

~~~~~~~~~~~~~~~~~~~

The weather was pleasant with warm sunshine and only a mild breeze, which was a rare day in Oklahoma. The winds could normally be outrageous in early spring months. Tessa was glad for Tina and Craig's sake the weather was calm for their barbeque that evening. She poured herself a glass of iced tea and, thinking how Jack would be there at any moment, she poured a glass for him as well.

On cue, her doorbell rang, and she punched the code to the security alarm and opened the front door. Jack strolled inside and accepted the offered glass of tea. He sat on the leather chair in her front room and looked worried. Feeling the heavy weights of fretful concern roll off his shoulders, he gazed at her sitting across from him. He hadn't been convinced she wasn't in any type of peril until he physically saw she was safe and sound with his own eyes.

"Thank you, Tessa. I needed this," he said, as he sipped from the tall glass. "Craig and I got some information from Randy Dillard that I wanted to apprise you of. Seems O'Brien and Dillard had a little venture on the side making extra bucks. They have been delivering laundered money to the Hayes brothers from a bank in Tulsa through a lady who worked at the bank. Jeff and Matt Hayes live between here and Mineral Springs.

When Dillard visited O'Brien in jail, he told him he wanted out of their arrangement. However, Randy had to do a little job for
~~~~~~~~~~~~~~~~~~~

O'Brien, or else he threatened to tell the feds about him. He blackmailed Randy into stalking you and looking for information connected with documents from an *eyewitness* of Marcy Phillip's murder. Randy appeared to be in the dark and clueless. I don't think he had time to gather too much information on you, but the interview with him creates a lot more questions. He also commented that O'Brien is angry with you for pointing us toward him. We've obviously got a mole in the PD. Someone's been feeding him information on the investigation. We need to figure out who stole my copy of your dream journal."

Tessa shook her head as she processed the information Jack had just given her. Comprehending O'Brien was focused on her, she cringed. Trying to lighten the atmosphere, she asked Jack if he were hungry and said, "All this speculating is exhausting. How about we have lunch? I made some club sandwiches and a Greek pasta salad."

They carried salads, drinks, and thick, deli-sliced sandwiches made with Tessa's homemade sourdough bread outside to the backyard patio. Sitting at the wrought iron table, they bowed their heads over the simple lunch. Bright pink petunias in clay pots fragranced the deck, and greenish-blue dragonflies dipped into the nearby bird bath in the lush flower garden. The couple tried to enjoy their meal, but the thought of the angry murderer with his stalking, flying monkeys felt like a dark cloud raining on their parade.

"That was delicious, Tessa. Thank you. It's so peaceful out here. I could lay down on one of your lounge chairs and go straight to sleep right now. Instead, I need to wrap up a couple things at the PD and check if the Chief or Lieutenant has those arrest warrants ready for the Hayes brothers."

He hoisted himself up from the wrought iron chair, sighed, and gave her a gentle kiss. They walked into her house, and Jack was relieved that Tessa reset the alarm on the back door without him reminding her. She walked him to the front, and he told her he'd be picking her up later at 5:45 to go to the Taylor's barbeque. Walking outside onto the front porch, he heard the electronic lock of the alarm system click on her front door. He smiled and felt reasonably assured she was safe.

Chapter Thirty

Chief Jerry Mullins of the MPD was frustrated he couldn't locate a judge in the county. Judge Jenson was supposed to call him back hours ago, but he hadn't responded yet. Evidently, everyone was taking advantage of the perfect weather and was unavailable. He was anxious to get the arrest warrants filed on the Hayes brothers. He'd been chasing them for the last two months. Every single time he thought they had solid evidence he'd be disappointed. The charmed brothers seemed untouchable, as though they were always a step ahead of the MPD.

He smiled as he thought how his detectives had done an outstanding job apprehending Randy Dillard and getting informative, incriminating evidence from him. The federal agents were pleased with the interrogation results as well. Besides information on the Hayes brothers, Dillard had given confirmation of a money laundering scheme out of a bank in Tulsa and a female accomplice named Melody. The OSBI was narrowing down that search and hoped to have her in custody soon. Perhaps then, they could finally determine who was the ringleader.

Chief Mullins was surprised the man they had behind bars in the federal facility, Inmate O'Brien, was part of the drug ring. Besides the assault charge on Officer Connors, the murder of Marcy Phillips and the other seven women he had tortured and killed across the country for three decades, they could now add money laundering to his long list of crimes. Chief Mullins prayed O'Brien would never be walking the streets again. He was a dangerous monster who deserved the worst punishment possible.

~~~~~~~~~~~~~~~~~~~~

O'Brien sat in his small cell in a Federal Transfer Center. It was a Federal Bureau of Prisons facility, and the courts and judges were in the process of determining if he would remain in Oklahoma or be transferred to New Jersey to face charges for the death of the first of his victims. No matter where he was held, or which crime for which he was going to trial, Daniel knew he couldn't stand being caged like an animal much longer.

He'd become more irritable, raging and screaming until he was threatened by the correctional officers to tone it down. He had trashed his cell, which ended up being worse for himself more than anything. For over twelve hours, he had no toilet paper and the thin, cheap mattress with its blue, torn vinyl cover provided no cushion or comfort on the hard, narrow bunk.

He missed the luxurious condominium in which he used to live, with the spacious rooms and elegant furnishings. His lawyer had informed him of Sandra leasing the home, and he'd been worried someone would find his stash of treasures in the hidden shelf. Sure enough, his ex-wife had noticed it and called in the Feds. The thought of anyone other than himself touching his trophies caused him to quiver with fury. *They're mine, and mine alone!*

He had seldom removed them from the clever hiding spot, and knowing he'd never see or fondle them again was more than he could fathom.

He was disappointed in his attorney, as well as Randy Dillard. Instead of getting information for him about the girl, Tessa Ryan, and the documents she'd given the police which incriminated him to begin with, Dillard had only screwed up. O'Brien wanted answers of who had seen him in 1992 at Crampton Lake.

He'd been informed from one of the correctional officers about Dillard flipping on him and Selena's brothers, Matt and Jeff. The correctional officer had a good friend who worked at the MPD. He kept the officer abreast of a lot of information. O'Brien paid the guard very handsomely for a burner phone that was smuggled to him. As soon as O'Brien had gotten hold of the contraband phone,
~~~~~~~~~~~~~~~~~~~~

he'd messaged Ivan Barnes and Selena, to give them a heads up about Dillard's betrayal. Knowing the Hayes brothers and their brilliant, but soul-less sister, he almost felt sorry for Randy. His disloyalty would be dealt with in an expedient, proper fashion.

The correctional officer, Jared, who had helped Daniel acquire the burner cell phone was a cousin to the Hayes brothers and Selena. Jared supposedly had friends in high places, and one of his high school friends was a son to a high-ranking court official. He'd been an excellent source of information for Daniel with the current events happening in Morrigan and Mineral Springs. He had informed Daniel that Sandra had moved into a swanky hotel after moving from the condo, and she was in the process of building a new house. That Sandra was moving into a larger, prettier home seemed unfair to Daniel, and he was being shuffled back and forth to prison facilities with tiny, nasty smelling cells. The rancid, putrid scent in the prisons with disinfectant odor mixed with hundreds of inmate's sweaty, unclean bodies created a pungent, repulsive, nostril burning stench. Evidently, most of the inmates didn't believe in brushing their teeth, and he'd noticed the few prisoners to whom he'd spoken had ridiculously, disgusting bad breath and gray, furry looking teeth.

With the help of Jared and the burner phone, Daniel had spoken to a few of his old friends who owed him favors. He didn't consider the thinly veiled threats as blackmail, but they were. He threatened to expose them of the secrets he was aware of, if they didn't help him. He'd been accumulating information on people with whom he'd dealt for years. He knew about many scandalous skeletons and illegal activities in some corrupt official's closets. He thought extorting favors from them was not going to be difficult, since he had kept documented evidence of their wrongdoings in a safe place. His girlfriend of ten years, ever faithful Melody, whom he'd convinced to move from Georgia to Oklahoma, was aware of the illicit information and had the secrets locked up tight in a safety deposit box in the bank where she worked. He had a plan to escape the rancid, foul smelling hole in which he'd been stuck. He also planned on paying back some of the people who had turned on him. *Retribution is mine.* He cackled as he thought of his revenge.

Chapter Thirty-One

Sandra needed extra therapy sessions with Lily after the discovery of Daniel's stash of horrors in the shelf unit. She was having a difficult time accepting the truth that the man she married and with whom she had lived was such a demented monster. While believing he had traits of a psychopath, being a serial killer was almost more than her tired brain could fathom. Reading the posts written by the members in the online support group which she frequented, she realized her ex-husband was far worse than the run of the mill sociopaths, which were monsters themselves. She adjusted her song choices on her iPad's playlist and turned up the volume. At Lily's office earlier, she had listened to the contemporary gospel music played by the radio station, *K-Love.* She knew her therapist was a strong Christian, and it wasn't the first time she'd listened to the uplifting tunes playing in the background of her sessions.

Instead of giving more thoughts to her ex-husband, she listened to the powerful voice of *Mandisa* sing *Overcomer,* and she chose to focus on her therapeutic project, with its phases of planning and building the many structures. Phase One was constructing her new home, and Sandra was excited to see the carpenter, Jacob Kiefer, was making excellent progress. To her delight, the move in date was two weeks ahead of schedule. She had already ordered and purchased most of the new furnishings and décor for the house.

Phase Two would be organizing the sanctuary-safehouse with all the legal red tape and necessary documentation. Sandra was grateful for her talented accountant and his newly hired assistant. She'd met with her skillful attorney, Jonathan Kane, who was dedicated to making the project successful. Jonathan had grown up with narcissistic parents, especially his mother, so he knew firsthand how painful and damaging having a narcissist in one's life could be, especially in one's childhood. Jonathan was even excited about helping Sandra choose playground equipment for the designated play area.

Phase Three was building the housing complex for the families, plus the clubhouse, and offices. The plans were ready, and groundbreaking was scheduled in a few weeks. Sandra knew the project would take months to complete, but she wanted everything done perfectly and knew taking adequate time was necessary. She was determined to make the organization successful.

Anxious to get moved and settled in her new house, she felt her emotional healing was progressing. She continued researching and educating herself about narcissists and sociopaths. Earlier, she had read in an article which had been posted in her support group how narcissists go through the same relationship patterns, over and over like an old phonograph's needle stuck on a record, replaying the same old tune. She thought how they all seemed to have the same playbook and felt they must belong to the same monstrous club. She read how narcissists and sociopaths wear carefully constructed masks but could remove them at the drop of a hat, just like Jekyll and Hyde, revealing their true colors underneath their fake smiles and charming behavior used to ply and deceive their victims.

Sitting down to research another article on her iPad, she read about the traits and patterns of their counterfeit performances. The first stage of the narcissist's behavior in a new relationship is what some call the *Honeymoon Stage*. Narcissists will pursue their prey, their victim, with a gusto. The *love-bombing* with hearts and flowers, flattery, massive attention, generous gifts, and placing their victim on a pedestal to make her feel extra special is part of the web of deceit used to catch their prey. They convince the victim of their total devotion and pretend to idealize her. Although most narcissists are men, some women are known to carry these destructive traits.

Once they have their claws in their prey, the chase is over, and the narcissist relishes his prize. In a cat and mouse game, they begin tearing down their prey's confidence with a stealthy concealed destruction. Covert comments, demeaning remarks, and belittling the victim in such an insidious fashion, the victim begins to believe herself as inadequate. The narcissist begins withholding all the compliments and flattery, and the victim goes overboard trying to impress her captor. The victim tries to regain the early *fairytale stage* by doing anything the predator wants, and the monster takes full advantage of the victim's vulnerability.

After months and sometimes years of the emotional abuse, the victim becomes depressed and confused. She can't comprehend why her amorous knight in shining armor stopped giving her adoration and love. What she doesn't understand is that her charming knight never loved her. A narcissist or sociopath is incapable of loving anyone. Everything, every action is all an act, which is extremely difficult for the victim to accept or even comprehend. Then comes the *devalue and discard stage* of the relationship. The narcissist has decided to trade in his victim for someone new, much the same as upgrading to a newer model car. The narcissist has no empathy… zero. He doesn't feel sympathy or emotions like a normal person, because he's mentally hard-wired differently. He, and those like him, are not normal, and there's no cure, or magic pill, or therapy that can change them.

Accepting that truth is one of the hardest things a victim can do. Understanding the person whom she loved did not love her back is devastating, and the victim painstakingly realizes the love of her life was a total fraud. That misjudgment of unrequited love is a tough pill to swallow. After the victim has been discarded, like an old worn out shoe, the narcissist moves on to his next target. The pattern repeats itself over again, and the narcissistic-sociopath leaves destruction and traumatic angst behind him, time and time again.

Sandra reread the article and thought to herself how the narcissists, sociopaths, and psychopaths must be racking up some serious negative points in the karma department. She thought of Daniel and shook her head. He was being paid back for much of his cruel behavior by being stuck in a small, disgusting cell. She smiled when the idea dawned on her that his days of destruction and reign of terror were over, although the pain and heartache he had caused so many victims and their families were forever irreparable.

Missing her friend, Tessa, she decided to call her and hoped she was doing well. She hadn't spoken to her in a few days and wondered how she and the handsome detective, Jack Parker, were getting along. She felt fortunate for all the help the young couple had given her.

She got Tessa's voicemail when she called, so she left a message saying she'd love to take Tessa and Jack to dinner when the timing was convenient for them. She enjoyed their company, and the affection and chemistry between the young couple was refreshing for Sandra. She wondered if she'd ever find love again, or if she'd even be able to trust a man or consider a relationship with someone new. She'd been lonely for many years. With Daniel gone over half the time driving a truck throughout the lower forty-eight states, loneliness had become her closest companion. Becoming a loner had created an independence in Sandra.

She was quite good at organizing and managing things, which was why she had been such an accomplished manager and businessperson. She had passed the reins of the restaurant to her assistant manager, Wanda, and now Sandra was beyond excited about her new enterprise and project. Tessa had informed Sandra that there were a couple of abused wives, patients she knew from Dr. Redman's office, who would probably be interested in becoming guests of the shelter Sandra was building. Tessa also told her that she'd love to be involved in some way with helping the battered women and the project of hope. Sandra considered Tessa a healer, and she knew they'd be successful creating a means for women to gain freedom from their narcissistic captors.

Freedom, healing, hope, and beginning an exciting new chapter in their battered lives were among the many opportunities Sandra wanted to offer victims of abuse. She prayed every day for guidance to achieve her goal, and she could feel God's presence in her life. She knew the people who were being placed in her path were sent to help her on her journey.

Chapter Thirty-Two

Tina and Craig's barbeque had been a welcome distraction from the recent developments of the disturbing cases. Tessa and Jack enjoyed the entertaining company of the other detectives and officers from the MPD who had joined them at the Taylor's. Chief Mullins was supposed to have dropped by, but he never showed.

The Taylor's home was an English Tudor design. The two-story house had been an inheritance from Tina's parents, and she and Craig had invested a lot of hard work and time into the two-acre property on which the home sat. Every few months, Tina would choose a project, and the most recent had been their backyard's outdoor kitchen and swimming pool. Craig had mentioned to Jack numerous times that he needed to remove the home and garden channels from his TV cable.

Lieutenant Johnson and his wife arrived at the party as Tessa and Jack walked up to Craig's front door. The Johnsons were an attractive couple. Lieutenant Darrell Johnson was a tall, handsome man with broad shoulders, and his wife was much younger than him who appeared of Asian descent. When he introduced the quiet woman, she kept her lovely almond shaped eyes lowered and gave them a gentle smile. As always, the Lieutenant was all smiles and cracking jokes. Between helping Craig grill burgers and steaks, Lt. Johnson entertained the crowd by jumping from the large, heated swimming pool's diving board with some elaborate flips and moves.

Craig teased his guest, "Lieutenant, should we start calling you *Aquaman*? You can stay underwater like a fish."

"No, I'm more like a dolphin. You can call me Flipper." He began making high pitched squeaks and clicking noises, sounding exactly like a dolphin as he skillfully backstroked to the other end of the pool.

The group of close-knit coworkers laughed at their comical superior officer. The rest of the evening was enjoyable, and most of the guests stayed late into the evening at Craig and Tina's successful barbeque.

~~~~~~~~~~~~~~~~~~

The get-together and spending time with Tessa had recharged Jack's battery. He was his ambitious, high energy self on Monday morning. Before he could grab his first cup of mud from the breakroom's coffee machine, Jack and the other detectives were called into Chief Mullin's office. He hoped the chief had good news. Unfortunately, after the detectives and a few officers had seated themselves, Jack noticed Lieutenant Johnson looked grim, and Chief Mullins looked tired with frustration etching his face. He began briefing them of the latest developments.

"I'm sorry to inform you all, but our witness, Randy Dillard, was found dead in his cell this morning. He hung himself. Sadly, this incident puts quite a wrinkle in our case." The Chief gave a long sigh.

He continued telling his crew of the circumstances and details of the predicament. Then he gave them more bad news. Chief Mullins ran his hand over his fatigued sixty-year-old face and continued.

"An hour ago, we received another report of cattle theft. This time, it's from the Ralston Ranch, ten miles west of town. The cattle are registered red angus, estimated value of five-thousand dollars per head, and there were forty head stolen. Once again, the herd was in a pasture without a lot of visibility. We've got guys on the scene now. This time, there were tire marks and evidence left behind which
~~~~~~~~~~~~~~~~~~

should give us insight to the kind of rig used to load the cattle." Chief Mullins assigned the men tasks, and the somber crew made their way into their own offices.

Craig and Jack were assigned a *cold contact* at the Hayes brother's address and residence. On the drive to interview the suspects, they spoke about Randy Dillard's demise, and they had doubts that he had hung himself. They suspected Dillard might have had some unwanted help. Craig told Jack he strongly suspected they had at least one mole in the precinct, maybe more than one. After going over all the latest incidents, Jack was inclined to agree.

Before they could further discuss the suspicions of moles in the MPD, a white Chevrolet pickup truck almost ran them into a ditch as it barreled down the narrow blacktop road. Craig and Jack looked at each other with the same instant realization that it was the Hayes brother's pickup. Jack made a U-turn in the road and quickly gave chase to the big white Chevy.

"I only saw one guy in the truck," observed Jack. His eyes were focused as the gap between the vehicles narrowed.

He flipped on the red and blue lights as he chased the speeding white pickup. Jack held his breath as he noticed they were headed toward an S-curve and hoped the white truck would slow down; however, the truck seemed to accelerate. Jack slowed his speed, and as he had feared, the white truck's driver lost control. The truck swerved; its right side veered onto the dirt shoulder of the blacktop. The ground was soft, and the truck was pulled toward the deep ditch trenched along the side of the road. Clumps of grass and Oklahoma red dirt spun into the air as the truck churned its way onto its side, bounced and then screeched, landing upside down in the ditch's sand-rock embankment.

Jack and Craig came to a quick halt behind the wrecked truck, with Craig calling in the accident to the MPD and requesting an ambulance. Jumping from the car, Jack grabbed a fire extinguisher from the trunk, and they raced toward the mangled mess of the wrecked Chevy. The wheels were still turning, and the engine was still running. Unsettled dust and hissing steam from the engine created a dirty fog. The smell of anti-freeze and gasoline began filling the air.

Craig ran along the driver's side of the overturned truck, searching for the driver, hoping he hadn't been injured or ejected. Jack wedged himself between the passenger side of the pick-up and the red sandrock embankment. They spotted the driver, a huge mountain of a man, who was unconscious inside the cab.

Craig checked for his pulse and told Jack, "The driver's alive!"

He had a long, bloody gash on his forehead and a large knot the size of a baseball was rapidly forming over his right eyebrow. Hot oil from the engine began dripping inside the truck's cab and was scalding the driver's upper left arm. They noticed tiny flames trying to ignite in the steaming engine.

"We've gotta move him, Jack. No time to waste!" Craig was able to wedge open the driver's door.

It took all the strength Jack and Craig could muster to pull and haul the large stocky man from the precarious heap. Jack lifted his fire extinguisher and doused the flames before they grew more dangerous.

Within minutes, an ambulance and fire truck arrived and began administering medical aid to the still unconscious driver and tended to the smoking engine as it caught on fire again. Craig held the driver's wallet and identified the big man as Ivan Barnes from Mineral Springs, thirty-four years old, and the address on his driver's license matched Matthew Hayes' address. The truck's registration read the owner of the truck was Matthew Hayes. Craig speculated Barnes worked for the Hayes brothers. He informed Jack of the information, and they waited until the injured driver was loaded into the ambulance and on his way to the hospital. Two Oklahoma State troopers had arrived and were already working the scene of the accident. Jack and Craig followed the ambulance transporting the unconscious man, feeling their own heart rates and breathing begin to ease.

Waiting in the lobby of the emergency room at the hospital, the detectives began gathering information on the driver. They worked on writing reports of Ivan Barnes fleeing and eluding, but they were interrupted from the attending physician. He approached the detectives in the lobby and informed them the driver of the wrecked truck was stabilized and awaiting lab results and a CT scan.

The tired looking doctor said, "Detectives, Mr. Barnes is still unconscious. I will call you as soon as I have further information."

When an officer arrived to guard the patient / suspect, Jack and Craig decided to return to the accident site to check for any evidence, and then they would continue investigating the Hayes brother's residence.

Arriving back at the site, a tow truck reading *A Rough Day's Tow Service* on the sides of its doors was chaining up the wreckage of the Chevy Silverado. The J-hook chain and pulley system loaded the crushed vehicle onto the flatbed of the tow truck. Jack and Craig did an extensive search of the area around the sandrock ditch, but other than a lot of broken glass and chunks of red plastic from the broken taillights, there didn't appear to be anything significant. They climbed into the Charger and drove the remaining miles to the Hayes' residence.

Pulling into the long driveway of a gray brick house, they noticed two large metal barns on the property which were at least fifty yards from the ranch style home. One was a seventy-foot long, red barn. The other was half its size; a white barn with a commercial type of roll-up door on its front.

Built sometime in the '80s, the ranch style house was barely visible from the road. The detectives walked up the concrete sidewalk to the front door, carefully observing the area. The place was surprisingly neat and appeared well cared for, with orange marigolds growing in a flower bed by the covered porch in front of the house. Jack had expected something dilapidated and surmised the tidy brick home would seem unsuspecting to most who looked at it. He thought it would have belonged to a farmer or rancher instead of dangerous, drug dealing criminals. He began to think they must have a wrong address.

Standing on a large doormat reading Welcome, they knocked on the front door adorned with a yellow forsythia wreath and rang the bell. A young woman in her mid to late twenties opened the door, and the detectives heard a crying infant from the next room.

"Can I help you?" she asked, looking extremely perturbed that the doorbell had woken the baby.

Showing her their badges, the detectives introduced themselves and asked if they could come inside. She was reluctant, but the increased volume of the baby's wails distracted her. She held the door open and gratingly said, "Please, come in."

As they walked into the home's entrance, she walked to the bedroom where the baby wept. They could hear her quietly soothe the child. Within a minute or so, the baby had fallen back to sleep, and the woman joined them in the front room.

"Please talk quietly, so my little one doesn't wake again."

Jack assessed the tidy appearance of the house, and there was a half empty laundry basket of neatly folded baby clothes. Most were blue colored tiny sleep shirts and plaid outfits indicating the crying little one was a baby boy. The young woman who joined them looked tired and haggard with dark circles under her eyes.

"How old is your little boy, ma'am? Is he teething?" asked Jack.

"He's seven months old, and yes, the poor little guy is cutting teeth and staying up most of the night. How can I help you, Detectives?"

Craig asked the woman her name, and she replied, "Jordan Randall."

"Do Matthew and Jeffrey Hayes reside at this address?" asked Jack.

She hesitantly answered, "Matt stays here with my boyfriend and me sometimes, but we haven't seen him for a few days."

Jack asked the tired young mother if she knew Ivan Barnes, and she replied with frightened eyes, "Yes, that's my boyfriend. Why? What's happened? Where is Ivan?"

Craig answered, "Ms. Randall, Ivan was in an accident. He wrecked the pickup truck he was driving and was transported to Morrigan Regional Hospital." Jack noticed Jordan's face pale, and she quickly sat on a rocking chair near the basket of laundry. "He's in stable condition and was having some tests and CT scans done when we left the hospital. Do you or Ivan Barnes own this property?"

Craig began writing in his small pocket-size notebook as Jordan replied, "No, my father owns the house. Ivan and I just rent it from him. My Dad is Kevin Randall. His phone number is 525-6414. I need to call my mother to stay with my son, so I can go to the hospital to check on Ivan. Are you finished with your questions?"

"Yes, for now… thank you, ma'am." Jack answered. He and Craig made their way back to the Charger.

Once the detectives were back in their car, Craig called Jordan's father and asked if they had permission to enter the barns and search the property. Mr. Randall asked them to wait until he arrived. He lived three miles away and would be with them in a few moments.

Less than ten minutes later, Jordan's parents arrived at the gray brick house. Jordan's mother hurriedly went inside to tend to her daughter and grandson, and her father walked to where the detectives were parked and stood beside the Charger. Mr. Randall smiled, shook the detective's hands, nodded his head toward them, and said, "Detectives, I'm Kevin Randall, Jordan's father. Is Ivan okay? Jordan told her mother that he was in a car wreck?"

He seemed to be a reserved, quiet spoken man. As the detectives informed him of Ivan's accident, Jack noticed the front door of the house open. Jordan hastily walked down the sidewalk to a late model SUV parked in the driveway. She was carrying a baby's diaper bag and seemed anxious to get to the hospital to check on her boyfriend.

Jack strode toward her and called out, "Jordan? Wait a moment, please."

She appeared nervous, standing beside the open door of her vehicle, and Jack asked her, "Are you taking your baby with you to the hospital, or is your mother staying with him?"

"Mom will stay here with my baby until I get back."

Jack looked at the light blue, diaper bag monogrammed with the name Jason and trimmed with navy and white cartoon elephants. He wondered why she needed to take it with her, if the child was staying with his grandmother. Jordan saw the inquisitive look on Jack's face as he gazed at the bulky diaper bag, and she bolted. As she threw the bag inside the SUV, small plastic bags fell onto the passenger seat. She jumped behind the steering wheel, but before she could turn on the ignition, Jack had pulled her out of the vehicle. Mr. Randall ran towards them, and Craig followed.

Craig pulled his weapon from his holster and ordered Jordan and Kevin, "Both of you, place your hands on the hood of the vehicle." Not moving, Kevin Randall balked and glared at Craig. He warned Kevin, "I said to put your hands on the hood of the vehicle. Mister, you mess with me, and I'm gonna cream your corn."

Jack checked the bags, filled with a white-powdery substance. He sadly looked at Craig and dully replied, "Cocaine."

Craig immediately called for back-up and requested Thor, the K-9 officer, to search the house and property. Kevin Randall glared at his daughter and yelled at her, "Idiot! What have you done?"

The quiet spoken gentleman from earlier was gone, and a loud, angry man began berating his nervous daughter. "Stupid… just like your mother."

Jack thought how the neat and orderly house and property looked normal and harmless from the outside, but deep inside, it held secrets and drugs. The attentive and caring mother of the baby boy, and the supposedly loving parents who came running to help their daughter and grandson, were anything but kind people. *Looks can be deceiving,* he thought, and wondered what else they'd discover when searching the property.

Chapter Thirty-Three

Much later that evening, Craig and Jack finished the paperwork and reports from the day's events and arrests. The most recent update on Ivan Barnes reported he was in a medically induced coma because of the severity of his head injury. He was responding well to medications, and they hoped he would be conscious and able to be questioned soon. Kevin and Jordan Randall had been arrested on numerous drug charges.

Jack was still amazed that the gray brick residence had turned out to be a stash house. Thor, the K-9 officer had been brought to the house, and a thorough search uncovered numerous drugs, cocaine and methamphetamines. There was also fifteen-thousand-dollars in cash hidden in the basement, and two 9mm guns, a shotgun, and plenty of ammunition.

Surprisingly, the metal barns on the property did not have any drugs in them, but they had noticed the barns were meticulously clean. Thor's animated reactions indicated there must have been drugs there at one time. Jack wondered if the Randalls had been tipped off that the police were coming, and perhaps there hadn't been enough time to empty the house. Hopefully, either Jordan or Kevin Randall, or Ivan Barnes would be cooperative and offer information in exchange for leniency.

Jack called Tessa as he was walking out of the station, and she picked up the call right away. She asked if he'd like to come by her house. She was anxious to hear about the case, and he sounded like he needed to vent.

Minutes later, he walked into Tessa's front room. She offered him tea or a bottle of water, and he chose water since it was late. He thought the teas caffeine might keep him awake. Although, even as tired as he was, he expected the day's events would probably trigger insomnia. He hated when he'd replay things over and over in his head, and the long day had been very eventful.

Cold rain had fallen on the town of Morrigan earlier that evening, and Jack had noticed large, wet paw prints on Tessa's front porch. "That was quite a rainstorm we had earlier, a real frog wash. I noticed paw prints on your porch. Are the German shepherds still coming to visit you?" She nodded and gave him a big smile.

"Yes, they come at night and stay on the porch, but they leave in the mornings. So, tell me the scoop on the case… at least, what you're allowed to tell me."

Jack normally wouldn't share a lot of information about ongoing cases, but he felt Tessa needed to know certain details since she was inadvertently involved. He updated her about the O'Brien case and the death of Randy Dillard. He mentioned Dillard and O'Brien were into money laundering, and a female accomplice from Tulsa named Melody was mixed in it as well.

"Wait… Did you say the woman's name was Melody?" Tessa felt the name sounded familiar to her for some reason and began wracking her mind trying to remember. She said, "Let me call Sandra really quick. I think she's mentioned something about a woman named Melody."

Tapping Sandra's number in her phone, she noticed Jack didn't seem quite so tired. He had recognized the look in Tessa's eyes. She was onto something.

After speaking with Sandra, she told Jack that she had a name for him. Melody Lambert was the woman with whom Daniel

O'Brien had an affair ten years ago. Tessa told Jack the story about the affair and how Sandra had discovered the woman's name and phone numbers. She thought Melody may have moved from Georgia to Oklahoma to be closer to Daniel, and she had worked for a bank when she lived in Georgia.

"Ha!" Jack huffed and laughed. "You're like the MPD's own personal secret weapon. I'll call Craig, so he can pass on the information." Within minutes, Melody Lambert's name had traveled from Craig to Chief Mullins and on to the OSBI. She would be brought in for questioning that night.

"Sandra also asked if she could take you and me out to dinner, her treat. I'd love to get together with her. Would you be able to make it maybe later this week?" Tessa asked.

Jack responded by pointing his thumbs up, and they planned for Friday evening to meet Sandra. Tessa texted their friend and asked if Friday would work for her.

~~~~~~~~~~~~~~~~~~

After Sandra agreed Friday was good for their evening dinner plans, she smiled and thought if she'd been lucky enough to have had a daughter, she wished she would have been exactly like Tessa. She'd never met such a brave and optimistic young person. Everyone around Tessa enjoyed her company and compassionate charisma.

Nursing a cup of hot herbal tea, Sandra returned to her online discussion before Tessa had called her. She, and at least a dozen other members of the group, their Sisterhood, were discussing the aftermath of being with a *narcopath,* a narcissistic sociopath. She always felt amazed, and horrified, of the devastation the *narcopaths* created for their victims. For the remainder of her days, Sandra would be eternally thankful for coming upon the support group and its founder, Karen. She shuddered to think how lost she'd been before stumbling onto the group. With time, research and educating themselves, Sandra and other members of the group, her sorority sisters, had traveled through an emotionally pitch black, frightening tunnel. Through therapeutic discussions within their group and taking lots of efforts to heal, they'd become enlightened and increased their strength. She felt she owed the group and would forever remain beholden.
~~~~~~~~~~~~~~~~~~

Sandra stretched and put down her iPad. She'd also been reading blogs of several of her new online friends. Her knowledge was expanding. All the bloggers had been victimized by mentally disordered bullies, sociopaths. The latest blog she'd read was written by a lady whose goal was to plant seeds of truth about personality disorders and spread awareness of the resulting destructive behavior.

The blogger included articles and informative psychological data and studies, and she wrote about her own personal experiences as well. One of the things Sandra identified with the blogger was that she'd been in a relationship with the abuser for over twenty years. Being with the sociopath had caused an alarming amount of health issues for the woman. Medical challenges were a factor to which many victims could relate. Not only was their mental health damaged, their physical health was also affected. The blogger wrote about her development of chronic asthma soon after she married her abuser. Her health continued deteriorating, and by the time she was divorced from her monster, she was taking ten different prescription medicines for multiple health issues.

The blogger told of her uphill battle, and Sandra was relieved when she read the woman was recovering her health. She encouraged the readers to focus on their health and make it a priority. She commented she had noticed a shift in her whole being when she began practicing self-care. From taking vitamins, an exercise regime, a healthier diet, to treating herself to pedicures, and practicing yoga, the blogger happily confirmed to Sandra and the readers how important it is to take care of themselves. Practicing self-love and positive self-talk were often mentioned in the Facebook support group.

Sandra considered herself lucky, compared to many others, that her most hindering physical health concern was the extra weight she'd gained due to her depression. Sandra was diligently working to lose fifty pounds, and the hotel's gym and swimming pool had become invaluable to her. Since she wasn't managing the restaurant anymore, she had plenty of time to devote to regaining her health. She had even added a gym area and swimming pool in the safehouse complex's blueprint. Another feature she thought might help victims heal was a walking path and bicycle lane which would wind through a wooded, picturesque area near the apartments.

Being physically active, and taking interest in her physical health, was also helping her emotional health, and Sandra realized more than ever how one affected the other. The many side effects of abuse touched every aspect of one's life.

Sandra had purchased one-hundred-and-sixty acres of undeveloped land, and she was becoming increasingly more excited with her project. She would wake up in the mornings with purpose and earnest passion to complete the building of the sanctuary of hope. By the time she was finished, she wanted the complex to be more than a shelter in the storm for the many women and children abused by narcissists and sociopaths. She wanted the sanctuary to be a place of inspiration, recovery, and healing both inside and out. She wanted to help people thrive and find their joy.

Suddenly, she realized she had found her own joy. She was happier than she'd ever been. She felt encouraged to know she had taken a horrible and painful life experience and was turning it into something exceptional, good, and productive. She remembered a quote she'd read earlier in the day written by Maya Angelou: "My mission in life is not merely to survive, but to thrive."

Chapter Thirty-Four

Selena Hayes was disheartened and very displeased, but she also knew the drug bust could have been far worse. Altogether, she'd lost over ninety-thousand-dollars in product, cash, and weapons, but with Daniel O'Brien giving them a heads up about rat Randy Dillard, they had barely had time to break down and move equipment from the labs. Until yesterday, they had a manufacturing lab set up in the bigger barn, and meth was stored in the smaller barn waiting for distribution. Most of the heroin and cocaine she'd provided for her clients came from Mexico or south Texas.

Worried that Jordan or her father, Kevin, might betray her, she decided to make some phone calls and remind the Randalls to keep their mouths shut. She had one of her men go to the Randalls residence and sneak some photos of Jordan's baby and mother through the windows. Selena knew Kevin could care less about his daughter or wife, but his grandson was his pride and joy. She'd use that weakness as leverage. She knew several inmates who had contraband, burner cell phones and were in the same facilities where the Randalls were being detained. She'd have her man who took the photos send them to the inmate's phones. They'd show Jordan and Kevin the photos and deliver Selena's message to keep quiet, or their family members would pay the price for their loose lips.

Selena had a client named Kelley, who worked as a nurse at the hospital, and she'd been keeping Selena informed of Ivan's condition. Ivan had always been loyal to her, but she knew the police would use his family against him, to squeeze information from him about her operation. She was bothered to put the hit on Ivan, but he was a liability to her now. He literally *knew where the bodies were buried.* She already had one of her men contacting the nurse, so he could get the necessary information to have access to Ivan, even if there was a guard at his room's door.

Selena was also relieved the cattle had been moved from the Randall's ranch. In the last two months, they'd been able to pinch one hundred and eighty head of cattle. Black angus, Herefords, and red angus cattle had been carefully chosen from a tri-state area. They'd deliberately focused on certain ranches, with brands with K's and R's. Kevin Randall had been rebranding and tagging the cattle to be able to sell them under his name, incorporating the old brands by branding over them. With him in jail, she needed to move the cattle to a different location. She had made calls to her truck drivers and ranch hands. They should be able to move the livestock within hours. They would finish rebranding them in the new location.

Trying to keep Matthew and Jeffrey out of trouble, she had her brothers working with the cattle. They were ordered to keep a very low profile. If they didn't do as she said, this would be their last time. She had a backup plan to deal with her bothersome brothers. She also had an associate, Octavio Martinez, who owned a section of land ninety miles south of where the cattle were currently being held. Octavio's six-hundred-forty acres was in a secluded area, and she'd chosen Octavio's ranch for the location's privacy. She'd make it work.

Selena Hayes was tired from juggling her businesses, but it was also an exciting challenge for her. Her burgeoning empire had lots of employees, and their clientele was rapidly expanding. People needed their medicine, and there was a strong demand for her product. As in Business 101, everything was all about supply and demand.

~~~~~~~~~~~~~~~~~~~~

Back at the hospital, Ivan's condition improved, and the doctor told Jack and Craig he was expected to make a full recovery. His medication would soon be changed, and the doctors would know more when he woke from the induced coma. The detectives stood in
~~~~~~~~~~~~~~~~~~~~

the patient's room, anxious to ask him questions. A uniformed officer guarded the door, and Jack wanted to be nearby when Ivan regained consciousness. Knowing it would likely be a few hours, Craig decided to leave and follow up on some of the evidence they'd found at the stash house.

Jack tried to settle into a hard, straight-backed chair beside Ivan's bed. The room was dark with the drapes pulled closed. Feeling tired from all the recent excitement, Jack felt his eyelids grow heavy, but he was instantly awake when a nurse came slinking into the room. She didn't see Jack sitting in the corner, and he noticed she looked at the patient with an annoyed, angry expression. Studying her stealthy demeanor, he observed her movements were rather odd and jerky.

As she crept near the bed, Jack said, "Would you like me to open the drapes or turn on a light for you?" She noticeably jumped, and his cop instincts picked up bad energy from her.

Turning on the bedside lamp, as well as the light over the bed, he studied the young woman. She had medium brown hair, was tall and gauntly slim. Dark circles under her surprised eyes, and the *deer in the headlights* look when Jack spoke to her triggered his gut reaction. He glanced at her name tag clipped on her nursing scrub's top which read, "Kelley".

"Kelley… how's our patient?" He watched her closely as she checked Ivan's blood pressure monitor and straightened the already neat bed linens. Her hands shook a little, and she avoided looking at Jack.

"He seems to be doing fine. He should be waking soon. I'll open the drapes." As she pulled the heavy drapes to the side and sunshine poured into the hospital room, he noticed the nurse's hands had a slight tremor. Jack looked closely at her eyes. With the sudden light in the room, he expected the pupils in her eyes to narrow; however, they appeared dilated. The doctor walked into the room and spoke to Jack.

"Good morning, Detective Parker." He smiled and continued, "Mr. Barnes still has some of the sedation in his system, so it might be another hour or so before we see him awake and responsive. It can take up to six hours after the last dose of the sedative."

Jack noticed Nurse Kelley carefully ease herself out of the room. She looked guilty of something, and he wondered if she was taking drugs. He also wondered why she had an apparent dislike for Ivan Barnes.

Shaking hands with the doctor, Jack told him he'd be glad to wait until the patient became conscious. Then he decided to ask the doctor a question unrelated to Ivan.

"Doctor Jackson, can I ask how often you require drug testing of your employees? I'm just curious."

"I believe employees are tested when they're first hired. After that, I'm not sure. I can find out what the hospital's policy is if you need me to," the doctor offered.

"No, that's okay, but thank you. I'll just sit here beside Mr. Barnes and wait till he wakes up. Thanks for your help." Jack answered, as he lowered himself into the uncomfortable chair.

The doctor left to finish his rounds in the hospital, and within a half hour, Ivan began moving his legs. Jack heard the suspect / patient quietly moan and noticed the monitor indicated his blood pressure and pulse rate were slowly increasing. Ivan Barnes was getting ready to wake up to a very different world from before the truck accident.

A different nurse, this one's name tag read Kathleen, hurried to Ivan's bedside and began checking his vital signs. He watched her go back to the nurse's station where she called Dr. Jackson, and he was in Ivan's room in moments. Jack squeezed himself into a corner to be out of the staff's way. He heard the doctor comment how the last scan indicated the swelling from the brain injury had significantly improved. Ivan thrashed, and the nurse administered an injection into his I.V. The patient calmed, and Dr. Jackson spoke to Jack.

"We need to give him a little more time. If you want to wait in the cafeteria or in the lobby, we'll call you as soon as he's up to answering your questions. It might be another hour or so. We'll need to monitor him closely, but he's coming around."

"Thank you, sir. I'll stay close by." Jack walked into the hallway and spoke to Officer Josh Simmons, guarding Ivan's door. He told him to be extra cautious because there could possibly be people wanting to silence Barnes before he could give the police incriminating information on the Hayes' organization. The officer nodded that he understood and assured Jack he would remain alert.

Jack walked to the nurse's station to see if Kelley was still on duty. He saw Nurse Kathleen standing with an older nurse who wore glasses, and they were staring at him. Her spectacled eyes squinted; then she smiled, and the older nurse said, "Benjamin Bratt! You look like a young, handsome Benjamin Bratt." She literally sighed, and Jack modestly laughed, feeling embarrassed.

He noticed her name tag and said, "Well, Sylvia… I have had a few people tell me I'm a brat before. Hey, is the nurse that was here earlier, Kelley, is she still here? She came into Ivan Barnes' room earlier."

"Hmmm, she shouldn't have been in there, unless Dr. Jackson asked her to check on the patient. That doesn't seem likely to me, though. She's supposed to be working in Radiology, helping with some ultrasounds. She normally doesn't work in this area."

Jack's S*pidey senses* went on full alert, and he thanked Sylvia as he quickly walked back to Barnes' room. Officer Simmons was carefully watching the hallway and everyone who walked by. Jack nodded at him as he walked inside. The monitors were beeping their normal rhythm and his vital signs looked good. With tired, sandpaper dry eyes, Jack studied Ivan. A huge, purple knot remained over Ivan's eyebrow, and a large bandage covered his lacerated forehead. His eyes were blackened with purple and beginnings of yellowish bruises. His breathing appeared normal. Feeling weary, Jack wished the man would wake up, so he could speak with him.

Considering Nurse Kelley's behavior, he got an idea, hoped he wasn't right, and walked into the hall.

"Hey Josh, can I ask a favor of you? I'd give my eyetooth for a strong cup of fresh coffee right now. Would you mind grabbing me a cup of mud in the cafeteria?" He handed the young officer a twenty-dollar bill. "Get yourself something to munch on, if you'd like."

Officer Simmons accepted the twenty and said, "I'm starving. Want anything besides coffee?" Jack shook his head and the young man sauntered down the wide hallway.

Jack closed the drapes, turned off the lights, and his eyes adjusted to the darkness of the room as he continued listening to Ivan's beeping monitors. In less than five minutes, the door slowly opened and a male of average height and size, wearing blue scrubs and a white face mask, sidled inside. Jack thought how he reminded him of a slithering snake, and he flipped on the room's light switch. The lurking man was quite surprised, and his eyes widened. His head was clean shaven. He wore surgical gloves and expensive Italian leather dress shoes.

Lurker-man didn't say a word, and neither did Jack as he stood in front of the door. The man glared at Jack over his facemask, balled his vinyl gloved fists and threw a punch, but the detective was expecting that move. He flipped the lights off and easily avoided the punch and the bald man's continued jabs. With a hard fist to the aggressive man's middle, Jack heard him grunt and struggle to catch his breath. He'd knocked the air out of him, and Jack quickly wrestled him to the floor in the darkness. Lurker-man was strong, but Jack had the element of surprise. He was able to overtake the bald man and pulled his arms behind his back. Suddenly, the room's light switch was turned back on. Nurse Kathleen strode into Ivan's room. She immediately took in what was happening and yelled to Sylvia to call for Security. Kathleen came running toward the men on the floor. As Jack struggled to cuff his wrists, Kathleen firmly stepped on Lurker-man's hairless head. A syringe was found in Lurker's pocket, and Jack carefully picked it up with a glove he'd removed from a box attached to the wall that was used by the hospital staff.

"Thanks, Kathleen… I think we've got him. I'm grateful for your help, though." Jack hauled the protesting man to his feet. Lurker-man tried throwing his bald head backwards to head-butt Jack. Instead, his round head sharply thumped against the wall, denting the sheetrock, and Jack suspected the stubborn man was seeing stars.

"Bruh… bet that hurt. Nurse Kathleen, how's patient Barnes?" asked Jack, as he looked at Lurker and shook his head.

"He's still resting. Can't believe he didn't wake up through all the commotion," she said and began studying Lurker-man. She pulled down his surgical face mask and said, "Hmmm, I recognize you. You were talking with Kelley. I saw you guys in the hall by the Radiology doors."

Officer Simmons and a security guard came running into the room. Jack asked the security guard to please check if Nurse Kelley was still on the hospital grounds, and if she was, to bring her to him. Officer Simmons pulled the cuffed man towards the door to remove him from the room and march him to his squad car.

"Hold up, Simmons." As the officer and bald man looked backwards, Jack held his cell phone, and sarcastically said, "Say cheese!" He took Lurker-man's photo, and then dropped the syringe into an evidence bag and photographed it as well.

He sent the photos to Craig's cell phone and texted, "Check out Ivan's uninvited guest."

Craig was nearby. He had been on his way back to the hospital when Jack messaged him. He walked into Ivan's room as the photos pinged their arrival on his phone, and he scrutinized the bald man being escorted by Officer Simmons. Jack handed him the bagged syringe.

"Good job, Detective," Craig grinned and proceeded to read the bald man his rights. He and Officer Simmons escorted him out the door and headed to the MPD.

Jack felt tired as he stood beside Ivan's hospital bed. "Please wake up, Ivan," he quietly pleaded. He felt relief to see Ivan's eyes slowly open, droop, and look directly at him.

Ivan looked confused and then angry when he saw he was handcuffed to the hospital bed. He yanked and loudly jangled the bracelets attached to the bedrail. His vital signs became erratic, and Nurse Kathleen and Dr. Jackson rushed into the room. They calmed him and told him where he was and that he'd been in a motor vehicle accident. He motioned to a plastic glass sitting on a tray next to his bed, indicating to them he was thirsty. Kathleen offered Ivan a drink of water with a curved straw. As he sipped the water, his eyes returned to Jack, and his first words were, "Are you a cop?"

Dr. Jackson noticed his patient's vitals had calmed. "Jack, my patient needs his rest. Please keep the conversation brief." He and Nurse Kathleen left the room. Jack turned on the recording app on his phone.

He looked at Ivan and said, "My name is Detective Jack Parker with the Morrigan Police Department. Do you remember driving a pickup truck and losing control of it? You were going too fast around an S-curve, and the truck flipped. Why were you driving so fast, Ivan?"

Ivan closed his eyes and groaned, "I'm a dead man. Where's Jordan and my baby?"

"They're okay. Ivan, why would someone want you dead? A man tried sneaking in here. He had a syringe, and I barely caught him in time. If you want protection, I'm sure that can be arranged, but you need to tell me what's going on."

On his phone, Jack clicked the photos of the bald man and the syringe. He showed them to Ivan who suddenly paled a lighter shade beneath his bruises.

"That's Terry Adler. He does jobs for Selena Hayes. She sure didn't waste any time." Ivan muttered, cursed and continued, as the monitor indicated his blood pressure was rising. "I've worked like a faithful dog for her… put up with her ignorant brothers and her hissy fits… and now, she sends Adler after me? Humph… The reason I was driving so fast in Matt's truck was because the diva was throwing one of her tantrums and demanded I get to her house ASAP. I've never met anyone who is so beautiful on the outside, yet ugly as sin on the inside. She has a black heart."

"Tell me more about Selena Hayes," Jack coaxed. "What kind of work did you do for her? Do you know where she is?"

"She and her brothers come from a very dysfunctional family. The mother disappeared when they were just kids. Their father was a cruel, ruthless monster. He introduced his children to the world of dealing drugs when they were young. After he passed away a few years ago, Selena took over the reins of the business. Drug sales increased rapidly. Business is booming, but she's in bed with some scary dudes from Mexico. God, she's an arrogant snob. She has her nose so high in the air, she could drown in a rainstorm."

Twenty minutes later, Dr. Jackson came into the room and checked his patient. He told Jack it was time to wrap up his questioning. As Jack walked out of Ivan Barnes' room, he noticed Officer Connors had assumed Josh Simmons post.

Jack nodded his head toward her and asked, "Officer Connors, do you know if the nurse, Kelley, has been located inside the hospital?"

She answered, "No sir, but a unit has been sent to her residence to pick her up."

Jack told her, "Thanks, and please be careful. The people after Barnes won't stop until he's dead or in Witness Protection."

Feeling exhaustion begin to take hold, he walked out of the hospital and drove to the police station where a ton of paperwork awaited him.

Chapter Thirty-Five

Tessa woke from her nap feeling apprehensive. She hadn't dreamed of anything, yet a sense of uneasiness wrapped around her. She rolled off the thick cushioned couch and slowly sauntered into her kitchen. Pouring herself a glass of ice water with lemon, she hoped to ward off a threatening migraine and took a pill to dull the ache in her right temple.

She kept thinking of her father, so she picked up her phone and called him. James Ryan answered his cell phone, and Tessa thought he sounded like he was on his hands-free device while driving. "Hi, Dad. Sounds like you're in your truck. Where are you?"

"Well… I don't know."

Hairs stood up on the back of her neck. "What do you mean, you don't know, Dad? What road… or highway are you on?"

"We're on Highway 59 heading south, but I'm not sure where we're headed. Vernon and I were checking on his cattle by the old Niles' home place when we saw two, big bull wagons loaded down with red angus drive right by us. Tessa, something felt wrong to me about them. I can't explain it, so we're following them. There hasn't been anyone at the Niles' farm for almost a year. Anyhow, we've got three-quarters of a tank of gas, so we'll see how far it goes." Tessa could hear concern in her father's voice. She also noticed how he referred to "something felt wrong to me," and she thought maybe some of her intuitive abilities might have come from her father as well as her Grandma Lucy.

"So, there's two cattle trucks going south? Dad, I'm going to have Jack call you, okay? Just in case…" Tessa felt alarm shiver up her spine.

"Yes, two big Kenworth trucks. We didn't recognize the logo on the truck's doors, and me and Vernon know all the outfits around here. These bull haulers were driving on back roads to get to Highway 59, and it just feels… off. There aren't any weigh stations out this way, so it's not like they need to avoid the scales."

"Dad, you guys be safe. Don't get too close to them. I'm going to hang up now and call Jack, okay?" She quickly called Jack and informed him about her father and Vernon traipsing after a couple of trucks hauling red angus cattle going south on Highway 59. She sent her father's phone number contact to Jack and tried not to feel distraught, but her gut told her something was very wrong.

After hanging up her call with Jack, she knelt beside her dragonfly chair and began to pray. Asking God to protect her father, Vernon, and Jack, she also prayed for the cattle. If these were the stolen red angus, the truck drivers might feel threatened or exposed, if approached. They might drive too fast, which could be hazardous for all involved.

~~~~~~~~~~~~~~~~~~~

Matthew and Jeffrey Hayes were traveling with the truck drivers moving the cattle to Selena's friend, Octavio's, ranch. Matthew was in the lead semi, and Jeffrey rode in the second one. Jeffrey had noticed the brown Ford pickup truck following them twenty miles back, and he called his brother to warn him that they might be being tailed. Matthew thought his brother was being foolish, and he ridiculed his younger brother, not taking him seriously.

"Quit being a paranoid drama king, *Norbert*." Matthew taunted. Cringing, Jeffrey stiffened and angrily hung up their phone call. He was sick of his brother's ridicule, and he still felt uneasy with the brown truck following so closely behind them.

~~~~~~~~~~~~~~~~~~~

Vernon looked irritated and said, "You know James, I'm beginning to wonder about something else. A couple weeks ago, I noticed a smoke plume near the Niles' farm. I just figured it must have been from the Tillman place south of there, but now I'm wondering. I could smell cowhide burning, like someone was branding cattle. That's a nostril burning stench you never forget, and I could hear cattle bawling, too. Living where we do, it's not unusual to smell and hear those cattle noises, but what if it was the rustlers?"

James thoughtfully nodded his head and handed Vernon his binoculars, which he kept in his truck for scouting deer and wildlife. He told him to write down the tag number off the cattle trailer. Vernon squinted through the field glasses, pulled out the Bic ink pen he always carried in his left shirt pocket and wrote the numbers from the trailer's back plate onto his left hand.

James' phone rang, and he quickly answered. "Hey there, James. It's Jack. Tessa gave me the low-down about the cattle trucks. Can you make out the trailer's plate number?"

"Yes, Vernon just now got the tag number. Let me see your hand, Vernon. He wrote the number on the palm of his hand. It's DK-3148. It's a Barrett trailer, and they've got cowbells hanging from the back bumper. The semi-trucks are both blue Kenworths with Longhorn logos on their doors. Want us to keep following them?"

"Tell me what mile marker you're near James, and I'd rather you fellas drop way back behind the trucks. Don't get too close, or they'll spook. I'll have some state highway troopers out there in a few minutes. Thank you, James, and tell Vernon, too. I appreciate y'all being so observant. Just be careful."

James told Jack the mile marker number he'd just driven by, and they hung up their call. James slowed his pickup, and the cattle trucks quickly pulled away from him and Vernon. The rigs continued making their way south down Highway 59.

Jack immediately made phone calls to have the semi-trucks full of cattle checked out. Knowing Tessa was probably worried, he decided to check on her and drove to her house as soon as he'd finished speaking to the Oklahoma Highway Patrol Department. Standing on her front porch, he heard the electronic unlocking of the front door and smiled, knowing she was being cautious and keeping her doors locked.

Tessa answered her front door, and the young couple wrapped their arms around each other. Even though it had been less than twenty-four hours since they'd last been together, they'd genuinely missed each other. He held her tight. *Man, I've got it bad for the girl.* Jack noticed the tension on her worried face and assured her the Highway Patrolmen would be on the scene of the cattle trucks on Highway 59 any moment.

"I hope so, Jack. I'm worried about my Dad." Worry lines pinched between her brows.

Tessa carried steaming cups of coffee for Jack and herself to her small dining table. She handed a freshly baked loaf of zucchini bread she had made that afternoon to him. The recipe was a new one, and she told him that he was her guinea pig. She hadn't tried any herself, because she had absolutely no appetite courtesy of her worry. Jack sliced the loaf and took a bite of the warm bread. He closed his eyes and appreciatively groaned.

"If you ever want to change careers, you should cook for a living. It's delicious, Tessa! Try it. Seriously, everything you've cooked that I've tried has been excellent, except the peanut butter dog biscuits." He offered her some of the bread, and she took a small bite.

She smiled, and said, "It's better than I expected it to be. When I get nervous, I cook."

He took a second slice and gave her one as well. Within fifteen minutes, both their cell phones rang. Tessa stood up and walked into the front room to give Jack space to talk to whomever had called him.

~~~~~~~~~~~~~~~~~~~

Recognizing her father's phone number, Tessa anxiously answered her own ringing phone. "Are you okay, Dad?"

Tessa's father assured her, "Me and Vernon are just fine, Daughter. We've got to give statements to the Highway Patrolmen in a few minutes, but I wanted to let you know the trucks were stopped by the troopers. They're certain the cattle are the ones stolen from the ranchers. I'll call you later after I get home, okay? I need to call your Mama."

"Dad, I'm proud of you! You guys did so good. I'll talk to you soon. Love you!"
~~~~~~~~~~~~~~~~~~~

Hanging up the call, tears of relief welled in her eyes, and she looked upward and thanked her heavenly Father for the good outcome.

Jack joined her in the front room a few minutes later. His eyes were bright, and he was smiling ear to ear. “They got them, Tessa!”

~~~~~~~~~~~~~~~~~~~~

Jack continued telling her about the now confiscated trucks and trailers full of stolen cattle. His excitement was contagious, and she was thrilled to hear the cattle rustlers had been apprehended. As Jack had suspected, the Hayes brothers were involved. He gave her a tender kiss, tasting the sweetness of the fresh bread from her lips. He touched his forehead to hers and told her he would be back as soon as he could.

“We’ve got cattle rustling, drug dealing, criminals to deal with, and I owe your father and Vernon a big steak dinner!” Anxious to question the Hayes brothers, Jack raced out of the house and drove to the police department.
~~~~~~~~~~~~~~~~~~~~

Chapter Thirty-Six

When Selena received a call telling her the cattle had not arrived at the ranch of her friend and business associate, Octavio Martinez, she could literally feel her temper rising. Her useless, feeble-minded brothers had probably messed up again. She tried calling Matthew, but the call went to his voicemail. She angrily paced back and forth in front of the tall windows spanning fifteen feet along the wall in her office. Gentle raindrops spattered the long windows, and the drizzly, gloomy clouds reflected her dark mood. Oklahoma's rainy spring was getting on her last nerve. She needed sunshine. A luxurious resort and a handsome cabana boy painting her toenails suddenly struck her as a necessary distraction. She decided to pack a bag and get out of town.

Searching through her tall armoire for her black and gold Fendi bikini, her phone rang, and she hesitantly took the call. She dreaded answering her phone.

"Kelley, give me some good news!"

"I wish I could, Selena... but things have gone from bad to worse." Nurse Kelley's voice trembled as she regrettably informed her boss of the botched job. "At the hospital, Adler got his butt handed to him from a cop, a detective named Jack Parker. Adler didn't have a chance to get near Ivan, and he got himself arrested."

Hearing Adler had flubbed the job on Ivan Barnes, Selena began throwing anything within her reach from the armoire. Hermes scarves and Dolce & Gabbana lingerie carelessly littered her bedroom floor.

"Where's my gold Fendi bikini?" she screamed, still searching through drawers.

"What? Selena, what should I do? I can't go home... there's a cop car parked out front of my house." Kelley frantically continued asking for instructions, "Should I leave town?"

Without answering Kelley, Selena hung up the call and muttered, "That's exactly what I'm trying to do."

She gave up her search for the gold designer bikini and decided to buy a new one later. After quickly packing, she rolled the Gucci suitcase to the garage, opened the trunk and carefully placed the suitcase inside the Mercedes. Looking forward to relaxing on a sandy beach and drinking vodka cocktails, she sighed, started the car and listened to its powerful engine purr. She loved her sapphire-blue roadster. Pressing the garage door opener, she shifted the car into reverse. As she slowly backed out, she stomped her brakes and felt her stomach lurch. There were three police cruisers with flashing blue and red lights parked in front of her house and blocking her driveway.

Uniformed officers, with raised guns pointed at her, began circling the Mercedes. They yelled at Selena to stop the car and put her hands where they could see them. She sat there for a minute, her mind racing to think of an escape, and her calculating gray eyes sized up the angry looking policemen. She decided to give herself up and shifted the car into park, turned off the ignition, and raised her hands in the air to surrender. An officer pulled her driver's side door open and ordered her to slowly get out of the vehicle and put her hands on her head. She complied and was already thinking of a plan her attorney and she could devise to extricate herself. Not once did she think of her brothers.

~~~~~~~~~~~~~~~~~~~~

Back at the police department, Matthew and Jeffrey Hayes were being questioned in separate rooms. The older brother, Matthew, was arrogant and obnoxious, but the younger brother seemed quiet and reserved. Jack kept a close eye on Jeffrey.

While questioning Matthew, Craig asked him if Selena Hayes was his sister. He ignored the question with the perpetual smirk he'd been wearing for the last ten minutes. With scowling eyes, and a curled upper lip, the insolent brother gave the impression
~~~~~~~~~~~~~~~~~~~~

he was smelling rotten eggs. Jack laid some photos on the table in front of Matthew. Jack pointed to the photo of a wrecked white pickup truck and asked if the truck belonged to him. Matthew looked disgusted and angry as he glanced at the wreckage in the photo. Jack placed another one next to the truck photo.

"Do you recognize this man?" he asked, pointing to a photo of a very bruised, comatose Ivan Barnes.

Matthew looked away, and Jack continued, "Notice, he's lying in a hospital bed? He was banged up quite badly in the truck wreck. Now look at this guy… he was sent to the hospital to silence your friend, Ivan, permanently."

Jack laid a photo on the table of a grimacing Terry Adler. It showed the bald man with his wrists cuffed behind him in Ivan's hospital room. The photo of Adler made Matthew sit up straight on the metal chair, and his upper lip began to uncurl. He looked at Jack and Craig with confusion glazed across his face. Clearly, he had not been privy to his sister putting a hit on Ivan Barnes, and he became extremely agitated.

"Is Ivan okay?" asked Matthew in a slightly humble voice, as he squinted at the photo of his battered friend lying in the hospital bed.

Matthew's arrogance had dropped a few notches, and Jack answered, "He's out of a coma and doing better, for now." He lay the photo of the syringe on the table. "I took this off Adler before he had a chance to use it on Barnes." Matthew sharply inhaled, then looked down his long, angular nose.

"I'm not going to say anything more. I want a lawyer." Matthew squeezed his thin lips tight, signaling he was finished with the conversation, but Jack could tell he was doing some serious soul searching. He seemed scared and uneasy.

~~~~~~~~~~~~~~~~~~~~

Jeffrey Hayes seemed to be the polar-opposite of his brother, and Jack likened him to his dog, Hank, that he'd raised when he was young. Hank was the runt of the litter, and the sibling puppies pushed him around. They wouldn't let him nurse from the mother dog, and he probably would have died if Jack hadn't taken him under his wing. He rescued Hank from the larger, bullying sibling pups and enjoyed having the loyal dog as his sidekick for fourteen
~~~~~~~~~~~~~~~~~~~~

years. Jeffrey had the same crushed and defeated mentality that Hank had before Jack saved him. He'd literally been a whipped pup.

Jeffrey sat at the metal table with his eyes cast downward, and Jack put the photos of the wrecked truck, Ivan Barnes, and Terry Adler before him. Studying each photo, Jeffrey's shoulders slumped even more, and he seemed to feel doomed. With sad eyes, he looked up towards Craig and Jack and began talking.

"Is Ivan dead? Did Adler kill him?" asked Jeffrey.

"No, he's alive, and Terry Adler is facing charges of attempted murder. Does Adler work for your sister, Selena? We know all about your sister's drug manufacturing and dealing, and we also know about her being behind the cattle thefts. We're aware you and your brother Matthew work for your sister. She's been arrested, Jeffrey. Selena and Matthew can't hurt you anymore."

Jeffrey almost smiled as his demoralized brain processed the information he was just told. Painfully remembering all the decades of his sibling's bullying and his sociopath father watching the abuse and laughing at his youngest son, Jeffrey was glad they'd been caught.

He pushed his shoulders back, lifted his underdeveloped chin with a determined air, and asked, "If I give you plenty of info on them, will they be kept in jail… not released? If I tell you everything I know, no doubt, I'll be next on Adler's list, or another of my sister's contractors. I want a deal giving me complete immunity and protection. I want a new identity, plastic surgery, a whole new life."

The proper authorities took all day to reach an agreement with Jeffrey's terms, and a signed and documented arrangement was finally concluded. Jeffrey was enrolled into a witness security program. He gave them damning evidence of his family's crimes and organization. Jeffrey would be assigned a new name, a new social security number, a new driver's license, and most importantly to Jeffrey, he'd be seeing a renowned plastic surgeon and orthodontist. This unexpected, fortuitous plan was the answer to Jeffrey's prayers.

The District Attorney's office was ecstatic and relieved Jeffrey had so easily given up everything he knew. Selena Hayes would be brought to her knees. Her organization would be totally dismantled after Jeffrey's testimony. Her days of wearing designer clothing, driving expensive cars, and living lavishly were over. She had become wealthy from selling her poison and destroying lives. The scales of justice had finally tipped... or so they thought.

Chapter Thirty-Seven

Sitting at a table with a view of the town's night lights, Tessa and Jack sat in the always packed, popular steak house with their friend, Sandra. All three were happy to see each other and anxious to catch up on the recent events. Famished, they ordered their meals and appetizers. The restaurant was dark and rather cozy, and the service seemed excellent with attentive servers. Tiny clinks from crystal glasses could be heard as the cheerful diners conversed. Tessa looked from Jack to Sandra and thanked God that her dear friends were feeling content and lighthearted. She felt blessed and thought how she was most happy when her loved ones were happy and successful.

"So, Jack, I hear you've had incredible, good fortune with the deal-making Jeffrey Hayes. Word around town is indictments on his brother and sister are imminent." Sandra said, looking pleased for the young detective.

Jack was elated, and replied, "Yes, and combined with Ivan Barnes' testimony, the Hayes organization will soon be a thing of the past. Of course, Tessa's father and neighbor, Vernon, are responsible for the return of the rancher's cattle. That was an exciting afternoon!"

Tessa beamed with pride at the mention of her father. "I'm so glad Dad trusted his instincts, and the cattle rustlers were caught. Dad and Vernon feel a bit like celebrities right now."

Sandra chuckled, and Tessa looked at her friend noticing a glow that emanated from her whole being. Sandra wore a flattering, navy blue Chanel dress with a boatneck design and pearl earrings. She wore simple elegance well. An enchanting type of contentment brightened Sandra's hazel-green eyes as she spoke of her ongoing project. What a difference from the woman she first met at the condo the day she escorted her to see her therapist. Building the shelter for abused women and children had given Sandra purpose, and the benefits would bless many lives in the years to come.

"We've finally decided to name the safehouse organization as *The Marcy Phillips Haven of Hope*." Sandra all but sparkled as she shared her news.

"That's amazing! Sandra, I'm thrilled for you, and you look so good, my friend. Honestly, you're looking beautiful! Are you visiting spas, or what's your secret?" Tessa had spoken from her heart. With the horrors of what the poor woman had suffered, that she was doing so well seemed miraculous.

"Well, I have lost a little weight. Twenty whole pounds, and I've been working out and swimming every day. Physically and mentally, I feel better than I have in years."

Jack finished his New York strip steak and patted his stomach. "That was the best steak I've ever had in my whole life." He declared with a satisfied smile.

The evening progressed with more warm conversation and scrumptious desserts. Jack ordered an apple crumb tart. Tessa indulged in creamy cheesecake, but Sandra was more reserved with a raspberry sorbet. After finishing their meals, all three felt indulgently full.

Sandra gave them the good news of her home's approximate finish date. She was anxious to move into her new house and decorate it with all the furnishings she'd ordered. They would be delivered in two weeks, and she told them she'd like to have a party shortly after she had settled. They were on the top of her invitation list. She would also invite Lily, her accountants, her attorneys, plus the contractors, Jacob Kiefer and his son Eric. Her eyes lit up when she mentioned Jacob. They had all become her beloved team and were supportive and excited to make the *Haven of Hope* successful. It had become an ambitious project of love.

~~~~~~~~~~~~~~~~~~~~~~~~~~

Jacob, the fifty-six-year-old carpenter, had become enamored of Sandra. Although he was trying to keep his admiration and feelings to himself, he thought she was one of the most beautiful women he'd ever known. Her generous, kind heart was what he'd fallen in love with first. She reminded him of his late wife. Sandra was the only woman he'd been interested in since his wife passed away over three years ago. He felt afraid to approach her. He hadn't dated since he'd courted his late wife in high school, but he knew he'd be working closely with Sandra on the project for at least another year. Maybe by then, he'd be brave enough to share his feelings with her.

~~~~~~~~~~~~~~~~~~~

In a federal prison halfway across the state, another man thought about Sandra. As usual, O'Brien felt as though he'd been cheated. He wallowed in self-pity and blamed everyone but himself for his current circumstances.

Selena's cousin, Jared, the correctional officer in the prison who had supplied him with a burner cell phone, informed O'Brien about his cousin's arrests.

The correctional officer was furious and cautiously told the inmate in a hissing whisper, "I can't believe Jeff could burn his brother and sister, his own blood. What kind of man does that? He gave them up for immunity… told the DA all the locations of the labs, everything, and he gave up a list of client's names, too. My buddy from high school, who was told from a reliable source, said that ole Jeff got a pile of cash to move to a different state. He's sitting pretty while Matt and Selena are sitting in stinking cages." Jared's face had reddened with anger.

O'Brien listened to the latest news with bulging eyes. Shaking his head, he replied, "I swear if I get out of here, I'm going after Jeff, or whatever his name is now. Can your buddy, your source, find out what his new name is? One way or another, I'm getting out of this dump. Don't think I can take it much longer."

"Yeah, my bud is working on that now… getting Jeff's new identity and location. If Jeff thinks he's getting out of this deal scot-free, he's got another think coming."

~~~~~~~~~~~~~~~~~~~~

Weeks prior, Daniel had phoned his old co-driver, his accomplice and partner in crime. With the phone he'd bought in prison from Jared, he had called his old friend's office, which had been a huge surprise for his fellow hunter. His old hunting buddy's reaction to the unexpected call was angry and intense. He threatened to have Daniel *shivved* in his prison cell if he dared to ever call him again. The old co-driver paid Daniel a visit in the prison the next day, and he made it clear that Daniel should never contact him again.

The disgruntled fellow-predator told him, "I'll do what I can to help you in here, O'Brien, but from now on, don't call me; I'll call you. I've got several contacts here in the pen, so I'll try to pull some strings for you." Daniel decided he wouldn't hold his breath.

Several of the people Daniel had contacted, requesting assistance, had ignored his blackmail attempts. What Daniel didn't realize was they weren't threatened by him. His insinuations of exposing them of what he knew of their corruption, affairs and unscrupulous deeds weren't severe enough to give Daniel much leverage. Mostly, his threats would amount to O'Brien's word against theirs. As usual, his grandiose thinking made him feel more important than he was. He mistakenly considered himself a big player. One of his girlfriends, Melody Lambert, had paid a price for believing Daniel's pompous deceptions. She was being held for theft and money-laundering, however she had made a beneficial deal with the DA for herself. Unbeknownst to O'Brien, she'd given them account numbers to the bank in the Cayman Islands where the Hayes' organization stashed the bulk of their profits.

~~~~~~~~~~~~~~~~~~~~

Daniel's contraband cell phone vibrated under his pillow as he lay on his hard, narrow bed. Carefully carrying it to a corner of the cell where he couldn't be seen, he accepted the call that read Private Number and cautiously whispered, "Hello?".

"O'Brien… it's me, Selena. We need to talk. The wheels are in motion. I've called in some big favors, so be ready. We should be out of these nasty cells within twenty-four hours. I haven't been here but one day, and I can't stand it. What is it with the stench of these places? Smells like a bunch of wet dogs." Selena complained.

Selena had plans for O'Brien. She needed someone who was ruthless, indebted to her, as well as expendable. Since so many of her associates were being arrested, to regroup and make some big adjustments in her organization was imperative. She also needed someone to help her locate and deal with her traitor brother, Jeff. Yes, Selena had big plans for Inmate O'Brien.

~~~~~~~~~~~~~~~~~~

He almost shouted with joy! He quivered with anticipation of freedom and was thrilled to be included in Selena's plan. The escape was going to happen, and O'Brien would do anything to be out in the free world again. He missed his comfortable home, his truck, his girlfriends, and he especially missed making Sandra crazy. He giggled like a little schoolgirl as he thought of all the mind games he'd played on her over the years.

"I'll see you soon, Sandra," he whispered, "and, I'll be paying your little Tessa a visit, too. She caused every bit of this mess by pointing the cops to me about Marcy when she gave that eyewitness paper to her cop boyfriend. She will get what's coming to her. Every bit of this trouble is Tessa Ryan's fault."
~~~~~~~~~~~~~~~~~~

Chapter Thirty-Eight

The Three *Amigas* hit their best time running the two-mile trail. They'd raced around the paved path with its sand plum groves and shady wooded edges. Breathing heavily, they made a beeline for their cars and water bottles. A couple of young college men, around eighteen or nineteen, had been checking them out, and the girls laughed because of the age difference. They began teasing each other, as they stretched their tired muscles.

They'd been meeting at the walking path, running four to five miles a day in the early mornings before going to work. Usually, they did so on Mondays, Wednesdays, and Fridays. Tessa felt she was in better shape than when she was in high school. She'd also been lifting weights in her garage every other evening, and she was satisfied with the results of her efforts. Rachel was more dedicated than she was, and she had the six-pack to prove it. Tessa hoped to catch up to her friend by the end of the summer. Her competitive nature kept her on track.

The friends waved goodbye to each other and agreed to meet the day after tomorrow. Before Tessa could buckle her seatbelt, her phone rang. She saw Jack was calling her, and her stomach quivered with butterflies.

Beaming, she smiled and cheerfully answered. “Hi, Jack! How’s your morning going?”

“Not good, Tessa. Not good at all.” Jack gave her the bad news that Daniel O’Brien had escaped from prison early that morning, and her fluttering stomach dropped like a bucket of lead.

He told Tessa, “O’Brien evidently had a lot of help from two corrupt correctional officers as well as other inmates. He was smuggled into the sally port and delivery area of the prison. When a grocery truck driver was making his delivery to the kitchen, O’Brien was snuck into the truck’s trailer. Cameras were tampered with, and the crooked guards are nowhere to be found.” Jack’s phone beeped. “Chief Mullins is calling me, Tessa. I’ll call you right back.”

The Chief had more discouraging news for Jack. He had just been informed that Selena Hayes had escaped from the Federal Prison in western Oklahoma. Heads would roll, because not one, but two, dangerous criminals had managed to break out of incarceration in a short span of time. They had underestimated Selena’s long reach into the prison’s and her many associates.

“Where are you, Tess? I have more bad news.” Jack cringed, dreading telling her.

“I’m on my way home, then on to work after a quick shower.”

“You might want to call in and request the day off. I know you don’t like doing that, but you don’t want to endanger anyone at the clinic. Selena has escaped from prison, as well. I’ll explain everything soon.”

Tessa thought she must have heard Jack wrong. *Selena has also escaped? That doesn’t seem possible, not from a federal facility. How has this happened?*

“Okay… I’m pulling into my garage right now. I’ll check all the windows and doors to make sure everything is all right here. I’ll call you back in a bit.”

Jack answered, “I’ve got to drop by my house to get something, and I’ll be at your place in a few minutes.” Parking in his driveway, he hurried inside his log house, pulled keys from his pocket, and made his way to the locked gun case. He removed his Glock from the case and grabbed a bag holding four boxes of shells, jumped back in the Charger, and synced his phone to the car’s onboard system.

"I'm driving to your house right now, Tessa. Can you open the garage door when I get to your driveway? I'd rather not advertise to O'Brien that I'm there with you. Is everything okay?"

"Yes, I'm fine… just in shock." Tessa thought, that was an understatement. The reality that she was in danger from the monster O'Brien had fully dawned on her. She didn't want to feel scared or intimidated, but she was.

Less than ten minutes later, she opened the garage door, and Jack parked his Charger beside Mabel. Tessa was glad to see him and met him at the kitchen door. The dark glint in his eyes startled her, and she thought he looked like a warrior ready for battle. She'd hate to be the unfortunate adversary going against her dark-eyed detective. He placed a black case on her kitchen table, and a heavy bag loudly clunked beside it. Turning toward her, he opened his arms wide. She didn't hesitate for a second and welcomed his embrace. They stood holding each other for a full minute. Then, sitting down at the table, Jack removed his pistol from the case. He methodically loaded two magazines with fifteen rounds of ammo each. He also checked his service gun. He was ready.

She told Jack she was going to take a quick shower since he was there. Minutes later, Tessa emerged from her bedroom wearing Levi's, a black t-shirt, and her *Ariat* western boots. She also wore her turquoise cross necklace from her Grandma Lucy. She often held the small pendant within her fingers when she was in prayer. She sat down on her couch to check the cameras.

Walking into the front room, Jack made sure every window had its blinds and drapes closed tight. Joining Tessa on the leather couch, he noticed her laptop was open and sitting on the turquoise coffee table. All four of the security cameras were shown on the computer screen in quartered sections. He lay the extra gun beside the laptop and began informing her of the details of Selena's escape.

"Chief Mullins just called and gave me more information about the escapes. Evidently, Selena had several family members and contacts inside the prisons that no one was aware of. Most of them were inmates who did her bidding, but a few were employed at the prisons. Some of her crew on the outside smuggled guns into the prison via drones where she was being held. Two correctional officers were wounded, but thankfully, no one was killed. She was behind O'Brien's escape, as well. According to information that was gathered from inmates when they were questioned after the escape,

O'Brien had indicated to several of them that he's after *you*. He's holding a grudge against *you*. In his twisted, warped mind, he's blaming you and Sandra for all his problems, but he's projecting all his hatred onto you, Tessa."

"How does he even know about me?" She slowly shook her head in disbelief, as Jack's phone rang. The call was from Craig, asking his partner if Tessa was safe. Tessa asked if they could bring Sandra to her house. She was worried about her friend.

Jack relayed the request to Craig, "Tessa asked if you could pick up Sandra and bring her to the house. Craig, do you think we should move Tessa and Sandra into a safehouse?"

Craig had already considered it, but he felt it was a bad idea. They still didn't know exactly who or how many moles were in the MPD, and he'd bet they knew all the safehouse's addresses.

Craig replied, "No, Jack. I think we'd be sitting ducks. Since you've got Tessa hooked up with a great alarm system, she'd probably be safer there for the time being. I'll go to Sandra's hotel and pick her up. We'll arrive at Tessa's from the back alley. I'll drop off Sandra at the back door and park my car down the block and walk back to the house. Have Tessa call her and fill her in of all the details. She needs to be ready as soon as I get there."

After hanging up with Jack, Craig called Chief Mullins and ran his idea by him. "Chief, I'm headed to pick up Sandra Dawson, and then we'll head back to Tessa's place. Jack has an outstanding security system set up for her, and I'd feel safer there than at a safehouse. I'm worried about whoever the moles are at the PD tipping off O'Brien. What do ya' think?"

"I agree completely, Taylor. It's time we smoked out these moles. Time to set some bait. I'll make sure to drop comments around the station that Tessa has been moved to the safehouse south of town. I especially want Reed and Warren to overhear the bogus info, so we can trap these rats."

"Good idea, Chief. I'll call ya' once I'm back to Tessa's with Sandra." He flipped on the car's red and blue lights and drove as fast as he could to Sandra's hotel.

By two o'clock, they were settled in at Tessa's home, and Chief Mullins called and informed them he'd have units driving by the house. There were two officers that he trusted, and he'd have them patrolling Tessa's neighborhood. He had purposely made a phone call to Jack, in front of Ben Reed in the breakroom, giving the address for the bogus safehouse. The bait was set. They didn't really expect O'Brien to try anything until nightfall, but they'd be ready if he did.

Being the attentive hostess, Tessa offered coffee, tea, and homemade cinnamon rolls she'd baked the day before to everyone. Earlier for lunch, she'd served thick deli-sliced roast beef sandwiches and cheesy fries. From her flat screen television mounted over the fireplace mantle, they watched news reports and updates of the prison escapes and paced the floors.

Craig shook his head, and said, "I feel bad for the wardens in these prisons. They're in major hot water over these escapes. I, personally, know several of the correctional officers and deputy wardens in these locations, and they're good people. There hasn't been an escape like this in many years, if ever, but the few corrupt officers and dirty staff are like bad apples… makes the whole barrel look bad."

~~~~~~~~~~~~~~~~~~~

Craig and Jack took turns watching the cameras on Tessa's laptop, and Sandra hoped to create a diversion to dispel some of the tension. She opened her iPad to show everyone the plans and photos of her new home being built. Sandra asked for Jack's friend, Curtis's phone number, so she could consult with him regarding an alarm system for her new house and the complex. She had an aerial photo of the one-hundred-sixty acres and asked for advice from the two detectives on the location where she was considering building the guest house complex.

She had purposely chosen a potential spot that was not visible from the main road and was on a lower elevation in a valley. The apartment complex would be completely concealed in a wooded area. Her concern was the guests could possibly have ex-husbands or ex-boyfriends pursuing them, and she wanted to keep her guests safe. Sandra showed them diagrams of the eagerly anticipated shelter with its duplexes, clubhouse, and grounds for future guests, victims of abuse who'd get a helping hand to overcome their trauma and have a fresh start. The group was glad she had a positive distraction to share with them, and the optimistic conversation of the project took the edge off their strained nerves.

Sandra's excitement was infectious, and Tessa was thrilled about the headway being made on her friend's new enterprise.
~~~~~~~~~~~~~~~~~~~

Sandra commented that the carpenter and his construction crew were exceptional. She told Tessa about the carpenter, Jacob, and what a kind man he was. Tessa noticed her friend's expression softened when speaking of the contractor, which gave Tessa hope that Sandra might find true love. She deserved it, especially after the emotional trauma and abuse she'd endured from O'Brien. She silently said a prayer that Sandra would be blessed with a loving relationship and hoped it would be with Jacob.

~~~~~~~~~~~~~~~~~~~~

Peeking through the blinds from her kitchen window, Tessa noticed there was a beautiful sunset gracing the dusky Oklahoma sky. The bright red sun dipped below the western horizon. Realizing that night was falling, she involuntarily shuddered. She felt angry with Daniel O'Brien and his threats; although she wasn't as terrified as she had been earlier. Mainly, she was furious at the monster who had caused so many complications and pain in hers and other's lives. She didn't underestimate the evil that emanated from him, and she even wondered if he had a soul. She prayed for a hedge of protection for her friends and herself.

Keeping the lights off, with the television's volume low to conceal the fact they were in the house, the atmosphere felt eerie. Tessa watched Jack and Craig's faces by the light of the television, and she was glad they were in her corner. She trusted these good people and prayed for their safety. Wondering if O'Brien would show up, she felt on edge. They'd been on lockdown for several hours. Craig's phone vibrated, and he answered. Putting the call on speaker, they all listened to Chief Mullins inform them of the latest developments.

~~~~~~~~~~~~~~~~~~~~

"Hope you're holding up okay. I know this has got to be nerve wracking for you. As we expected, Ben Reed and his partner, Gary, took the bait. We had several officers at the safehouse watching for them. There's a couple of other officers I've been suspecting are dirty as well, but only Reed and Warren were caught. I'm sure when they don't check in with O'Brien and Selena Hayes,

O'Brien will head toward Tessa's house. Stay safe and keep me updated."

After receiving the information that Reed did indeed go looking for them at the safehouse, probably scouting things out for O'Brien, Jack knew they'd be seeing the murdering psychopath that night. He'd been having flashbacks of being in Afghanistan for the last hour. Preparing for an attack from O'Brien, his past battles and missions were haunting him. He watched Craig, moving from room to room in the little house, keeping an eye on the camera images on the computer, and being alert. He felt comfort knowing his partner had his back, and Tessa held his extra Glock ready to defend herself and Sandra.

~~~~~~~~~~~~~~~~~~~~

Sandra watched her friends and tried to ward off the panic creeping up her spine. She had hoped she would never have to see Daniel again, but she had a foreboding feeling that tonight she'd be laying eyes on his ugly face. She held Tessa's aluminum baseball bat in her right hand. It wasn't a gun, but it could do some damage. Sandra was terrified of guns, yet she was glad Tessa was holding one. She tightened her grip on the bat. She wouldn't allow her monster to hurt her friends. Glancing at Tessa, she noticed she had her eyes closed and realized she was silently praying as she held her turquoise pendant in her left hand. Sandra closed her own eyes and began praying for protection from the evil ex-husband searching for them. They were his prey, but he was in for a surprise when he found them.
~~~~~~~~~~~~~~~~~~~~

Chapter Thirty-Nine

Daniel fumed when he was notified Ben Reed and his partner, Gary Warren, had been taken into custody. He angrily punched himself on the right side of his head with his hairy fist and cursed his old co-driver. He'd always considered Ben Reed to be overconfident, even when he'd taught him how to drive a truck many years ago when he'd worked for the same Topeka trucking company as O'Brien. He knew Ben and Randy Dillard had been drug users themselves, and he'd warned them numerous times how the cocaine effected their judgment. Recently, Randy had mentioned to O'Brien that he was worried he wouldn't pass Thomas Trucking's upcoming drug test. Since he'd run his mouth to the feds, Selena's dirty minion cops had silenced Randy. There would be no more drug tests for the cocaine addict.

Since Tessa and Sandra had not been taken to the safehouse where Ben had foolishly been caught, Daniel wondered where the women were. He made calls to the two MPD officers who had helped him and Selena in the past, in exchange for money.

"Find her… find out where she's holed up. Put out feelers for any information that can be found. I promise you'll be handsomely rewarded if you can get me an address where Tessa Ryan is staying."

As he hung up the call, he said aloud in a sing song voice, "Come out, come out wherever you are, Tessa… wherever you are..."

~~~~~~~~~~~~~~~~~~~~

The night skies were growing darker by the minute, and the group was feeling fraught and nervous. Tessa handed everyone bottles of water, and they continued staying alert. Sitting beside Jack on the couch, she rested her head on his shoulder for a minute before going back to watching the backyard camera on her phone. She walked to the kitchen and sat at her small table, feeling grateful for the guardian eyes of the cameras.

On her phone's screen, she noticed two large shadows fall over the sidewalk by the back door. She gasped, suddenly remembering her nightmare when O'Brien had his two flying monkeys stalk her. Jack had also seen the shadows on the camera monitor, shadows which should not have been there. They soon realized they were from a couple of burly looking men. He motioned to Tessa to come into the front room and put a finger to his lips indicating she shouldn't say anything. With her heart pounding loudly against her chest, she quietly walked towards Jack.

He and Craig slowly made their way to the backdoor and noticed the doorknob twist back and forth. Someone was checking to see if the door was locked. On the computer screen, the backyard camera revealed the two men in the darkness. One was hunched over to eye level of the doorknob attempting to pick the lock. He appeared to be jabbing something inside the knob.

Continuing to watch the cameras feed on the computer screen, Tessa and Sandra noticed another dark figure slinking beside the front porch. The looming shape seemed to slither up the front steps, and Sandra and Tessa looked at each other with wide eyes. It was O'Brien, holding what looked like a crowbar. His brazenness of walking up to the front door amazed them, but perhaps his direct approach was what no one expected. They heard low growls that became louder by the second. The Angel Dogs were warning the evil man of their presence. He quickly but quietly scrambled away from the front porch and creeped along the south side of the house approaching the long window to Tessa's office.

Tessa worried about the safety of the Angel Dogs and was tempted to open the front door to move them inside the house, but
~~~~~~~~~~~~~~~~~~~~

their growls quieted. Like a major league veteran, Sandra held the bat in both hands, ready to come out swinging to defend herself and her friends. Practically standing back to back, Tessa held the gun which felt foreign to her. She had shot her father's rifles before, but she wasn't familiar with the Glock, and the grip felt too big for her hands. She decided she'd be more prepared if there was a next time. Dates with Jack at the shooting range were on her agenda. The women watched the quartered cameras on the laptop's screen, rapidly interspersing glances at the long window where they knew the vile man lurked.

O'Brien slammed the window with the crowbar shattering the glass, and simultaneously, the two men by the backdoor began ramming their big bodies into the door trying to get inside. The alarm system began making a shrill beeping noise, and Tessa felt as though she were in another of her nightmares. With her heartbeat hammering in her chest, she purposely walked into the office and pointed the gun toward the window.

As her boots crunched on the broken glass littering the hardwood floor, she yelled, "Leave us alone O'Brien! If you come into my house, I will shoot first and ask questions later!"

Tessa and Sandra listened to him loudly curse as the rosebush's sharp, bloodletting thorns tore his flesh. The beautiful, but deadly roses were proving to be a hazard for the predator as he hunted the women, causing him several minutes of frustration. Nevertheless, O'Brien bent his head down, plowed through the long, thorns and finally launched his bulky body toward the office. He became entangled in the curtains and cursed again.

~~~~~~~~~~~~~~~~~~~~

When the brawny men began pounding on the backdoor, Craig surprised them by yanking the door open. With their pistols locked on the intruders, he and Jack began yelling at the two men to get on their knees. Wearing sporty jogging suits and gold chains around their necks, they looked like men who professionally bludgeoned people, or maybe extras in an old *Sopranos* mobster scene. The man standing the furthest in the shadows jumped backwards and began running. Craig took chase as Jack held his gun aimed directly at the other man.
~~~~~~~~~~~~~~~~~~~~

Jack's angry, dark eyes fiercely warned the intruder as he instructed the big man to get on his knees and put his hands on his head. The thug had tattoos on his neck and arms making him look like a human doodle pad. For a second, Jack could tell the intruder considered running, but the dark, threatening glare from Jack made him think otherwise. With his gun still drawn, Jack handcuffed and quickly led him to the garage, locking the tattooed man in the back seat of his Charger. He could hear Craig yell at the other man in the alley and realized his partner had overtaken the other thug. Craig had apprehended the goon and was marching him back to the house.

~~~~~~~~~~~~~~~~~~~

O'Brien crawled over the splintered office window, shaking loose from the now destroyed curtains and blinds. Tessa pulled the trigger on the Glock, and the deafening roar made her ears ring. The flash from the muzzle revealed O'Brien's right arm jerk, and she realized the bullet had grazed him. Moving closer toward her, she saw he looked in pain, but he kept advancing. Tessa squeezed off another shot, effectively winging his upper left arm, but unfortunately, the bullet didn't stop him. He was close enough to reach her.

Sandra shrilly screamed, and Tessa saw the gleam fan across Daniel's hideous face as he realized he was terrifying his ex-wife. He reveled in causing fright and fear. His obsidian eyes looked demon possessed. Jack came racing into the front room after hearing screams and shots loudly ring out from the office. He flipped on the light switch and was horrified as he watched O'Brien step toward Tessa and violently grab her by her hair, pulling her to him. Tessa tried pulling his arm away from her neck, but his firm grip was unyielding.

Jack felt terror-stricken as he saw the madman wield a 9mm gun in his left hand. With her being held so close to Daniel, Jack was unable to get a safe shot to stop him, but he trained his revolver on the bloody man the best he could. He noticed O'Brien's left arm leaking blood from an apparent gunshot wound from Tessa. His craggy face was covered in blood, causing his evil grin to look more garish. Multiple, deep lacerations on his forehead bled profusely.

~~~~~~~~~~~~~~~~~~~

Wiping the streaming blood from his eyebrows with his left forearm, Daniel looked at his ex-wife and demanded, "Unlock the front door, now."

Sandra looked uncertain, and he cursed and bellowed that he'd break Tessa's neck if she didn't open the door immediately. Sandra unlocked the front door with tears streaming down her face. Her insides were churning with a multitude of emotions. Not only did she fear for Tessa's wellbeing, but she was also furious to the point she was shaking. She continued to clutch the baseball bat and prayed that God would protect her young friend.

"Sayonara, losers." O'Brien wore a confident smirk.

Jack kept his gun aimed at Daniel, but the psycho kept pulling Tessa back and forth, hiding behind his captive. Craig hurried into the front room, blanching in horror when he saw Tessa being pulled out the front door by the bloody maniac.

~~~~~~~~~~~~~~~~~~~

Sliding backwards, O'Brien pulled her outside away from her friends. Tessa knew she couldn't spare a second. She couldn't be taken by O'Brien. It would mean certain death. His tight grip around her throat caused her to choke, and she felt the barrel of his gun in her back. She could hear the monster breathing heavily and felt the dampness of his sweat. The coppery smell of fresh blood from his wounds sickened Tessa.

Fighting the paralyzing panic and nausea that threatened her, she continued to pull at his arm from around her throat and gasped trying to catch air into her constricted lungs. She suddenly began to remember her self-defense class and all Tony Andrews had taught her. She silently said a prayer for mercy and strength and heard her Angel Dogs on the front porch loudly growl and bark at the evil man.

The dogs distracted O'Brien's attention from her onto them, and Tessa knew it was perhaps her only chance to escape his murderous vice. As hard as she could, she stomped her boot heel onto the top of O'Brien's right foot. At the same time, she elbowed him in his thick gut with all her might and twisted her body out of his grip. She turned and faced him, took a step back, and quickly
~~~~~~~~~~~~~~~~~~~

kicked between his legs like she was kicking a game winning field goal.

Daniel bent over, howling in pain. Sandra ran forward, swinging the baseball bat. A metallic sounding thud was heard as the aluminum bat caught his chin. Stumbling, O'Brien landed hard on his back on the porches concrete floor. His gun slid out of his reach. Looking like a silver flying streak, the Angel Dogs landed on top of the murderer. One of the large dogs grabbed O'Brien's right arm within its strong jaws, and one of them bit into his left thigh and shook its large silver head stilling the psychopath's movements. The smaller dog straddled O'Brien's chest, snarling as its sharp teeth hovered closely to the now terrified man's jugular vein.

Tessa seemed to be watching the scenario in fast motion. She heard Jack and Craig yell at O'Brien to "Don't move! Stay down!" and the three Angel Dogs retreated to Tessa's side.

~~~~~~~~~~~~~~~~~~~~

Hunched over, the monster rose to his feet. With his left arm hanging limply, now completely immobile, O'Brien made a last-ditch effort and swung his beefy right fist, barely missing Craig. Sandra swung the bat again, catching the madman in the ribs. He loudly grunted and fell to the concrete face-first. As he was handcuffed and hauled to his feet by the detectives, he wore an extremely shocked and pained expression.

"That one was for Marcy." Sandra calmly told O'Brien.

Sandra didn't take her eyes off her ex-husband's flabby, bloodied face. Their eyes locked, and she glared at her abuser until he broke eye contact and lowered his gaze. He spit out a broken tooth, and frothy blood oozed out of his swelling mouth. He couldn't stand to look at her, and he realized she was no longer afraid of him. He had lost his power over her forever.

Craig looked at the deep gashes on O'Brien's forehead, chuckled, and asked him in his composed, slow drawl, "Danny boy, how did you get all mangled up like that, man? You've done been thrashed by these gals." Craig continued laughing at him, and O'Brien visibly drooped.

~~~~~~~~~~~~~~~~~~~~

Tessa slowly walked to one of the wicker chairs on the porch and sat down. Her silver angels joined her, sitting at her feet and looked at her, checking to make sure she was all right. Her heart continued its rapid thudding as she reassured them with gentle whispers in their ears and tenderly hugged them. She felt the tension from their strong bodies ease.

"Thank you, my angels. Thank you, Lord, for protecting us all tonight," she softly said, as tears threatened to leak from her blue eyes. She continued stroking their silver heads with her shaking hands.

Tessa had no doubt that God had sent the beautiful dogs to protect her. She felt intensely humbled. Jack slowly stepped toward them and sat in the other, nearby wicker chair. He stared at her in awe and respect, as she thanked the large dogs and told them she loved them. The three silver warriors stood, and he suddenly realized how huge they were. With a graceful fluid movement, the dogs walked down the porch steps and onto the sidewalk. They didn't look back as they moved away from Tessa and her friends, disappearing into the night.

From the other end of the street, Tessa saw red and blue swirling lights grow larger and louder as police cars and an ambulance quickly rolled closer with their sirens blaring. She felt relief knowing they were there to take O'Brien and his henchmen away. Jack stood and held his hand out to her. He pulled her close to him, and she didn't know if she wanted to cry tears of joy or give a loud warrior's shout. She thought the brave dogs' courage must still be lingering in the air. Jack could feel it, too.

Tessa's neighbors had begun wandering outside, looking toward her house in curiosity and watched the squad cars and ambulance come to sudden stops. Chief Mullins hopped out of his sedan and hurried onto Tessa's front porch. Taking in the scene, he exchanged grins with Craig. Feeling relief for Tessa and Jack, he gazed upon the young couple wrapped in each other's arms. On the other end of the porch, holding the dynamic baseball bat, Sandra continued piercing O'Brien with a withering scowl, and O'Brien avoided her stare.

With surprise, Chief Mullins studied the bleeding convict, and casually commented, "You're looking green around the gills, Inmate O'Brien. Looks like someone opened a can of whooping on you."

Craig softly chuckled, and added, “Chief, this dude picked the wrong gals to tangle with.”

Chapter Forty

The next few days seemed to slow in pace, and Tessa found a sense of peace. She and Sandra were especially relieved to know O'Brien was awaiting extradition and was being transferred out of state to a maximum-security prison where he would sulk in solitary confinement awaiting trial.

From O'Brien's contraband-burner cell phone, Chief Mullins was able to obtain phone numbers for the other crooked police officers in the MPD. The dirty officers were now federal prisoners. Selena Hayes had been tracked to the Mexican border, and there were rumors that she'd vowed to never step foot on American soil again. Her promise seemed likely since there were also rumors that the Mexican drug cartel was not happy with Selena. Her future did not look healthy. Her accomplices from the prison breaks had been caught and were facing long prison sentences.

Numerous moles had been identified. A corrupt Judge Jenson and his drug addict son had been arrested. One of the police department's janitors had also been taken into custody. He had been the eyes and ears for Ben Reed in the police department, and he admitted to stealing Tessa's dream journals from Jack's desk which had been delivered to O'Brien from Randy Dillard. He had also started the rumor that she was the eyewitness of Marcy's murder. From the lowest to the highest-ranking officials, Chief Mullins had cleaned house, and the Morrigan Police Department was running in an orderly fashion again.

Lieutenant Darrell Johnson had retired and moved to an island off the coast of Florida. He told Chief Mullins he'd had enough excitement and was ready to enjoy sunshine and fishing full time. The Lieutenant had only been at the Morrigan Police Department for five years, however, before that, he'd worked in law enforcement in Tulsa. He told the Chief his twenty-five years of service were enough for him.

Chief Mullins had pulled Detective Taylor aside and asked if he would consider a promotion to the vacant position. Craig would miss working closely with Jack, but he had confidence in the young detective. The future Lieutenant Taylor knew his partner had grown in leaps and bounds the last few months.

~~~~~~~~~~~~~~~~~~~

A few days after O'Brien was returned behind bars, federal agents were summoned. O'Brien wanted to make a deal. He was willing to give the agents information of his accomplice in two of the murders, which included Marcy Phillips' death. In exchange for the name of his partner-in-crime, O'Brien asked that the death penalty be removed from his sentence.

Chief Mullins and Detectives Taylor and Parker had been invited to attend the interview between O'Brien and the federal agents. The men from the MPD patiently waited, ready to observe the meeting from the other side of the two-way glass adjacent to the interrogation room.

O'Brien shuffled into the room, escorted by two muscular correctional officers, and his handcuffs were removed. He was then cuffed to the long tables built-in wrist restraints. Under the harsh overhead lighting, the fluorescent bulbs gently buzzed and illuminated the inmate's sallow complexion. He was pale beneath his blackened eyes and bruises. His swollen jaws and chin were dark purple from Sandra's batting practice. Both of his arms were bandaged from gunshot wounds courtesy of Tessa. His forehead bore multiple dark angry looking lacerations bestowed to him from the
~~~~~~~~~~~~~~~~~~~

pernicious rosebush. O'Brien's normally aggressive demeanor seemed unusually docile, but no one underestimated his ability to turn into a rabid maniac at any moment. He tried to appear humble, but he was not that good of an actor.

Special Agents Morris and Carson introduced themselves to the meek acting inmate. Agent Morris placed a tape recorder on the table, clicked it on, stating the date and time.

"So, Inmate O'Brien, would you like to tell us why you called us together for this meeting? Do you wish to have an attorney present?" asked Special Agent Carson.

Softly, O'Brien said, "No need for a lawyer. Lawyers have done me no good so far. There's something I want to get off my chest." His eyes did not match his words. His steely-blue leer was anything but remorseful. "I didn't kill the woman in 2014 by myself, or Marcy Phillips either, but you all know who my partner was. You know my old co-driver, my fellow hunter, quite well. He's made promises to help me, but he hasn't lifted a finger."

O'Brien confidently gazed at the two-way mirrored glass, seeming to know the men were watching the interview.

Agent Carson, showed no expression, and replied, "Again, are you certain you don't want an attorney? I strongly advise you to have representation before you speak further."

O'Brien shook his head and said, "I told you no. I don't need a lawyer. I don't need anyone."

"Fine. Your hunting partner… are you referring to Randy Dillard? We know he was your co-driver for quite a while before he became a truck dispatcher at Thomas Trucking. Randy is dead, O'Brien. Your information is a day late and a dollar short."

"No, I'm not talking about Randy. That spineless piece of dirt was gutless. He could never have joined me on my hunts. He wasn't worthy. He was nothing but a half-witted meth head." O'Brien sneered and let his words soak into the listening ears. He seemed to enjoy having an audience, and he continued staring at the mirrored glass. "I'll give you the name of my hunting comrade if you get the death sentence taken off the table."

The agent nodded and said, "We'll see what we can do. No promises, but I'm sure the state's District Attorney will take your information into consideration. It's been established that you once worked with Ben Reed in the early '90s in Kansas. Since he's already in custody, I'm not sure if naming him as your former co-driver and accomplice will help your cause."

O'Brien's eyes darkened. His lisp became more pronounced, and he smirked, "I'm not talking about Ben Reed. That incompetent *Barney Fife* is unworthy to go hunting with me. He was using more and more *blow* every day. Bet you didn't know that. Right, smart-aleck detectives? Your co-worker is an addict." O'Brien began recounting the night Marcy was murdered in 1992. Instead of looking at the federal agents, he glared at the mirrored glass wall during the whole spiel, as he sneered and scoffed.

"I got Marcy to the lake all by myself. The dumb blonde had parked in the darkest corner of the parking lot at the bar. I messed with her car's battery, so it wouldn't start. From there, it was easy to grab her and go. My hunting partner met us at Crampton Lake. He also did an outstanding job of destroying evidence, on both cases, that came up in the months … and years, after our hunts, which is why both of our kills remained unsolved for so long. Avoiding arrest is easy when you have someone on the inside watching your back."

O'Brien raised his voice, his eyes riveted on the glass. "You all know him well, you especially, Chief Mullins. My hunting comrade is your buddy, Lieutenant Darrel Johnson. Ole Lieutenant is an experienced hunter, and he's been staying busy for years… right under your noses."

O'Brien looked amused. He loudly howled and started snickering at Agents Carson and Morris, who somehow continued to show no emotion.

"So, let me get this straight. Randy Dillard and Ben Reed never hurt anyone physically while accompanying you on any of your… *hunts*? However, retired Lieutenant Darrell Johnson helped you murder Marcy Phillips in 1992, as well as the woman, the cashier from the truck stop found in 2014 in western Oklahoma? Darrell Johnson tampered with evidence from the 1992 murder as well as the 2014 murder, and he's committed other crimes? You're also saying both Dillard and Reed were drug addicts? Is that correct?" asked Special Agent Carson.

"Yes! Can't you understand English, man?" O'Brien bellowed, becoming impatient and angry.

The federal agent wasn't intimidated by the madman's rage. In a calm voice, he answered, "I'm sure the Oklahoma District Attorney's Office will appreciate this new information. Perhaps the death penalty will be taken off the table at the trial for the deaths of the Oklahoma victims."

O'Brien leaned back in his chair, looking smug.

"As for the state of New Jersey, as well as the other state's you committed murder, I doubt they will care. My guess is that you will receive the death penalty from each of them. Your betrayal of your hunting buddy, your accomplice in these horrific murders, won't matter to them in the least." The satisfied expression on the agent's face infuriated O'Brien, and the agent continued, "Officers, please escort Inmate O'Brien back to his cell and prepare him for transport to New Jersey this afternoon."

The two federal agents calmly stood to their feet. Special Agent Morris picked up the recorder, and they walked out of the room. The murderer's mouth fell open, revealing several broken and missing teeth. He was dumbfounded and screeched. "You can't do this! I can't live like this!" raged the brutal psychopath.

One of the officers, leading him out of the interrogation room, replied, "No worries, Inmate. You won't be living much longer anywhere, accept maybe in hell."

Feeling shell-shocked, Chief Mullins, Jack, and Craig walked out of the interrogation room's observation area. O'Brien glanced at them. The defeated killer's face had turned an ashen gray.

"Who saw me that night? The night at the lake with Marcy... who was the witness that caused me to be caught?"

Craig responded to the killer's question, "Marcy told us... through Tessa. Marcy identified you as her killer."

He held his head low as his shackled ankles and wrists made loud clinking noises, shuffling away from the men of the Morrigan Police Department who had put him behind bars.

Craig nodded his head as he watched the madman, and said, "Looks like Lady Karma has found that fella's address, and Tessa and Sandra gave her directions how to get there."

Taking small, restrained steps due to the tight shackles, O'Brien tottered and slogged further down-range into the depths of the prison's bowels. Deep, angry voices of other inmates yelling at each other echoed throughout the narrow hallway as he was returned to his cell.

With frustration, Chief Mullins gruffly remarked, "Darrell Johnson. Well, I didn't see that coming. How could I have missed that? I vaguely remember Reed commenting that he and Johnson worked together in Topeka years ago, but Johnson hid his ugly truth very well… apparently for decades."

"I remember Lieutenant Johnson's name being on O'Brien's visitor log. I didn't think anything of it at the time. I was more concerned about Randy Dillard's name being listed," commented Jack, as he frowned and slowly shook his head in disbelief.

Looking grim, Craig said, "I'm having a hard time imagining happy-go-lucky Johnson as a vicious murderer, but I hope both of the monsters are prosecuted to the harshest extent of the law. Guess we'd better visit with the feds and see what we can do to help apprehend Johnson."

~~~~~~~~~~~~~~~~~~~~

On the long drive back to the MPD from the federal prison, Chief Mullins and the detectives were in deep thought, and it was unusually quiet inside the sedan. As they were pulling into the police station's parking lot, the Chief's phone rang. He put the call on speaker phone, and solemnly answered, "Chief Mullins."

"Chief Mullins, it's Special Agent Morris, and I have some news for you. Darrell Johnson was located near Sanibel Island, Florida. When he was approached by four of our agents, he attempted to escape. He tried to flee using his new thirty-foot Mako fishing boat, but he isn't a very good captain. He ended up crashing into a marina, and with the boat's fiberglass hull, he sunk like a rock. Our agents are still searching the bay for his body. I'll contact you as soon as we have more information."

Chief Jerry Mullins was disappointed Johnson hadn't been taken into custody, and replied, "Thank you for the intel, Special Agent Morris. Please, let me know if I can be of further assistance."

After the Chief hung up his call, Craig commented, "I sure hope they can find Johnson in that marina. Chief, that guy is like Aquaman. When he was swimming in my pool at the barbeque, he was obviously an accomplished swimmer. He could hold his breath underwater longer than anyone I've ever seen."

Chief Mullins groaned and replied, "Well, isn't that extra special?"
~~~~~~~~~~~~~~~~~~~~

Chapter Forty-One

A few days after the ordeal with O'Brien, Tessa was extremely happy to return to her home. Thanks to Jack and his friend, Curtis, her house had been cleaned and repaired, removing any trace of the psychopath. Dr. Redman had encouraged Tessa to take a two-week-long vacation, and she graciously accepted. She spent time with her family, with Jack, and with Sandra during the first few days.

She helped plan Sandra's housewarming party and project, and Jack had surprised her with plane tickets to Seattle for a four-day weekend. Jack had boasted of the city's beauty, and the young couple were anxious for the short jaunt.

With her fondness for cooking, she was also collaborating with Sandra on menus using many of her favorite recipes. When the *Marcy Phillips' Haven of Hope* accepted the first guests, there would be lots of delicious dishes available. She and Sandra were making a detailed list of supplies and grocery items to stock the enormous food pantry. Utilizing her love for cooking, she'd be contributing to Sandra's beloved project, and that gave Tessa joy.

~~~~~~~~~~~~~~~~~~~~

Many of her evenings were spent with Jack, and they had grown closer in mind, body, and spirit. Jack felt a profound, loving tenderness toward Tessa and prayed for guidance in approaching her with his love. In his heart, he knew she was the woman he'd been waiting for all his life. Their strong chemistry was powerful, and they cherished every moment they spent together. He felt privileged to have found such a beautiful, courageous young woman, and he was excited to return to Seattle with her by his side for an impromptu, long weekend.

Jack was eager to have dinner with Tessa that evening. He'd planned a special meal and another surprise for her at his home. The oven timer indicated he had enough time to drive to her house and pick her up.

Minutes later, as they drove back to his log home, he kept glancing and smiling at the blue-eyed girl sitting next to him on the seat of his pickup truck. She sent smiles back at him and fidgeted with the turquoise pendant with its long chain hanging from her neck.

"Jack, has there been any more news about Darrell Johnson? He's been on my mind today."

"No, Tessa, not that I'm aware of. His body was never recovered from the boat accident, and I can't stop thinking how he was quite a talented swimmer. Remember how he could hold his breath underwater at Craig's barbeque?" Jack looked uneasy.

Tessa frowned and shook her head. "You know, it isn't hard to believe that O'Brien is a psychopath. His evil is written all over him, but Darrell Johnson was so likable. Makes me wonder how many other charming, charismatic monsters are out there."

Once they arrived at his home and walked inside, she was drawn into the log house's kitchen by the enticing aroma of the spicy pasta dish and baked bread that emanated from the oven.

"Oh Jack, it smells just like *Marco's* in here!" exclaimed Tessa, as she breathed deep.

They hadn't been to their favorite Italian restaurant for a couple of weeks, and she'd been craving pasta. From the oven's
~~~~~~~~~~~~~~~~~~~~

warming drawer, Jack placed the food on the countertop. Tessa helped him carry silverware, dishes, and the steaming lasagna to the dining room table. As she sat down in the ladder-back dining chair across from Jack, who she had noticed couldn't seem to quit smiling, she stopped and looked curious.

"Did you hear something, Jack? I know I heard something," she said, straining her ears for the odd noise she heard from the back of the house.

"Oh, I think I know what it might have been. Hold on, stay here while I check it out."

Grinning like a Cheshire cat, he left the table and strode toward the hallway off the living area by the bedrooms. A minute later, he ambled back into the dining room carrying a fluffy two-month-old, silver German shepherd puppy with a big pink bow tied around her neck. The pup looked at Tessa and excitedly whined, trying to squirm from Jack's arms. Tessa's eyes rounded wide, as big as saucers, and her mouth fell open in shock. She gasped, stood up, and Jack handed her the wiggling ball of fur.

"Oh Jack… oh! I can't believe it. You got a puppy! What's her name?"

"Yes, I got a puppy, and she's for you. You can name her whatever you'd like."

Tears of joy began to sneak out of her eyes, and she cuddled the little dog, feeling the pup's soft fur tickle her chin. She beamed with pure delight and began laughing.

"Look at her big ears! Oh, she's precious! What shall we name her? Where did you find her?" Tessa couldn't keep her eyes off the adorable silver pup.

~~~~~~~~~~~~~~~~~~~

The evening could not have gone better. All three of them snuggled on Jack's couch and began watching a movie on the huge, flat screen television. Feeling relaxed, content, and almost comatose from the excellent pasta dinner, Tessa couldn't keep her eyes open. Ten minutes into the beginning scenes of *I Can Only Imagine,* Jack heard gentle snoring and looked down to see Tessa and the puppy had both fallen asleep. He cradled the dark-haired beauty in his arms, listened to her breathe and sighed. Besides feeling devotion, Jack felt admiration and deep respect for his Ninja girl. He cringed
~~~~~~~~~~~~~~~~~~~

thinking how close he'd come to losing her to the monster who now sat in solitary confinement over a thousand miles away. Inhaling the sweet peachy scent of her hair, he silently vowed to always protect her.

~~~~~~~~~~~~~~~~~~~~

Falling into a deep slumber, Tessa began to dream. Through a thick foggy haze, she saw a beautiful, black-haired woman with kind brown eyes and a gentle smile come into clear focus. The woman began speaking in a language that Tessa had never heard before, and she wondered how she could understand the woman's rhythmic words.

"*Semi-hotta*," said the woman. Tessa understood it to mean "my pretty girl*."*

Tessa responded, "*In-ko*", which meant, "Grandmother."

She wondered how she knew how to speak the cadent-rich language. The woman smiled, and Tessa saw three silver dogs join the woman, standing at her side. She knew they were her Angel Dogs.

Tessa felt as though they were old friends, and she had been missing them. She said, "*Wa-kan-ta shon-ke's*", which meant "Spirit Dogs*"*. Looking at her grandmother, Tessa told her, "*Pi-de di-e, In-ko*", which meant "I Love You, Grandmother."

Her Grandma Lucy told her she loved her, too, in her native Quapaw language. Tessa understood her every word. Her grandmother and the three silver warriors slowly drifted away from her until Tessa could not see them any longer.

Waking from her blessed dream, Tessa smiled and opened her eyes. She touched the turquoise cross around her neck, enclosed the pendant within her hand, and gave a contented sigh. The puppy was looking directly at her and started barking.

"Hello, little Lucy," she responded to the adorable dog. The puppy yelped and barked happily at her new name, and licked Tessa's face.

Jack kissed the top of her brunette head and gently embraced her. "Did you sleep well? You took quite a long nap."

"Yes, I feel rested…and safe." Tessa turned to face Jack and looked into his dark eyes. She felt their souls connect, and her heart beat faster.
~~~~~~~~~~~~~~~~~~~~

~~~~~~~~~~~~~~~~~~~~

Jack felt himself melting as he gazed at the girl of his dreams. "Tessa… I know we haven't known each other long, but I know how I feel. I love you, and I feel very blessed to have you in my life. I love you, Ninja-girl."

He felt her blue eyes pull his spirit closer with a kind of invisible, strong thread.

Lacing her fingertips within Jack's, happy tears slowly leaked from her eyes, and she said, "Jack, you had me from the very first day we met. The moment you took off your Ray Ban's, flashed me your sexy grin, and showed off your dimples, you had me. I love you, too, and I can't wait to see where God leads us next."
~~~~~~~~~~~~~~~~~~~~

THE AWAKENING SERIES - BOOK 2

Awakening to Peace

(*Excerpt*)

"What are you looking at, Big Boy?" asked Tiffany Connors, as the twenty-five-hundred-pound black Angus bull glared at her, looking quite agitated and combative.

Obviously, the enormous animal was not happy with her presence in the pasture where he and his heifers resided. The herd of cattle had been lying in the pasture's tall bluestem grass when Tiffany drove up to the work site. Although they were used to seeing the white pickup truck pull into their stomping grounds and park beside the gigantic wind turbine which had recently been erected, the herd was unhappy that she had disrupted their afternoon slumber.

Tiffany decided to call her supervisor to ask about the quarrelsome bull. "Hey there, Phillip. I have a quick question about the ginormous black bull at Site 32. Is he just cranky and harmless, or do I need to carry a big stick?"

"According to the landowner, Curly Bill won't hurt a fly, but he's definitely big. Be careful when patrolling the site." Phillip didn't seem too concerned.

"Well, he'd better stay in his own lane. Who would name a bull Curly Bill?" She studied the beast as he swatted at flies with his tail and continued to glare at her.

Phillip chuckled and answered, "The farmer told me the bull had been a pet when he was young, and his son loved to pet his curly topknot on his head. Hence, Curly Bill."

Tiffany shrugged and said, "Hmmm, well, okay then. Gotta put my phone on the charger. I'm about out of juice. Talk to you later."

Sitting in the company-owned truck parked beside the towering turbine, she inspected the site area. She noted in her work report that everything was fine and undisturbed at Turbine Site #32. Tiffany listened to the swishing thud of the turbine's rotating blades. The rhythmic, loud swooshing sound had a repeating pattern every three seconds. Tiffany counted to herself, *One, two, three, swoosh... one, two, three, swoosh...*

She worked part-time for the wind energy company as a security guard. Her weekends were busy, inspecting and driving from one wind turbine site to the next. Dozens of soaring, white wind turbines dotted the rolling hillsides and rural pastures. With their circulating blades collecting energy from the abundance of Oklahoma winds, they converted the wind to electricity.

Her weekdays were spent at the Morrigan Police Department where she worked as a uniformed police officer. She loved her job in law enforcement, however the salary wasn't enough to cover her most recent project. When the job of working as security for the wind energy company was offered to her, she gratefully accepted the position.

Tiffany's coworker, Detective Jack Parker, didn't share her gratitude. He was not a fan of the invasive wind turbines. With good reason, Jack was extremely perturbed. One had been installed quite close to his home. She had listened to his valid complaints with sympathy. She wouldn't want to live near one either. The turbine which she was currently parked beside was only a short distance from Jack's log house.

She watched the cows slowly chew their cud and was relieved the bull had become disinterested in her. Tipping her head sideways, she listened to an unusual sound that floated to her through the truck's open window. Unable to discern its origin, she stepped from the white truck and began walking around the site, straining her ears for the location of the odd noise. Tiffany studied the base of the turbine and made her way to the bottom of a set of aluminum steps, leading to a platform and an entrance to the tower. A green, square-shaped metal transformer sat beside the tall monstrosity, and the door which the wind energy employees used to enter the turbine was arch-shaped. With her ears perked, she slowly climbed up the six steps and stood beside the door on the small platform. A padlock on the door prevented her from entering the tower.

"Hello? Is someone in there?" she loudly asked.

A thump and groan answered Tiffany from inside the turbine. Someone, or something, began banging on the door.

"Oh snap! Hey, hold on! I'm going to call for help. I'll be right back!" she assured whoever was inside, and she hurriedly stumbled down the steps and ran to the company pickup.

Out of breath from panic and with a huge dose of adrenaline, she pulled her cell phone from the truck's console where it was charging. She tapped Jack's number and prayed he was home.

"Jack? Are you at home or near your house?" she practically yelled into his ear when he answered her call.

~~~~~~~~~~~~~~~~~~~

"Yep, I'm in my workshop. I'm waiting on Tessa to get here, then we're going to the gym. Why? What's wrong?" Jack immediately noticed Tiffany's distraught tone of voice, which was unusual for her. She was normally quite laid back and cool headed.

"I'm at the windmill site behind your house, and I can hear someone in the turbine. They're locked inside. Can you bring some bolt cutters and call the PD? Something feels mighty wrong to me about this. Please hurry!" she pleaded.

Jack walked outside and gazed at the wind turbine near his home. The circular white tower ascended three-hundred feet into the air. The round wide base from the foundation gradually narrowed towards its peak. On the top, there were three massive blades, fan style, attached to a rotor.

"On my way," he assured her and hung up the call. Jack tapped his phone and rang Lieutenant Craig Taylor.

"Craig, can you get to my house right away? Connors just called me. She's patrolling sites for the windmill farm, and she heard
~~~~~~~~~~~~~~~~~~~

someone from inside the turbine behind my house. Evidently, they're locked inside. I'm not sure what's going on, but I'm headed there now to check it out. Connors seemed oddly riled up about it."

Jack felt his heart race and his *spidey senses* kicked in. Grabbing the red-handled bolt cutters from a hook on the wall over his worktable, he dashed to his pickup truck parked beside his shop.

He wondered if an employee had inadvertently been locked in the tower. He knew there was a ladder built inside which led from the base to the very top. The wind energy employees would climb the ladder inside the cylinder-shaped turbine to service the generator and gear box located inside the shaft which controlled the blades and rotor. *What if the person inside isn't an employee?*

~~~~~~~~~~~~~~~~~~~

Tiffany quickly made her way back to the base of the turbine and heard more thumping sounds bang on the arch-shaped door. She skipped up the steps to the platform and glanced around the pasture. Nothing seemed amiss out there, except for the cantankerous black bull. He seemed to sense something was awry in his neighborhood, and he was not happy as he threw his head sideways.

A cloud of red dust billowed from the dirt road leading to the #32 turbine site, announcing Jack's arrival as he screeched to a stop near Tiffany's company truck. He leapt out of his blue pickup and ran toward the wind tower. The domineering black bull had decided to protect his turf. The angry bovine bellowed a loud warning to Jack, letting him know his territory was off limits.

He pawed the ground and lowered his head, and Jack knew things were getting ready to get serious. He could see the whites of the animal's eyes, and the massive creature seemed to tuck his chin downward. He moved between Jack and the trucks. Jack's choices were now limited on which way he could run to avoid the enraged bull. He was at least fifteen yards from the steps leading to the tower's doorway and trying to get back to his truck was not an option. Noticing the steps and platform leading up to the tower door were made of aluminum, he thought how the brutish bull would make short order of them quickly. He needed to keep the bull away from Tiffany and whoever was trapped inside.

~~~~~~~~~~~~~~~~~~~

From atop the platform near the turbine's door, Tiffany observed the raging bull cornering Jack. Feeling horrified, she began to yell and wave her arms in the air, trying to distract the mad beast. Jack made the mistake of trying to make a run for it. He sped by the platform, tossing the bolt cutters to Tiffany, and circled around the turbine's base toward the front.

With the aid of the cutters and another surge of adrenaline, she managed to snap the padlock in two and yanked the tower's door open. The foul odor and what she saw inside the darkness caused her stomach to lurch and bile rose in her throat.

~~~~~~~~~~~~

Jack looked over his shoulder as he raced to the other side of the turbine, making a beeline for the now opened doorway. The beast was closer than he realized, and Jack suddenly had a newfound respect for rodeo clowns. He hoped he and Tiffany could wait in the turbine tower until Craig and help from the PD arrived. The aggressive bull bellowed again, and slobbery saliva drooled from his hairy chin as he tossed his head sideways. Cold fear clutched at Jack's heart. Disturbing loud snorts and grunts rumbled near his ears. Terrified, Jack frantically thought, *Feet don't fail me now!*
~~~~~~~~~~~~

A Note from the Author

Debbie Ellis

Through prayer and with God's grace, I've progressively healed from decades of narcissistic abuse. Joining online support groups, where I've met hundreds of amazing women with similar experiences as my own, has given me incentive and courage to share my story, even if it's only through my book's characters. Writing has become part of my journey, and I hope my stories help create awareness of personality disorders, such as narcissism and psychopathy, as well as domestic violence.

I've always loved reading, and writing has always been a passion, especially of mystery and suspense, romance, and laced with God's messages. Striving to give others hope by sharing knowledge, experiences, and my own hopes and dreams, I write.

The first book, *Awakening from Terror*, is a fictional novel, however the story has a lot of truth woven throughout the pages. Reading between the lines, my own personal experiences, as well as some of my dear friends, can be found tied into the book's storyline. Sadly, many of my experiences are quite similar as other victims. The disordered abusers have comparable characteristics and reading someone else's unpleasant experience with a sociopath feels familiar. That factor has created a kind of sisterhood, a kinship among members in our FaceBook support group, creating a bond of unity in recovery. Love and empathy are shared, and those healing powers become a chain reaction of tenacity, wisdom, and empowerment. I will forever be grateful and indebted to my sisters in our FaceBook group family.

I decided to write a series of books called *The Awakening Series*. Book Two, titled *Awakening to Peace*, is another novel with a message that is heavy on my heart. There's a myriad of books to be written. As they flourish and develop in my mind, my fingertips itch to put them to ink and paper.

I'm anxious to put my thoughts into a new storyline, continuing the adventures of Tessa and Jack from Morrigan, Oklahoma. While writing has been therapeutic for me, I pray my books will be entertaining for my readers. Thank you for reading my novels.

Made in the USA
Columbia, SC
21 October 2022